# THE CHRISTMAS

Rebecca Funke

*The Christmas Gift*
*Not all gifts fit under the tree*



**Author's Webpage: funkenovels.com**



Cover designed by Estella Vukovic
Interior design by Sandra Jurca

Printed in the United States

First Edition

Print ISBN: 978-0-578-97500-9

*To Jackson,*
*my own inspiration behind Mason.*
*This story wouldn't exist without you.*
*With all my love, forever and always ∞*

CHAPTER 1

# Tuesday, December 6, 2016

*"Let's be naughty and save Santa the trip."*

— GARY ALLAN

## (19 DAYS UNTIL CHRISTMAS)

THIS MORNING'S SNOW FLURRIES have led to full-fledged anarchy in my living room. Both Susie and Noah march around the coffee table shouting, "No more school! No more school!" They move their arms up and down as if holding their invisible picket signs.

Noah breaks out of the march and heads outside. He walks past the coat rack and opts to just wear his inside-out pajamas—a tradition he does before bed to ensure a snow day. He scoops up a mist from the porch. He shouts, "The snow is packing! We can have a snowball fight!"

My gaze does not turn to Noah. Instead, my eyes stay fixed past the wilting herbs on the kitchen sink's windowsill onto the early morning sky. It's still dark, but the Christmas lights that line the neighborhood homes brighten the block in shades of red, green, and gold. All the houses except for ours. "It's just a light mist. You don't even have a school delay because of it. Come on inside, Noah." My hands continue to swirl the sponge around the already cleared-off plate as if possessed by the scene in front of me. *Did the Gencos buy an inflatable Jesus manger for their yard, or is my lightly caffeinated brain just imagining things?*

I maneuver the dishes in the overflowing drying rack to find space for this new plate. Arguably it would be easier just to clear out the drying rack, but we don't have time. Perhaps the easiest option would be to call the plumber to fix the dishwasher that has been unused for months, but that seemingly easy task always falls off on my daily to-do list.

Today, I need to go to their school early for a mandatory PTA check-in. The PTA moms always want to stop and chat, but I need to get out fast so I can still get to work on time. Stratford Junior seems to be keeping track of when we come and go these days. I'm always one of the first ones in, but I usually need to leave early to get the kids. The rest of the staff have a partner or nanny to do that for them.

I am already worrying about what these PTA moms will want to talk about. The parents in charge of the PTA love to ambush the rest of us, average non-good-doer parents, with unrequested tips on doing our jobs better. If the PTA group finds something I did 'wrong', they like to point it out and explain how it'll lead to my children's eventual death or imprisonment. I wonder if they noticed I brought a dessert with refined sugar for the last bake sale. Or even worse, did they see it was from the grocery store bakery, and I repackaged it to look homemade? Being a single mom is difficult, but one positive is that the PTA group criticizes me less than the other moms—or at least to my face. In exchange for their lowered expectations, I get their depressed looks, like they're watching those Sarah McLachlan animal cruelty commercials. Perhaps I should attach a 1-800 number to myself so that they can call to make donations in exchange for their gawking.

My thoughts are interrupted by the ear shuttering, cold-blooded screams of my youngest. "Mommmm! Noah put snow down my shirt!"

I search my to-go mug for another sip of energy, but nothing comes out. How have I already finished it? This was supposed to be enough for the whole morning. I breathe and accept I must address the chaos behind me. "Noah! I can't do this today." Noah continues to run, and Susie starts to cry. I need to find a reason for him to stop, but I can't find one.

He breaks into a sprint, chasing his now screaming baby sister. "Get him to stop, Mom," Susie demands.

He stops only for a second to take off his pajama top, swirling it around like a lasso. Where does this boy get his energy? Clearly, it's not from my side of the family, or it skipped generations and never came to me.

"Santa won't like this behavior," I say. He must still care about Santa's judgment of the situation, even if he doesn't care about my mental exhaustion this morning. "You don't want to be on the naughty list just a matter of weeks before Christmas, do you?"

"Santa barely gets me anything anyways!" Noah says as he continues to run.

Well, that feels like a punch to the gut. If I remember correctly, I had to special order the Nerf gun he asked for last year. Sure, he doesn't get a whole mountain of gifts like some of his classmates, but he still gets a respectable mound. And even then, I always get the gifts he rants about all year. Quality over quantity, right? "Well, maybe because of events like this, he shortened your list," I say, trying to silence the irritation in my tone.

Noah stops, takes a long pause, and looks at me. "Fine. But I still don't want to go to school." He runs towards the couch and throws his body at the cushions. He points out the window. "It's snowing outside, and I wore my pajamas inside out. That always works! We should have school canceled."

And thank God school isn't canceled. I didn't have childcare plans for today while I went to work. But I also know this is confusing for Noah. He is his father's son, a boy that believes in folklore and hopes for magic even in the darkest of places. And I know school is difficult for him, and I'm sure all the extra tutoring sessions only make it more frustrating. I set down the butter knife I am using to prepare their lunches and wrap my arms around Noah. "I'm sorry, Noah. I know you were looking forward to a snow day. But it's already 7 AM, and there isn't even a posting for a delay, so we need to go in, and we need to go soon because of that PTA meeting I told you about."

Susie snuggles herself onto my other side and smiles up at me. "I like going to school anyways, Mommy." She turns towards the stairs and joyfully skips away.

Noah unfolds his arms and slowly follows his sister, "Fine. I'll go get ready."

I smile, feeling just a tiny ounce of victory this morning. I return to making their sandwiches as I think forward to Christmas morning. I have barely prepared anything. We haven't even put out the Charlie Brown-esque Christmas tree that I got in a yard sale three years ago. Does my comment about Santa mean I need to get them more gifts to prove that he really is watching? I already got each of them a few presents, and I won't have the time to go shopping again. And I guess, more pressingly, I don't have any extra cash to spend.

I shake away the stress and head upstairs. I wish I could love Christmas as much as my kids do, but I just can't. All I can think about is the money wasted on wrapping paper that will get thrown away and the presents that will be in next year's garage sale. And then there is the additional small talk about every person's Christmas plans and the endless debate about whether we should be saying 'Happy Holidays' or 'Merry Christmas'. Even the extra donations to anybody that stands out in the cold with a Santa hat and a bell can make me frustrated. I know that one makes me sound like a less hairy Grinch, but I can't help feeling like it's just another demand of the season.

But maybe the Grinch was onto something. Perhaps this is the year I can cancel Christmas. I mean, I'm not a monster. I will still do the basics like get gifts from Santa and put up our small artificial tree. I just can't do the rest of it anymore. Granted, I haven't been doing that for several years, not since Mason.

Mason had a way of making Christmas truly magical for the family. He would wrap each inch of the house with Christmas lights, fight the natural elements to chop down a Christmas tree and start snowball fights, drawing in all the neighborhood kids. Without Mason, we no longer do these things. Our house remains dark. The fresh sap of a live Christmas tree has been replaced by the scentsicles sticks. And the snow remains untouched, waiting instead to melt into the already-dying grass.

I head to the bathroom to freshen up my face. My skin looks irritated. Are those pimples? Aren't I old enough to no longer have pimples? I wash my face and then grab my crusty cover-up to mask these irritations. I examine my various brushes and palettes of powders and paints. Each stroke of makeup is essentially the same as the day before, with only slight color variations. I opt for a subtle look. Something to show I'm presentable but discreet, the classic no-makeup look created with loads of makeup.

I force myself into one of my mundane suits that have gotten too tight and then go to collect Noah and Susie. I notice Noah is wearing cargo shorts but decide to let it go. Someday he will learn. Susie is wearing a flowery dress and stockings I set out for her last night. Somehow she managed to get it all on herself this morning.

We rush outside to my rusted baby blue Honda Civic parked in the driveway. Both inside and out, the car has an elderly charm, slow yet somehow graceful, earning her the endearing name Bonnie. When I turn the key in Bonnie's ignition, her muffled speakers play classic Christmas hits. Immediately, I turn the unwanted noise off.

"Turn it back on!" Susie demands.

I look in the rearview mirror. Susie's green eyes sparkle. *Damn is she cute? How could I ever say no to her?* "Sorry, honey. Natural habit." I forcefully press the radio button back on.

Our first stop is picking up Noah's closest friend, Marcus. Marcus has been Noah's best friend since preschool. Marcus's dark complexion and calm demeanor contrast that of my son. To an outsider, they seem like unlikely friends. But the commonality of getting bullied at school bonds children together in unpredictable ways.

With Marcus secured, I hear Noah ask, "Do you have the plans?"

I look back in the rear mirror. Marcus is rustling through his backpack and pulls out a pile of papers. "Do you think this is going to work?"

"Of course, it's going to work, Marcus! I just know it!" I admire my son's confidence. Like his high energy, I wonder where he got that quality.

I chime in, "What are you two planning back there?"

"Oh, don't worry about it, Mom. It's no big deal."

When stopped at a light, I look back again, trying to see the drawings they are discussing. I see pages with hand-drawn maps of the house and others that trace possible entrances into what looks like our home. *Is Noah creating some plan to break into his own house?* I look at one picture that is peeking out from the bottom of the pile. I notice a stick figure with a red suit and a half circle attached to the stick frame representing the figure's belly. *Is that Santa?* I look more closely. *Is that a noose around Santa's neck?* I try to focus back on the road. "Are those pictures of Santa?"

"Mommmmm, stopppp! These aren't for you to look at!" Noah demands as if I'm the embarrassing one in the car, not him and Marcus, who are discussing their hand-drawn images of attacks on an elderly man in a red jumpsuit. I shake it off. Noah is starting to get to that age where being a momma's boy isn't cool. I need to learn to accept that, but I can't help wishing that time will stand still and leave him to always be my little boy.

I turn my attention to Susie. "Do you have any fun activities at school today, Susie?"

Susie continues to look out her side window as her legs swing back and forth. "Yeah. We get to pick our class pet. I want a pony, but the teacher says a pony is too big, so I'm sad."

I smirk. Over the past year, Susie's obsession with ponies has grown exponentially. She has never ridden a horse or pony and has only seen one a handful of times, but that's the only thing she asks for anymore. "I think Ms. G is right," I respond. "Where would the pony play? She wouldn't have any pony friends."

Susie's attention moves from the window to the front of the car. "But I would be her friend!"

I chuckle. "And you would make a great friend to the pony, but there's still not enough space. Did the class pick a different animal?"

"Yeah. Everyone wants a frog, but I think they're gross."

"Why do you think that?"

"They're so slimy and sticky. I don't want to play with that. I want to play with a pony!" She pauses. "Do you think I'll ever get to ride a pony, Mommy?"

I look into the rearview mirror. Susie is strapped into a hefty car seat to protect her. She seems so fragile from here. I can see the blue veins under her soft white skin. I remember the scab she got on her knee from falling on the driveway this past weekend. I wasn't there to protect her, and she cried and cried all day just from that one scratch. My attention returns to the road. "I don't know, honey. Maybe someday . . . Maybe when you are older."

With my attention on the road, I notice a mist of snow that's illuminated by the streetlights and passing cars. I grip my hands firmly on the wheel, making slight adjustments to avoid the numerous potholes that have never been fixed. I notice the snow melts when it touches the ground. Each snowflake dissolves into the shallow puddle, briefly experiencing its uniqueness before melting with the rest. Like it was never a snowflake in the first place. Cars pass me as I slow down. Diligently, I watch for areas that might have frozen over. I fear the invisible black ice, the conjoined snowflakes. A singular danger that can take control. I know all too well the threat a road like this can bring to a family.

I pull into the school lot and park in the back corner. I take one final breath as I unclip my seatbelt. “Everyone ready?”

Noah and Marcus unstrap themselves, and I go to help Susie. The boys run ahead, but I grab Susie’s hand and walk toward the school with her. I spot Marie, the PTA president, standing at the school entrance like a guard for Buckingham Palace, protecting the treasured volunteer sign-up sheets.

“Hey, Rach! How are you doing, sweetie?” Marie’s tone resembles an owner rewarding their dog for a new trick. Marie fits all the stereotypes for the leader of a PTA group. Big house, big diamond ring, big breasts, and, of course, a tiny waist, further accentuated with a tight Lululemon-meets-winter-wonderland outfit, like a modern-day ice queen.

I want to look down and pretend I don’t see her, but I know that will cause more drama than good. I need to show her that I'm doing great . . . regardless of whether it's true. I increase the octave of my voice and prepare a response that will provide no insight into how I'm actually doing.

"Hey, Marie! Just feeling God's blessing today, being able to help the school!" Immediately, I feel stupid for saying that. I don't see this as a blessing. It's just an extra bullet on my never-ending to-do list. I don't even know if I believe in God. I attempt to put on a good show since I'm paying almost ten thousand dollars a year to this school. I just want my kids to blend in. I don't want to make their lives any harder than they already are.

"Well said. God always gives us what we need," Marie responds as she flips her curled hair behind her shoulder. Did she get a morning blowout for this meeting?

I stop my eyes from rolling and instead nod my head. I internally question the legitimacy of her response. Does God always give us what we need? I need extra cash to support my family, but I have yet to receive an envelope of money addressed *to Rachel from God Above.* I attempt to end the conversation by going to the sign-up sheets inside the school entrance. As I turn away, I hear Marie continue.

"Also, Rachel, I noticed you haven't brought in any gifts for the giving tree." She lowers her head and cocks it to one side. "You have picked a tag, right? I would hate to see one of those kids not get the gift they wanted because of our delays."

*Shit*. I remember getting the letter about this, but I have yet to figure out where this giving tree is. "Oh right, can I write a check for it? How much is it again?"

She huffs in disgust. "It's a toy drive, Rachel, not a check drive. You need to get a gift and then wrap it for the child you pick on the giving tree."

I force my customary fraudulent smile, which always hurts my cheeks. "Oh right, of course . . . Where is the—"

The conversation is interrupted by a Nerf bullet hitting Marie square in the face. "I gotch you!!" Noah shouts as he runs to pick up the evidence.

The light pressure of the foam cylinder is almost enough to knock Marie down. She stumbles back, then stares directly at me. "What was that?" she demands.

My face becomes dark red. I curl my lips in and widen my eyes in shock. "I'm so sorry, Marie!" I look down and grab Noah's small pocket-sized Nerf gun from his hands. "Noah! We have talked about this! No violence! You need to apologize to Marie right now."

Noah frowns. "I was just playing."

"But Marie never agreed to play with you. You can't just go around hitting people with Nerf bullets. You need to apologize."

Staring at the ground, he turns to Marie. "I'm sorry."

"Look at me when you apologize," Marie demands as she widens her own eyes. *Who is she to order how my child gives an apology?* I want to tell Noah he doesn't have to do anything she says, but I take a breath. Instead, I nod to Noah, letting him know to comply with her wish.

He slowly lifts his head to Marie. "I'm sorryyyy."

"Thank you for the apology." Marie's eyes narrow in on me as if lasering her judgment onto my soul. I grab Noah's hand and shuffle inside, giving her a couple more "sorrys" as I walk away.

When we are safely inside, I hug Susie, who runs off to her classroom. I tell Marcus to go ahead without Noah, who stays with me. I kneel to be eye-level with Noah. "Noah, why did you hit her with a bullet?"

"I don't know . . . I just thought . . . " He pauses and looks to the marbled floor.

"You thought what?" While part of me, of course, found the slightest amount of humor in Marie's reaction, I still worry that this is pointing to a bigger problem for Noah.

"I just wanted to protect you. She seemed mean."

I shake my head. "First, Noah, you do *not* need to protect me. It's quite the opposite. I need to protect *you*. And second, she was fine and pleasant. And third, no more violence, or I'll need to take away your Nerf guns, okay?"

His eyes widen. "Don't do that!"

"This is strike one. Two more strikes and no more Nerf guns."

"But . . . " He begins to stammer and looks like he'll cry. I don't want to make him cry.

"Hey, look at me." I lightly press on the bottom of his chin to move it up. "You are okay, just no more violence, okay?"

"Okay."

I hug him and then stand back up. "You head to class, and I will find those sign-up sheets." *And the damn giving tree*, I think to myself. He happily runs towards Marcus, who's waiting outside their homeroom door marked MRS. BUSHNELL'S 3RD GRADE CLASS.

When I look to my left, I see folding tables with the sign-up sheets taped on as if to prevent a parent from stealing the paper list for themselves. I notice that most of the roles are filled. There are three options left: volunteer for a week at lunchtime, support the fund to get a class pet, or help with the Christmas pageant props and practice for Pre-K and Kindergarten, the class that Susie is in. The first is a non-option since I work, and I fear the second option could get pricey, and I am already worried about all the extra expenses of Christmas. So the last one it is. And it might just be fun.

I sign my name and notice there is only one name above me. Karen. Unlike Marie, Karen is one of the least judgmental people I know. My son could have hit her with a hundred Nerf darts, and she would just laugh the whole time. The other moms joke that she could be a juror for a serial killer, and she would find nice things to say about the person. Karen's downfall, though, is her aggressive high energy, making it hard to spend large amounts of time with her. She must have access to some kind of insanely potent Ethiopian coffee. Or maybe she has some soundproof box where she gets uninterrupted sleep, unlike the rest of us. It's most likely the sugary, delicious cupcakes from the local bakery she owns called Pixie Dust Cupcakes.

Even though Karen has more cheer than a squad of high school cheerleaders, the other moms can't stand her. My theory is that they blame her and her tempting cupcakes for the extra pregnancy weight they can't lose. I look down at my belly. There is definitely a Pixie cupcake or two that has contributed to this still being here.

But most realistically, I think we are all a bit jealous of Karen. She has a Disney-designed husband and perfectly behaved children. Her husband runs a tech startup and makes millions. It must be nice to have that level of financial freedom.

In this case, I'm excited about Karen's high energy. I hope she can run the practices, and I can hide in the background making the props and costumes. Honestly, having something to create would be great. I haven't had a big art project in a while, something I find myself missing frequently.

I head back to my car, successfully avoiding the PTA moms that are now huddled in the front of the school, engrossed in conversation. I slip into my car and head to the office. My mind goes back to Noah and Marcus's drawing. *Is this going to be the last Christmas Noah will still believe in Santa? Is it time for me to tell the truth?* I decide, perhaps partly out of selfishness, I want him to have one more Christmas where he believes in some of the good parts of the season. Maybe I should try to make this Christmas extra special for him and Susie. If only I had the time and money to do it. If only I had Mason.

CHAPTER 2

# Afternoon of December 6

*"A lovely thing about Christmas is that it's compulsory, like a thunderstorm, and we all go through it together."*

— GARRISON KEILLOR, *LEAVING HOME*

"RACHEL, YOU ARE TAKING NOTES, CORRECT?" Stratford Senior asks.

I flinch, not expecting to be called out by Stratford Senior in the company-wide meeting. My mind was drifting, thinking of miscellaneous things: *Did Noah forget his lunch in the car? Did I lock the door before we left this morning? When am I going to get the rest of the Christmas gifts? What about the Christmas bonus for work? Doesn't that get handed out by now?*

During the first week of December, Stratford Senior will do a 'review' with each employee and give us our Christmas bonus. Typically, the review with Stratford Senior is more of a discussion about his latest golf games. He must be delayed in doing this. I shake those thoughts and try to focus on the meeting.

"Yes, definitely," I respond with fraudulent confidence.

I flip through my yellow legal pad to find a clean page, noticing more doodles and squiggles than actual notes. I know it's a childish habit, but I swear that it helps me think better.

The partners and associates collect around the glass conference table while my fellow paralegals and support staff sit on the stiff, modern couches that line the outside of the room.

Stratford Senior heads the conference table. His legs spread wide as he leans back, arms crossed behind his head. His grey whisks of hair are positioned artfully to hide his crusty scalp. It's rare to see Stratford Senior in the office. He believes business is about relationships, so he must spend his time in "the field," which translates to the country club, the nine-to-five home for the wealthy elite in this town.

His son, Stratford Junior, sits to Stratford Senior's right. His thick, dark hair is slicked back, providing a professional yet 'I'm-wealthier-than-you' vibe. In the decade that I have worked for the Stratford Legal firm, I have yet to see Stratford Junior slouch in a chair or lay his elbows on any table. His name is stamped across the building and on every document that leaves this office. I would have assumed he'd feel more comfortable breaking that shield of sophistication as his father did. It's not like he could ever get fired from the firm.

I observe the collection of austere yet familiar ties adorning my male colleagues' necks. I wonder if they notice my unornamented collar, my isolated femininity in the office, that I share the same button-down shirts, but my neck remains free to exposure while theirs are embellished with gold and swirls.

I cross my legs and feel my pencil skirt inch too far from my knee. I tug it down and feel the seam digging into my stomach. Tonight, when I change into sweatpants, the valley of red across my belly will remain, reminding me of my day at work.

Stratford Senior lifts his legs and rests them on the conference table as he leans back in his chair. "I don't have much time. Let's start with an update on the GM case."

Stratford Junior turns only his head to look at Stratford Senior. "We are in the final weeks of litigation with GM. It's unclear how the judge will rule. Jeff has developed a strong case against our client. And the judge seems swayed by his overall charisma."

Stratford Senior huffs. "I'll have to give Jeff a hard time when I see him . . . or better yet, when is the next time you will see him, Rachel? Give him a hard time for us, won't ya?"

My shoulders curl in as I look up from my notepad. I produce a nervous laugh. It's strange to have my family mentioned at work. In this room. With these people. I guess it's one of the downfalls of being hired by one of my dad's golf buddies. And it's only worse now because of the GM case that my dad is leading.

I wonder what my dad is thinking. About this case. About this law firm. About me. Before I knew how to string words into sentences, my parents were already demanding, "What do you want to do when you're older?" My answer used to be a ballerina, but I was always pressed to find a more realistic goal. Were the ballerinas performing the Nutcracker each year transplanted from another world? Certainly not human. And certainly not a human comparable to me, a simple girl from Novi, Michigan.

I remember sitting on my father's lap. His fingers danced across the keyboard, his voice rehearsing a rhythmic speech that I couldn't understand. I remember saying, "Daddy, I want to do what you do!" For the first time, I found an answer that drew his eyes away from the screen and onto me.

"That would make me very proud," he said.

I know it's embarrassing, but I still wonder, even in my thirties, if I make him proud. What does my dad think of my work? What does he think of the case I built against his own? I'm sure he feels confident that he'll win, but did my arguments at least challenge him? Did I impress him?

Stratford Junior continues to review the GM case when Senior interrupts him. "I just want to be clear. We must win. If it means late nights, so be it. If it means more coffee for the office, just let me know. Anything to win. Understood?" Stratford Senior stares directly at his son.

"Understood," Stratford Junior responds.

"Good. While we are gathered, I want to inform everyone of a possible new client." In unison, our eyes widen, and our postures straighten. The team has worked on the GM case for over a year. We are all ready for something—anything—new. Stratford Senior continues, "The company is called Myopic Therapies, owned by my buddy, Garrett. A hell of a guy! Anyways, his company is being sued because of some patent for extracting microbes from bacteria."

As I write Stratford Senior's words, I question the legality of this patent. I remember reading cases about patenting living DNA. I take a swig of coffee, hoping it'll power me to remember the name of the case.

I finish typing, and Stratford pauses, giving enough time for Brian to assert himself into the conversation. Brian sits on the opposite side of the table, yet I can smell his cinnamon-spiced cologne from here. I wonder if the numerous women he dates ever feel an urge to buy a cinnamon roll after a night of that smell. Just being near him in the office is enough to make me crave anything with sugar and cinnamon. I shake my head, trying to remove my overpowering vision of cinnamon rolls frolicking in my mind, a much more tempting image than having to spend a night with him.

"Interesting case," notes Brian. "We will be up against Molecular Pathology v Myriad Genetics."

Damn. How did Brain just have that on the tip of his tongue? I guess that's why he is the lawyer, and I'm not.

"Exactly," Stratford responds. "They ruled that you cannot patent naturally recurring DNA. We need to dissect that ruling and find a loophole for our client's patent. Brian will take the lead on that. I'll send you what I have so far from Garrett."

"Of course," Brian responds.

I write down Brian's name as the lead for the case, secretly wishing it was mine. Even if I had been able to answer before him, I can't lead the case as a paralegal. I guess it's just the recognition I want. Knowing that I can provide here. The reward for being first and the power that comes with it.

Stratford Senior continues, "That's all for me. I need to leave for an important client meeting at the club." He turns to his son. "Win us the GM case." Next, he turns to Brian. "And good work today, Brian."

Stratford Senior leaves the office, and we all stay to hear how the work will be divided. Junior assigns me five cases to review. When I go to my computer and open the PDFs, I notice it's a total of 500 pages. I pull my body closer to my desk and begin my day of reading. I drag my finger on my trackpad every couple of minutes, making uniformed yellow highlights on each document page as my own thoughts continue to whirl through my mind. *Why did Noah hit Marie with his Nerf bullet? What did I do wrong as a mother?*

## CHAPTER 3

# Evening of December 6

*"I will honour Christmas in my heart, and try to keep it all year. I will live in the Past, the Present, and the Future. The Spirits of all Three shall strive within me. I will not shut out the lessons that they teach."*

— CHARLES DICKENS, *A CHRISTMAS CAROL*

LIKE MOST NIGHTS, I can't fall asleep. My body feels numb, my nose as icy as the peak of a mountain. I roll over and reach my hand to the other side of the bed but am met by the empty, wintry sheets. I squeeze my eyes tighter, forced to remember my reality. I curl my body in closer, trying to create my own warmth. I try to empty my mind, but I can never escape the companion of loneliness at night. I observe the emptiness in this king-size bed that once held two.

I turn to my phone, resting on the nightstand. It's 1 AM. My fingers automatically navigate to my emails. I see the list of emails from work. One was sent an hour ago from Stratford Junior summarizing the role each of us will need to take on the Myopic case.

I continue down the list. The following email's subject line reads Proud MSU Art Program Alumni, Please Donate Now. I swipe left to delete. It's not like that degree did me any good.

Next are random promotions and newsletters that form padding around the occasional email that needs to be opened.

Spanx: You CAN'T miss this deal!!

I start to swipe left to delete, but then I feel a growl from my belly that's sagging onto the bed. Maybe I should check out that deal. I open the link. Even with the discount, these modern-day girdles cost about four times more than I want to pay. How did I even get on this mailing list?

I leave my mailbox and open Instagram. Instead of emails asking for a response and promotions that have little relevance, I'm met with photos of people that I can only half recognize. I never post these days. What would I post? I go to work, pick up the kids, feed them, wash them, and repeat day in and day out.

I scroll past the blurbs of text and focus on the images. Faces that mark my past. It's crazy to think that I shared words, hugs, and experiences with these people at one point. With each image, I see a new life I could have had if I made different choices.

What if I had kept dating Tommy, the star quarterback from high school? It looks like now he is a successful hedge fund manager with a wife that is infinitely more attractive than me. She certainly doesn't need any modern-day girdles, even after giving birth to their five Oshkosh model-ready children. What if I did move to NYC with the rest of the MSU art majors to try to really 'make it'? Would I be living in Skylar's rat-infested four-hundred-square-foot apartment on the outskirts of Williamsburg? Or would I be another star of the program like Bennett with his own art gallery and studio in Brooklyn?

There are also posts that make me question how old I have gotten. I notice the gray hairs in pictures of people I went to high school with and images of my third cousin flaunting her matured feminine features, no longer wearing the cute sparkly bows and princess dresses I remembered her wearing the last time I saw her.

And then there are the posts that parallel past moments in my own life that I wish were mine again. The family Christmas photos with both the mom and dad. The vacations to mountain peaks, new cities, and hot water springs. The husband who plans an elaborate dinner on a random Wednesday night just to show his wife that she is loved.

My finger lifts from my screen at a photo of a husband and wife flipping a coin into the Trevi Fountain in Italy with the caption *Our wish is coming true: we are expecting April 2017!!!* Even for this woman that I can't remember, I'm excited about her news. I double-tap the photo, sending this woman a digital heart to show my happiness for her.

But even when I look through all these alternative lives that could have been mine, there is only one life I wish I could still be living: my life with Mason. I remember my time in Italy, taking that same mandatory tourist photo at Trevi Fountain with Mason. I think of the number of carbs we ate as if preparing for a marathon each day and the gelato we shared on the Spanish Steps. I remember the thrill of having my arms wrapped around Mason's waist with my pregnant belly resisting against his back as we navigated the small cobblestone streets on a Vespa. I now think about how dangerous it was to be on a Vespa, especially pregnant and in a foreign country with different driving habits. At the time, though, I felt safe. I long to be back there with Mason, regardless of how frivolous it was to be taking those risks. With Mason, things always felt right. I can't help wishing he was back in this bed with me.

I swipe out of Instagram and go to my messages. At the top of the list is Rick. I smile and click to message him.

How was your day, babe?

After Mason, I never expected to date again, especially not a client from the office. After our work meetings, we started getting coffee together, then some lunches, and after months, Rick mustered the courage to ask me out for dinner over a year ago.

Almost immediately, I see the three dots. I flip onto my back and set my phone on my stomach as I wait for his response. With the phone screen off, the room becomes dark, a sanctuary from my 'what ifs' that cycle through my mind every time I can't sleep. I can see nothing else in the room. The dresser and mirror across from the bed have vanished from my eyes. The rocking chair next to the artificial tree has disappeared. The once white walls and ceiling seem the opposite now. It's all dark until the phone pings and the screen lights, bringing the truth of the room back into view.

Thanks, babe. Why are you up so late?

Is there ever really a reason to be up this late? As I think of a response, I look around the room. I can now see the sticky notes plastered on my mirror with various reminders for the morning. I notice the overflowing laundry bins that I have been promising to wash for weeks. The pile of books next to the rocking chair I read to Noah and Susie when they can't fall asleep. My reality is illuminated. I turn my phone screen off and roll back to the other side of the bed. I'm met again with the sheets' coldness. My body aches with loneliness. I look back at my phone and finally decide to make a call. I can't be alone tonight with these thoughts.

"Hey, can you come over?" I whisper.

"But it's so late?" I hear in a groggy tone.

"Please . . . I need you."

"What about the kids?"

"We'll figure it out in the morning. I just can't be alone right now."

There is a pause. "Okay . . . I'll be there in ten."

I return my phone to the nightstand. The room becomes dark again. The coldness of the bed grows. He will be here soon.

CHAPTER 4

# Wednesday, December 7, 2016

*"I stopped believing in Santa Claus when I was six. Mother took me to see him in a department store and he asked for my autograph."*

— SHIRLEY TEMPLE

## (18 DAYS UNTIL CHRISTMAS)

"MOMMY!!!! NOAH HIT ME!!" I hear screaming outside my door. "Let me in!!" Susie demands.

Startled, I look at my alarm clock. Shit! I overslept. I roll over and meet the warmth of Rick's body. *OH SHIT! How do I hide him from the kids?* This isn't the way I want my kids to meet Rick.

I violently shake him. "Rick, wake up, wake up!!"

He grumbles. "No good morning?" He rolls over and tries to engulf my body with his strong arms.

Though tempted, I resist. "Get up! The kids can't see you!" That seems to spark his motion. "Quick, just hide in the closet!"

He searches the ground for his clothes. "Are you serious?" he asks.

My neck snaps back towards him as I wrap myself in my robe. "Yes, Rick! I'm serious!"

Unable to get his pants on, he instead collects his items and rushes to the closet. "Thank you," I whisper as I hurry to unlock the door.

"Mommy!! Why couldn't I open the door?" Susie asks.

"Uhhh . . . I'm not sure, sweetie . . . It must have been jammed . . . I'll have to look into that." I notice tears streaming from her eyes. It is only 7 AM. How is she already crying? "So, what did Noah do this morning?" I ask.

"Noah hit me with his Nerf gun!"

Noah runs out of his room. "No, I did not!"

"Yeah, you did!"

"Nat-ah!!"

"Yah-hah!!" Susie insists back.

This could continue back and forth all morning. "Noah, don't hit your sister. This is strike two for you."

"But I—" Noah shouts.

Noah has always been high-energy but not violent. *What has gotten into him that he's resorting to violence? Is it because he doesn't have a father figure? It's been almost four years. Why is it becoming a problem now?* I won't be able to debunk it this morning, so I reply, "Noah, not today. Let's just get ready and go. We are already running late."

"Fine!" He stomps away. I notice Susie smile as she skips to her room.

"I want you both dressed and downstairs in three minutes, okay?" They scurry back to their rooms, and I go into my closet, almost forgetting that Rick is hiding there. "Babe, I'm so sorry," I say.

He wraps his arms around me, untying the rope around my waist. "Maybe one more round before you go?" he says as he kisses my earlobe.

I softly resist and remove a suit from the hangers. "Rick, no. I need to go. Dinner tonight, though?"

He unwraps his arms and lowers his head like a defeated dog. "Okay, fine. Tonight then." I quickly peck his lips and run out to start our days.

---

The legal team is gathered around the conference table. Stratford Senior is busy with clients at the country club, so Stratford Junior starts the meeting. "We need to discuss the closing arguments for the GM case." He reviews the outline for his speech as the associates provide critiques.

"Be sure to mention Dr. Veverka's testimony," Brian mentions.

"Rachel, can you pull that up for me?" Stratford Junior asks.

I frantically search through the papers in front of me but shake my head. "It's at my desk."

Stratford Junior's eyes stay fixed on his legal pad. "Go get it, then."

I jump from my seat and go to the main office area that holds the cubicles for the twenty or so supporting staff members. Small beams of light sneak through the conference room door with me, creating a reflection on the large metal letters spelling out STRATFORD AND STRATFORD LEGAL FIRM at the front of the office. Next to the sign is the front reception desk that has been decorated for Christmas. I notice the Santa figurine that holds a dozen untouched candy canes. The figure seems misplaced. Santa's joyful bellow. The bag of gifts for others. The vibrant red suit with no necktie. This office seems like no place for a man like Santa.

I grab the papers and scamper back in, trying to be as invisible as possible. With one ear, I listen for demands that might be relevant to me, while the other half of my brain thinks about this morning. *What is going on with Noah?*

Minutes into the meeting, my pocket vibrates. I take a peek and see the call is from Noah's school.

I anxiously rise from my chair and mouse out of the conference room.

"Hello," I answer. "This is Ms. Taylor. Is everything okay?"

"Hello, Ms. Taylor. We need you to pick up Noah. He was creating a disturbance in class today."

My eyes widen, and my head jerks back. I turn around to make sure no one can hear my conversation. "What happened?" I ask in a quiet tone.

"Ms. Taylor, your son hit another student in the class."

I shake my head in disbelief. "That can't be possible. My son wouldn't do that." After I say that, I think about this morning with Susie and Noah fighting. That's just typical sibling behavior, right? But that doesn't explain yesterday with Marie. Maybe my son did do this. Maybe he has become too violent. *What did I do to fail him?*

"Ms. Taylor, your son has been dismissed from class, and you need to pick him up."

Immediately, I respond, "Okay, I'm on my way."

I go back to the conference room to grab my laptop and notepad, hoping no one will notice my entrance and then sudden exit. I don't want to explain this to any of them. They wouldn't understand.

"Where are you going, Rachel?" Stratford Junior asks. I guess I can't go unnoticed.

"Uhhh . . . It's my son . . . I need to get him from school right now."

"But what about this meeting?" he asks.

"I'll send you my notes when I get back home. Stratford, I'm so sorry." I grab my things and rush out the door. I know Stratford Junior disapproves of my decision. But I have no choice. My son needs me.

---

When I get to the school's office, the secretary greets me. Her desk must be from when the school started in the 1950s. Based on her deep wrinkles and puffed-up white hair, like a poodle resting on her head, she might also be the same secretary. A crucifix hangs behind the desk and an inscription saying, "*God, grant me the serenity to accept the things I cannot change, the courage to change the things I can, and the wisdom to know the difference.*" I certainly need God to help me with all three of those things today.

Noah is sitting on a plastic chair. His legs are lifted onto the seat, pulled close to his chest. "Are you okay, Noah?" I ask.

Noah doesn't respond. He gets up, his head hangs low, with his eyes fixed on the floor. "I want to go home, Mommy."

Typically, I would push back, but I have never heard this pain in his voice. I have a million questions whirling through my mind to ask Noah. I decide to hold back. Instead, I say, "Okay, honey. Let's go home." I reach for his hand, and he willingly takes hold.

I turn to the secretary and ask, "Did Mrs. Bushnell provide any context on what happened?"

The secretary nods. "As I said on the phone, Noah became violent—"

Noah interrupts, "That's not true! I—"

I turn to Noah, "I know, baby. We can talk about it at home, okay?"

The secretary's eyes dart between Noah and me. "What I was going to say is that Mrs. Bushnell will be calling you later this afternoon to review what happened and discuss the best disciplinary action moving forward."

The car ride home is silent. Noah stares out the window, and I ruminate on what has made Noah violent. When we get home, Noah immediately runs up to his room. I follow close behind. Noah curls himself into a tight ball on his bed.

"Noah, can you tell me what happened today?" I ask.

He pulls his legs closer to his chest. "I don't want to."

I sit on the edge of his bed and put my arm around him. "I know it's hard, but I need to know what happened so that I can help you."

"It wasn't even my fault! It was all Gus."

Gus always seems to be the main villain in most of Noah's stories. Ironically, he's the son of Marie, the PTA president. Perhaps that's why parents join PTA—to ensure their children don't get kicked out. Maybe it is time for me to join if Noah keeps acting out.

"Okay. Can you tell me what Gus did?"

"No."

"Noah." I maneuver myself to get a view of his face. I see a small tear on his cheek. I wiggle my hand onto his face that's protected by his knees and wipe it away. "It's okay, Noah. You can tell me anything. I'll always love you. You know that, right?"

"Yeah, I know," he whispers.

"Can you sit up so I can see your face?"

Delicately, he unwraps his arms from his legs and adjusts himself so that his back is against the headboard. "I just can't take it when they are mean to Marcus," he says.

"What did they say to Marcus?" I ask. I try to have soft eyes to let him know he can trust me.

"We had to talk about our favorite Christmas tradition in class today, and Marcus talked about making cookies on Christmas Eve and how they pick the best cookie and leave it for Santa with some almond milk cause they figure Santa needs a break from all the dairy."

I know they leave almond milk because Marcus's mom has a severe lactose problem. If they put out whole milk, her frequent gas the next morning while opening presents might give away that she is the real Santa. But there is no reason for Noah to know this fact quite yet, so I continue to nod as Noah tells his story.

"And before Marcus even finished his story, Gus got up and called Marcus a loser for still believing in Santa Claus. And I stood up and told Gus to stop it. And then he called me a loser for being friends with the poor kid in class, and he just kept laughing at Marcus, and I don't know, I just got really mad, and I pushed him. I know I shouldn't have, but I just wanted him to stop. And . . . "

As Noah continues to ramble about what happened, I attempt to keep track of my questions and concerns as they arise. *Did Gus get sent home too? Why didn't Mrs. Bushnell step in sooner? Is Marcus okay? And why would Noah think it makes sense to push him?* Noah can have problems focusing in class, but he never hurts other people. Why would Noah do that?

I also feel conflicted. Should I tell Noah the truth about Santa? Not only would I take away the magic of Christmas, but I would also take a part of Noah's memories of his father. Mason always made Christmas special for him. Taking Santa from Noah feels like taking away a piece of Mason that he still holds deeply. Plus, Noah is still young, and most kids his age still believe. Except for, of course, Gus, who had to ruin it for all the other kids. I decide it's the wrong time to tell Noah the truth about Santa, especially in this heated moment.

Instead, I interject, asking, "Honey, but why would you push Gus? You know that you should never resort to violence."

"I don't know. I'm just sick of Marcus getting picked on in school. He is my best friend, and he was crying, and the kids were pointing and laughing at him, and I needed to do something to get Gus to stop, and words weren't working, so I guess I tried to push him to get him to stop."

"Noah, I'm proud that you wanted to stand up for your friend but hurting someone is never the right way to do that. You could have gotten really hurt, too, if Gus hit back. You never want to put yourself in harm's way."

"But that's what Daddy did," Noah responds.

My lungs seem to lock, and the air stops flowing. Noah is right. Mason was known to put himself in dangerous situations to help others. He always found a way to be a hero, but that braveness is also why he is no longer with us.

I think back to January 6, 2013. I was home with the kids. Noah was on the floor playing with the latest Nerf gun that he got for Christmas. Susie was falling asleep on my lap as I watched a Christmas movie that was still playing on TV. I remember thinking that I would force Mason to watch the rest of it with me when he got home as punishment for being gone for so long.

I was nervous that something terrible might have happened to Mason, but I attempted to rationalize my fears. I told myself there was nothing wrong. He was supposed to pick up my prescription and head home. He probably just ran into someone he knew while at the store. Mason always seemed to know someone when we went out together, so why would today be different? If anything, since I wasn't there, he would stop longer to talk to the person.

We all jumped when we heard an unexpected aggressive knock on the door. Noah looked to me to see what he should do. I smiled, letting him know it was okay. It was probably just a late-night delivery. I lifted Susie into my arms and approached the door. I cracked it open, looking down to see what package we got. Instead, I found two pairs of dark combat-like boots. My eyes moved up. I noticed the badges attached to their light brown uniforms.

My knees became weak. I wanted to collapse, but I couldn't. I needed to protect Susie. I felt transported to a scene in a movie where you cry for the main character knowing that such a day would be unlivable. But I was forced to live in that unlivable scene. My anxiety had always convinced me of the worst outcomes in every scenario. I had spent years training myself to stop those negative thoughts and accept that the worst case will never happen. But that day, the worst did happen. My anxiety was right. My husband was late to return home because he was dead.

To the uniformed men, I quietly said, "Give me a minute," and closed the door.

"Who is it?" Noah asked.

How could I respond? *It's two men in uniform that are about to announce a truth that will take us a lifetime to understand.* I decided to lie. I wasn't ready for them to know their father wouldn't be coming home tonight. That he would not be there to read their nightly bedtime story. And that, for the rest of their lives, their father wouldn't be there for any of the small or large events that defined their lives. That this moment would mark them forever.

"Oh, it's just a friend. Let me take you both upstairs to bed. It's past your bedtime anyway." I carried Susie up, and Noah followed close behind.

After putting them to bed, I returned to the door and stepped outside with the two officers. They quickly verified my suspicion: Mason was found dead. Immediately, I regretted allowing Mason to get on his motorcycle. It was the damn bike that killed him, I thought. The officers said that he was found eastbound on route 164, heading home from the grocery store. Eyewitnesses reported a young girl whose car was broken down on the side of the road. Steam was fuming from her engine. They said she was standing next to the car in tears. Mason reportedly pulled to the side of the road to help. I remember thinking that sounds like Mason.

The officers explained that Mason was leaning over the front of the car, examining the engine when the accident happened. The woman was inside, trying to start the engine, when another vehicle hit a patch of ice. Spinning viciously, the car slammed into the side of the railing and skidded right over the car, pinning Mason between the vehicle and the guardrail. Emergency vehicles were on the scene immediately and rushed him to the hospital but, unfortunately, nothing could be done. Mason was gone. Both other victims were also taken to the hospital. I never figured out what happened to them. I always wondered if the girl survived, but I was lost afterward. I never found the time to track her down.

Noah is right. Mason put himself in harm's way to help another person, and that decision led to his death. Perhaps that's the reason I don't want Noah to do the same. My response sticks in my throat. "Yes, honey, you are right. Your daddy did have a way of being a helper. And it sounds like you did that for Marcus by standing up for him. But you know your daddy would never become violent to defend someone."

"I know." Noah pauses and looks down. "I don't want to go back to school tomorrow."

"Why?" I ask as I wrap him closer to me.

"Gus is going to make fun of my Christmas tradition."

"What do you plan to present?"

"Well, we don't really have any traditions anymore, but Mrs. Bushnell said I could talk about a tradition with Daddy."

My heart seems to stop with Noah's words. Sure, I don't go to the extent that Mason went to make Christmas special, but I still try to do the basics. "Why do you feel that we don't have any Christmas traditions anymore?"

"It's just since Daddy died, we don't do the same stuff."

Noah is right. We don't do the same things. Is it because I don't feel like I have time, or is it just too painful to do them without him? Maybe this is the year I try to put in the same effort Mason always did. Mason would want that for the kids. "I'm sorry, Noah. I should have been better and kept the traditions alive. What have you missed the most that we used to do with Dad?"

He looks back into his lap as if ashamed of these feelings. "I don't know, like getting the tree and stuff, I guess."

"Hey, look at me, Noah." I pull his chin up and look into his eyes. "You can always tell me about these things or let me know when you are missing Daddy. You know that, right?" Maybe Noah has been acting out simply because he misses Mason.

He looks directly at me. "I miss Daddy . . . I miss him a lot."

I lean in and embrace Noah. Behind him, I squeeze my eyes shut, locking away tears I want to shed because of his pain. I wish I could better protect my son. That I could go with him everywhere in the world as his shield. That I could take his pain for him. I pull back and look straight into Noah's blue eyes, the same shade as Mason's eyes. "I miss him too."

I place my hands on his shoulders. "What do you think about us bringing back some of those traditions for this Christmas?"

Noah's face lights up in a way that I haven't seen since Mason's death. "Really?"

"Yeah, how about we go back to the Christmas tree farm this year? And we can put up Christmas lights on the house? And we can go to the mall, and you can pick out all the gifts you want for people? Would you like that?"

Noah's smile widens. He gets up and starts to bounce around the room. "Yes! Yes! Yes!"

I stand up as well, feeling relieved to see him smiling again. "Now, just because you got out of school today, you still need to be ready to go back tomorrow."

"Do I have to?" he whines.

"Yes, mister! And I need to get back to work as well, so why don't you start some of your homework?" We head downstairs, and both sit at the kitchen table. Crumbs from this morning's quick breakfast still linger on the wooden table. I eye my coffee maker next to the browning bananas, and I debate if I will need a coffee to keep my mind focused on my work rather than my whirling concerns about Noah. *Is he acting out because we are getting closer to Mason's favorite holiday? Is it because Noah doesn't have enough male role models? What am I doing wrong?*

I rub my hand across the table's finishing, finding it strange to be in the same house that I had bought with Mason. Though I have changed some decorations, his presence can still be sensed in small details throughout the home. For instance, this table. I place my hand on the inner side of the leg nearest me. I can feel his misplaced router holes recalling his promise that building our furniture will be cheaper than buying new, or even used, items. We quickly learned while it might be more affordable, it was a lot harder than either of us bargained for.

I look at Noah, his feet swinging from the chair. He grips his golden number two pencil and writes his name on the top of his problem sheet. He cocks his head as he processes each math problem. I wish Mason was here. He would know what to do. He would make our Christmas magical regardless of money or issues at school. Plus, this is probably the last year Noah will still believe in Santa. Mason would want it to be remarkable. I decide this is my last chance to give Noah the Christmas Mason would want for him. I know I need to go all out. I need to do everything in my power for Noah and Susie to feel the magic of the season that Mason effortlessly created each year. I think back to the last Christmas we had with Mason.

## — 2012 —

"Okay, gang! Who is ready for the official Taylor Christmas tree hunt?" Mason announces like a bellowing Santa himself.

Mason is dressed like a lumberjack with the same red hat as Santa, further complemented by the scraggly beard he refuses to shave. His right arm hangs free after months in a cast. I notice, though, as he lifts the saw and the bundle of cords into the car, he seems to rely mostly on his left hand. I assume his right arm is still in pain, but he wouldn't dare complain about it today of all days.

In the car, Mason leads the group in Christmas carols. Susie and Noah happily shout along even though they don't know the words. I look over at him. How did I get so lucky to find this man? I stare at him as he confidently sings "All I Want for Christmas Is You," giving Mariah Carey a challenge even on the highest of notes.

And how true those lyrics are. I reach to squeeze his leg. He turns his head just for a second to look at me. That one second fills my heart with love. No touch. No words. Just one look speaks more than a sonnet and feels as deep as a compassionate kiss. One quick look, and then his eyes are back on the road, but that's all I needed. Just his presence. His gaze. His comfort.

When we get to the barn, we head straight to the hot chocolate. We ignore the kids performing on the main stage and Santa handing out candy canes in the crowd. The hot chocolate was the top priority.

Before taking a sip, Mason wraps his hands around the mug, closes his eyes, breathes deeply, and smiles. "Do you smell that, Noah?"

"Smell what?" Noah jumps up to try to get closer to Mason's cup, causing his hot chocolate to splash on his mittens. They are both unfazed.

"Hold your mug right under your nose, then close your eyes and breathe in deeply."

Noah follows along. "It smells like chocolate."

"Awh, not just chocolate, though. Magical Christmas Chocolate!"

"Really?!" Noah starts to chug his cup.

"Not too fast, Son," Mason says while trying to get Noah to lower the cup so he doesn't burn his mouth. "You will want to savor that magic!"

Noah adjusts the cup's angle, so a small amount enters his mouth. "Dad! I taste it! This is the best hot chocolate ever!"

Mason smiles and nods in affirmation to Noah. Mason looks at all of us. "I think it's time to find our tree."

Both Noah and Susie roar with excitement, and I smile with pride. We exit the barn, and I look at the pre-cut trees leaning against it. "Some of these look nice," I say, hoping to save Mason the hassle of getting on the snowy ground and manually cutting a tree with our dulled saw.

"We can't get one of those! Half the fun is getting to cut the tree!" Noah demands.

"I have to agree with Noah on this one," Mason says. He looks to me to ensure I agree before we continue. I nod. I would do anything to keep my family happy.

"Let's head this way then," I say. We navigate the field and reach the far back that has tall pine trees.

"Do you like any of these, Noah?" I ask.

Noah, hand in hand with Mason, looks up to his dad for the answer. Mason shakes his head. "Not yet, Mom. Let's keep going."

We continue past the pines to an open field. No longer is the ground embossed with the steps of the families before us who are also searching for their tree. We continue past the open area to a part of the farm that no longer looks labeled for sales. Mason and Noah's steps are synced as I closely follow behind with Susie in her stroller.

Suddenly Mason stops. "Over there! I think our tree might be over there!"

"Where, Daddy? Is it that one?!" His finger, wrapped in a mitten, lifts to point to a tree in the distance.

"Yes, Noah! That's the tree!" We dash over until Noah stops in front of one tree, a beauty standing nine feet high and five feet wide. "Oh, man! This is it! This is the family tree right here!" Mason announces.

Noah's eyes are glimmering. "Sure is! I love it!"

"Isn't it a little big, sweetheart?" I ask.

He takes another look. "Sure, we can get it to fit, though."

"Are you sure? How are we going to get it into the house?"

His eyes radiate with charm. "Believe in the magic of Christmas, Rachel!"

I smile and say, "I believe in you." And I do believe. I believe in Mason, in the life we are building. I believe we can conquer anything together, even a tree too big for our living room.

Mason leans towards me, resting his lips on my forehead. I lift Susie into my arms, and Noah comes to hold our legs. Intertwined as a family, we simply stare at the tree in front of us. "It really is the perfect tree," I say.

CHAPTER 5

# Evening of December 7

*"I once bought my kids a set of batteries for Christmas with a note on it saying, toys not included."*

— BERNARD MANNING

THAT NIGHT, I agree to meet Rick for dinner. When I arrive at his house, he embraces me tightly and says, "Hello, beautiful!" Rick's stocky build is covered by a wool button-down and a puffy vest, a nice contrast from the suits he wears at work. He looks like the man on Brawny paper towels; both are strong, reliable men in my life. I burrow my face into his shoulder, cushioned perfectly by the vest. I feel like crap, but I didn't think it was fair to cancel on Rick last minute, especially after forcing him into my closet this morning to avoid introducing him to the kids.

Rick kisses me on the top of my head. "Everything okay?" he asks.

"Just a long day." I pull my face back and look into his eyes. I know I am feeling stressed about Noah and how to make this Christmas special, but I feel no need to talk to Rick about it.

"I have something for you," he announces as he grabs a fresh bouquet on the entrance table. For this man, there is no limit to the number of flowers to buy a woman.

"Oh, thank you, Rick." I grab the flowers, unsure where I should put them. With my other free hand, I reach for his. "So, what do we have planned for tonight?" I ask.

"What do you think about Italian tonight?"

"You thinking Luigi's on Maple?"

"I was thinking Olive Garden? Is that okay?"

I smile. "Sounds great."

In the past, I suggested that Rick and I go on an international trip, perhaps Europe, to start. I still follow all the discount travel blogs I used with Mason and see deals come and go every week. Rick, though, prefers the local comforts here in Michigan. He believes that all the luxuries of the world can be found right here in Novi. For instance, why spend thousands of dollars to go to Italy when we can drive ten minutes to the Olive Garden? So tonight, we are testing this claim. Does Olive Garden provide all the same quality of food and luxury as Italy? I already know the answer is no, but I still love Rick's idea, and it's nice to follow someone else's lead for once.

When we arrive at the Olive Garden, Rick gets out of the car and runs to the other side to open my door, a true gentleman.

Spiral-cut pine bushes line the restaurant entrance and lead us to the double oak doors. To the right is an authentic Italian garden with a bench. For now, though, the plants are dead, the stone water fountain is off, and the birds have migrated to a warmer home. It has all the charm of Tuscany, only if you have never been to Tuscany.

We sit down at our table. I lovingly embrace his bicep and jokingly say, "It already feels like Tuscany with this beautiful booth and a tablet to take our order."

He smiles. "Well, perhaps you just went before tablets got big in Italy. There could be tablets at every restaurant now in Tuscany."

"I guess we will need to go to verify if that's true." I wink at him as he leans in for a kiss. We reach for each other's hands and peruse the menu on the tablet. We debate if we should split a traditional spaghetti and meatballs dish. We could share a single noodle until our lips meet like *Lady and the Tramp*. Or should we be more adventurous and get the shrimp carbonara pasta? We settle on splitting the iconic "Tour of Italy" dish to taste the various Italian cuisines that Olive Garden offers.

Rick starts the conversation. "So last night was fun. Definitely unexpected."

I feel awkward addressing last night, but I know we should. "I don't know what got into me last night. And this morning! I'm so sorry about having you hide in the closet."

"I understand." He pauses and grabs both my hands. "But Rachel, it's been over a year. I think it might be time for me to meet your kids? What do you think?"

I look away. I know he's right, but Noah and Susie have never seen me with another man except for their father. I don't want to hurt them. And what if they end up loving Rick and it doesn't work out between us, or what if they hate him? Or what if Rick doesn't like them? He decided not to have kids in his first marriage. He says he is open to kids, but what if he meets them and decides it's not for him? Perhaps I have been hiding my kids from him because I am afraid that could be the end for us.

But then I think about Noah's outbreak today at school and him hitting Marie with a Nerf bullet. I think about the conversation we had about Mason. Maybe Rick is that father figure Noah is missing?

"Come on, Rachel," he continues, "I don't know how many more times I'll want to hide in the closet. I think it's time."

My eyes turn down to my hands resting on my lap. My ring finger is empty. The tan marks of my wedding band have vanished. I look at my watch, which ensures my timeliness. I twist it so the face is centered on my wrist. I look towards Rick. "You're right . . . let's start small, though."

"Small is good with me. Maybe this weekend?" he says as he squeezes my hands.

I search the room as if the answer will appear within the frescoes painted on the walls. I breathe in. I know it's time. "What about Saturday? We were planning to write letters to Santa. Would you like to join?"

"That sounds great. What do I need to know beforehand?"

I give him the rundown on Susie and Noah, their quirks and triggers. Soon, though, the conversation dies out about the kids. We both sip from the straws in our plastic cups as our eyes wander around the room. I study the other couples in the restaurant. Some are engaged in conversation, and others are on their phones. At least we aren't that bad.

"Anyways, I wanted to ask you about the stuff in your closet."

I grimace. "Oh God, I feel so bad about that! I'm sorry!"

"Yes, I'm not a fan either, but soon that won't be a problem. I did want to ask about something I found though—"

My cheeks start to blush as I cut him off. "I know I need to get rid of Mason's stuff."

"Not that . . . I actually didn't notice that. I was just going to ask if you want me to hang up the paintings you have in there?"

My cheeks turn an even deeper shade of red. I almost forgot about those being hidden in there. "Oh, those? Did you look at them?"

"No, they were all flipped to face the wall. Do you need me to hang them up?"

I feel some relief that he didn't look. "Uh . . . I think I'm good, but I'll let you know."

“Where did you get all of them?”

I feel my face heating up. I don’t want him to know about my past. “I . . . I just collected them.”

Our food arrives, and we return to our typical friendly banter. When that runs out, we comfortably sit in silence, with an occasional acknowledgment of how good the food is. While I smile and nod, my brain reminds me of the sensations I had in Italy. The delicate creaminess of the gelato melting onto my tongue, the rough edges of the al-dente pasta hand-rolled by the store owner’s grandmother, and the wine that sprouted flowering orchards in my body. I can’t help thinking about my time in Italy. The time I spent with Mason.

---

When I return home, I find my mom curled up on the couch with a worn paperback book. Her glasses are perched on her nose, and her body is covered in at least five blankets like a reptile forced into the cold Michigan winters. And I’m sure even the several inches of polyester and cotton covering her isn’t enough to keep her warm.

Her head pops up from the book. “So, how’d it go, sweetheart?” Even after an evening with the kids, her 1950s-esque bob—the one hairstyle she learned from her own mother that she has never dared to change—is still perfectly voluminous and quaffed.

“It was good.” I pause. “Yeah, it was nice just to get away.”

"Rick is such a good man." My mother has always liked Rick. Rick's parents and my parents happen to be close friends since they are members of the same country club. After Rick's divorce, my parents kept pestering me to join them at the country club, but I refused to go. It felt strange to be set up by my parents. Rick started coming to the Stratfords for some patent needs. I tried to resist, but he was kind to me. For my mom, I think she felt that Rick could provide me stability, something she thought I never had with Mason. Rick is strong. Reliable. Simple. All qualities my mother finds essential in a man. While she has never said it, I know she approves of Rick more than she ever did of Mason.

I take off my coat and place it with my bag on the entrance hooks. "Thanks for watching the kids, too. Any problem getting them to bed?"

"Noah was a bit lively, but we managed. Susie, of course, was on her best behavior." Her attention returns to the book. She doesn't budge from the couch as if I'm walking into her home.

I sit on the end of the couch next to her. "What book are you reading?"

"Oh, just another mystery novel. The author is coming out with a sequel next month, so I'm rereading the series."

That sounds like my mom. Since I can remember, I have always seen a mystery novel in her hand or close by in her purse. I have offered to buy her an e-reader, but she wouldn't dare cheat on her paperbacks like that.

"Sounds fun! Thanks again for helping tonight. I'm pretty exhausted from the day, though, so I think I'm going to head to bed."

"Is it okay if I just stay for a little bit longer? I want to get through this chapter before I leave."

"No problem." I head upstairs and go into my room, dark and silent. I mindlessly begin my nightly ritual. Ripping off the cage around my breasts and the suffocating skirt around my waist, I wrap myself in a decadently soft robe. I go into the bathroom and remove my makeup, the shield that blocks others from seeing my sagging eyes and wrinkling skin.

With the lights on, I see the laundry bin overflowing, the scattered clothes on the floor, and the closet door that's slightly creaked open, revealing some of the canvases on the floor. I turn off the light and burrow into my king-size bed. I try to sleep, but I'm worried about my mother downstairs. *When will she leave? Will she remember to lock the front door?* I stare into the darkness and wait to hear the distinctive hum of her Audi SUV. After it pulls away, I wait a few more minutes, then turn on the lights to head downstairs. First, I go to the front door and give a firm tug. My mom did lock the door. I shouldn't have been so worried. I turn to go back to bed but notice my purse, a reminder of all I need to do still. I grab the bag and go to the kitchen, turning all the lights on.

I decide to make a game plan on how I can afford the most magical Christmas. I know I need to keep a tight budget. Don't get me wrong, I love the gingerbread boys and cinnamon spice lattes of the season, but it seems each year the Christmas customs get more expensive. I start by writing down the list of expenses.

1. *Santa's gifts for Susie and Noah ~ 300*
2. *Gifts for Mason's parents, my parents, my aunt, Mason's cousins ~ 250*
3. *Gifts for the school teachers and office workers ~ 100*
4. *Donations ~ 200*
5. *Cake for the big family party ~ 150*
6. *Meals for Christmas Eve and Day ~ 100*
7. *Christmas tree, decor, wrapping paper ~ 100*
8. *Christmas cards ~ 100*
9. *Misc ~ 200*

I try to provide a generous estimate of what I would spend for each item, which comes out to about $1500. Where does someone just find this money lying around? Mason was always in charge of budgeting, and I have done a lousy job since then. Plus, we're still recovering from the unexpected cost of Mason's death and funeral. Since he didn't have life insurance, we accrued quite a financial blow that I'm too embarrassed to tell my parents about. They always demanded he get life insurance, and, at some point, I just lied and said he did. Now we are paying that cost.

Luckily, I have the yearly Christmas bonus from work that should cover the expenses. Usually, it would have hit my account by now, but it hasn't, so I just need to muster up the courage and ask Stratford Senior about it. I take a breath and remind myself it could be worse. We don't need to fly or get hotels during the holidays, and my mom is hosting the larger family Christmas party.

The reality is that I don't want to make sacrifices for Christmas. I want to go all out. If a neighborhood kid comes to my house selling ten-dollar rolls of gimmicky-looking wrapping paper, I am ready to buy it. If a random person wants to give me details about every family member flying in for Christmas, I am all ears. If I need to buy a damn gift for a giving tree, I am ready to make the purchase. I want everything to be perfect for Susie and Noah. I want them to pick out a live tree and run through the white aisles of Target to get gifts for their teachers and friends. I want them to have every damn detail of the holidays without worrying about the cost. I will find a way.

CHAPTER 6

# Saturday, December 10, 2016

*"The smells of Christmas are the smells of childhood"*

— RICHARD PAUL EVANS, *THE CHRISTMAS BOX*

## (15 DAYS UNTIL CHRISTMAS)

BEFORE THE KIDS ARE AWAKE, I lay out two dozen new boxes of LED Christmas lights that I purchased on my way home last night. It's still dark outside, but I want to string the lights before Noah and Susie wake up, so I can surprise them and the whole street. No one will be thinking of me as the neighborhood Grinch this year with the number of lights I bought.

I start stringing the lights at the top of the house. I put in my headphones and walk up the ladder leaning against the house. The old hooks Mason used have rusted, so every couple of feet, I add a clip and weave the lights onto it. I start to get into a groove when I feel a sharp pain in my back. *Did a small bird just run into me?*

I grip my hands on the ladder and twist my back to look down for any evidence of a bird. "Noah?"

He's still in his pajamas and doesn't have a jacket or shoes on. His bare hands are gripped on what seems to be his largest Nerf gun. "Get out of here!" He yells.

"Noah, it's me," I shout down.

"Mom?" He hesitantly lowers his Nerf gun to his side. "Why are you on a ladder?"

I notice his shaking hands. His face is wet with tears. I climb down the ladder and embrace him. "I was trying to surprise you with Christmas lights. What are you doing?"

"I thought . . . " He barrels his face into my chest. "I thought you were an intruder. I heard someone outside, and I couldn't find you in your room, so I decided I needed to protect Susie."

His face is consumed with worry. I pull him in closer. My plan to bring him and Susie a joyous surprise backfired and instead made him scared. I'm not off to a great start with making this the best Christmas ever. "Come on, let's go back inside, Noah. Everything is okay."

---

Later that morning, my mom arrives to go Christmas tree shopping. Now, my mother would say Christmas starts during the first week of Advent, like most good Catholics. For other families, it begins with the irresistible Black Friday deals. Stores declare Christmas can start as early as October as they continue to sell Halloween decorations, and radio stations seem to limit themselves to November first. For Mason, Christmas officially began when we picked out our Christmas tree. Since Mason and I were both kids, we had gone to the only tree farm in Novi, Michigan, Mathess Tree Farm. Once we figured out Mathess farm was a key part of both of our childhoods, we combined that into our own family tradition.

When my mom comes in, I ask, "Where is Dad? I thought he was coming today?"

"He needed to finish up some loose ends for the GM case, so he can't come today."

Did our latest additions to the case become a threat for him? His absence from these events is also typical, so perhaps he was just looking for an excuse.

We pack the kids in my mother's SUV. I just hope I can do better with this activity, especially since this is what Noah specifically asked for. It needs to be perfect.

Once we arrive, we enter the main barn and are greeted with every detail of the season. A blend of tree sap and hot chocolate meets my nose at the entrance. In the right corner of the barn is a long line of families waiting to take a picture with Santa, better known to the parents as Mr. Mathess, the farm owner. To the left of the open space is a slightly raised stage with rows of benches for the audience. A group of young ballerinas performs while the audience snaps pictures and sips on warm beverages. The Christmas lights, strung carefully through the rafters to avoid the bird's nest still there from the spring, illuminate the whole barn. For the last thirty years, everything has been the same. My senses indulge in the buffet of Christmas nostalgia.

"Do you remember dancing up there, honey?" my mom asks as she squeezes my arm. "I remember how cute you were in those little outfits."

I simply respond, "Yep." Instead, I think about when she made me stop ballet after my grades started slipping. God forbid a third-grader might get a B in their history class. Perhaps childish, but it's something I still resent my mother for.

We make our way to the hot chocolate and coffee, and we each get a cup. After one sip, my mom says, "Wow, somehow this gets worse each year! It can't be that hard to make a decent cup of hot chocolate."

"Yeah, I don't like it either," Noah responds with a soured face. He pushes the cup towards me. "I don't want it."

"That's strange," I respond, "You used to love it. In fact, you would demand we start with the hot chocolate every time."

"I don't like it anymore!"

"You know, your father's favorite part of this farm used to be this hot chocolate."

"Really? Why?"

"Here, take one more sip, and as you do, keep your eyes open. Look at the lights strung throughout the barn. Notice how the smells of the trees blend with the chocolate. Your daddy always said that makes it taste even better."

Susie and Noah follow my instructions, and Noah says, "It tastes the same."

I can't explain it like Mason. Perhaps it was his enthusiasm that made us fall in love with this simple hot chocolate. Why can't I replicate that energy for our kids? Instead, I try to find another reason why Susie and Noah should drink it. "Well, let's not waste it, okay?"

"Fine," he says.

We head outside, and my attention shifts to the infamous Douglas fir section placed strategically in front of the barn. Douglas firs are truly pristine with their short and tight bristles that never leave a mess and their strong fragrant smell that will diffuse through both floors of a home. This luxury tree comes at a high price, so I need to distract Noah and Susie from this area. Farther back are the less expensive and higher maintenance white pine trees. I'll need to lead the group there.

"Okay, kids," I say. "Why don't we start from the back and work forward because if we get a tree far away, then we can use the farm tractor to get back to the barn. How does that sound?"

"Race you there!" Noah shouts as he begins his sprint to the back of the farm.

"Noah! Be careful!" I shout as I jog in his direction. I look back at my mom. She seems unphased as she pushes Susie's stroller.

I follow Noah's direction, passing multiple families searching for their perfect tree, the family centerpiece for the holidays. I see a young couple strolling side by side. Her one hand embraces his, the other on her pregnant belly. I notice dads with their children. One has his daughter on his shoulders, allowing her to look across the entire field. Another man is lying on the ground, moving the saw back and forth at the tree's base. His family is surrounding him, waiting to announce "Timber!" Each group forms a complete family.

From a distance, I hear Noah shout, "Mom, I found the tree!"

My attention focuses on Noah. He seems to be right on the border of the Douglas firs and the pines. I just hope he picked a pine. I doubt I have gotten that lucky, though.

"It's lovely, honey," I say. The tree is twice the size of Noah. It's perfectly round and full, with no visibility to the trunk. Each branch is long and sturdy, making them suitable for heavy ornaments. Noah is right. The tree is perfect.

I bob my head around, trying to find the price tag. Of course, they put it inside the tree, forcing you to really work to get the price. I collapse my fingers together and strategically navigate around the branches to the price tag. Even through my gloves, I feel the needles prodding me, questioning me if it's even worth finding the label. When my fingers reach the tag, I flip it over to reveal the price, *$130*. My eyes widen. How can a tree that will be dead in a month be so expensive?

I keep my face hidden in the tree as I try to deliberate. I want to give Noah and Susie the perfect Christmas, but this tree is a lot more than I budgeted for. I remind myself that this might be the last Christmas Noah will still believe in Santa. But there must be another tree for half the price that will bring Noah and Susie just as much joy. Wouldn't they want that extra money spent on gifts anyway? I look down at the snow and respond. "Yeah, it's nice, but what about those trees over there?" I try to sound enthusiastic. "Maybe we should look in that area before we decide?"

Noah's face transforms. His eyes widen, and his lips pout. I know this face too well. I know how to say no to his seemingly irresistible bright blue eyes.

I hear my mother coming from behind with Susie. "I have to side with Noah," she says. "This tree is perfect."

My eyes dart between Noah and my mom. I know I said I want to go 'all-in' for Christmas, but this is legit 'all-in.' I didn't realize how expensive these customs have become over the last four years. I feel this need to defend my opinion. "Yes, it's perfect, but it's also expensive," I say calmly.

My mother responds, "Well, I think you should get it anyway."

Why does she need to go against everything I say? I step over to my mom and whisper, "Mother, you're supposed to be on my side."

She whispers back, "Don't you think your son *deserves* this tree?"

Of course, he deserves this tree, but there must be some compromise. Part of me wants to buy it, but, on principle, I want to stand up to my mother, who constantly pushes her agenda regardless of my own thoughts. I look at her with stern eyes and say quietly. "It's too expensive, Mom."

"Then let me buy it."

I hold my eyes back from rolling. What a typical move for her. She just throws money at any problem. "I'm trying to teach my son a lesson right now on the value of a dollar."

"Well, I want to buy it, so I will. End of discussion."

I lightly tug on my mom's coat, trying to make some distance from the kids. "Mom, I don't want to get into this right now. I want to get a more affordable tree, and I need you to respect that."

"Don't you think your children have been through enough? Rachel, it's your obligation as their mother to provide them with the most magical Christmas possible, and I see you are finally willing to do that for them."

My head jerks back in shock. "What do you mean?"

She tilts her head and looks at me. "Honey, you must realize that you have . . . slipped a bit since . . . you know . . . But I'm glad you are getting back into the holiday season. Really, I think it's great! I just want to support you on that!"

I shake my head, trying to remove my frustration for what my mother is implying. "Mom, I just want to spend less on the tree, okay? I'm sure there is another tree that will bring them the same amount of joy for less."

She leans closer to me. "Are you having money problems? Are the Stratfords not paying you enough? You know Daddy still goes golfing with Stratford Senior. He can get you a raise. I want to buy this tree, so you don't need to worry about this. Consider this my Christmas gift for you."

I know she will still buy me something for Christmas regardless of this tree. But I also know she'll just keep pushing regardless of what I say. I definitely don't want my father to intervene and try to save me as if I'm some damsel in distress. But at the end of the day, getting this tree will bring joy to Noah and Susie, which is what this is all about. I need to just accept my mom's generosity and move forward. "No, Mom, it's fine. I'm fine. Let's get the tree and head home."

"Well, no need to be a little sour grape, right kids!" she bellows, bringing Noah and Susie back into the conversation. "It's Christmas! It's the season of joy!"

When we return home, I instinctively go to get the vacuum to clean up the tree's-worth of bristles that will fall on the ground. But, as promised with the expensive Douglas firs, the carpet remains clean, and the fresh scent of pine permeates the room. I sit on the couch with my mom. Our bodies turn towards the bay window where the tree is placed. Next to the tree is a large plastic bin with layers of ornaments. Each ornament captures a memory. A wooden key for when we bought this house. A shell that reads Myrtle Beach 2012. A dove dancing around a bell for our wedding. Some memories are wrapped delicately in bubble wrap. Others lay freely on the pile.

Noah and Susie are in charge of decorating. They pick up each ornament and decide if that memory is worth displaying on our pristine tree. Noah trots over to the couch and hands me an ornament. "Where should I put this one, Mommy?"

The round ornament is embossed with a family photo that we took months before Christmas because of an irresistible Groupon I found. Each family member is dressed in their favorite Christmas sweater and a pair of dark wash jeans. Noah, who is five in the picture, has his version of a smile. An outsider might interpret it more as a growl. Susie is still a young toddler in the photo. Her eyes are wide with intrigue, and her small curls of soft blonde hair are decorated with festive green and red bows.

My eyes shift to Mason. His arm is in a sling because of a careless mistake on his motorbike just weeks beforehand. I remember being upset during this photoshoot because he seemed to make the kids rowdier intentionally. It was nearly impossible to get one shot where everyone smiled, had their eyes opened, and their clothes properly on. I look at the picture now, wishing I knew that would be our last Christmas together as a family; I wouldn't have gotten so upset. I feel disloyal now, even thinking about the bad, allowing it to sit in my most precious memories of him.

Susie wiggles her way into my arms to look at the ornament. "Is that Daddy?"

"Yes, sweetie, that's your daddy," I respond to Susie. I look to Noah, who is still standing in front of me, waiting for my answer. "I think this ornament should be front and center." I know this is what Noah wants to hear. He skips back to the tree and places it as high up on the tree as he can reach.

"Mommy, do you think Daddy can see our tree from heaven?" Noah asks.

I close my eyes deeply. "I sure hope so. He would be so proud."

CHAPTER 7

# Evening of December 7

*"Don't get your tinsel in a tangle."*

— UNKNOWN

THAT NIGHT, AFTER MY MOM LEAVES, Rick comes over to help us write letters to Santa. The more I think about it, the more I feel that Rick could be exactly what Noah needs right now. He could provide the calm Noah is missing. The role model that he has lost. I don't want to put too much pressure on tonight, but I have a lot of hope.

When he walks in, his arms are filled with supplies. In one hand, he has a bouquet of flowers, and in the other, a box of cookies from a local bakery. "Hello, gorgeous," he says as he leans in for a hug.

My heart swells. It's nice to be reminded of my femininity. To be affirmed that someone in this world finds me special. Attractive in their eyes. I softly smile and respond, "Thank you. And you look very nice as well." I wink in his direction, trying to appear flirtatious, even though I feel bloated from the day of treats.

Susie and Noah can see Rick in the entry, but they don't stop playing with their toys. I take one huff and say, "Kids! Don't be rude. Come introduce yourself to our guest."

They both get up from the floor and move toward the front hallway. From a distance, Noah waves and says, "Hey." Although Noah has a lot of energy when he is comfortable, he becomes shy around new people. Susie follows suit.

"Noah and Susie, this is Rick, a very, very close friend of mine that I want you to meet."

"Is he your boyfrienddddd?" Noah asks with a strong emphasis on the word boyfriend, causing Susie to giggle.

It feels awkward to have a boyfriend as a grown adult. For goodness sake, when I was Noah's age, I was coming home telling my mom I had a boyfriend. Rick feels more than a boyfriend. Not a husband or life partner quite yet. But something else. To keep it simple, though, I say, "Yes, Noah, Rick is my boyfriend. We have been hanging out when Grandma watches you, and he wanted to meet the two of you."

Rick adds, "Your mom has told me so much about both of you." He leans down to get closer to their eye level and hands a box of cookies to Noah as a peace offering. "She also told me you like this bakery, so I thought I would bring something from there as a treat while we write letters to Santa."

Noah's and Susie's eyes widen. Susie runs towards him and says, "Thanks," giving Rick a tight hug, almost pushing him to the ground. Noah follows behind, saying, "Hey, I want some!"

I knew the cookies would be a success. I grab the box. "Yes, after dinner. Let's first wash our hands, okay?" Noah and Susie jump with excitement. I look at Rick. We smile and reach for each other's hands as we follow behind them. As they run ahead, I kiss Rick on the cheek. "Thanks for coming today. It means a lot to me."

He winks. "Me too."

We gather around the table, all happy to eat. Noah and Susie scarf down their pasta as if it's their first meal of the day. Rick asks, "So, are you excited to write letters to Santa tonight?"

Both violently shake their heads up and down, continuing to take forkfuls of pasta to their face. I remind them no one is going to take their food.

The room becomes silent, except for Noah's loud chewing. That is something I need to work on with him. Rick looks at me as if he's out of questions to ask. In fairness, Rick has no experience with kids.

I try to keep the conversation going. "Do you guys think you will be on Santa's naughty or nice list?"

Noah bounces up from his chair. "Susie will probably be on the naughty list cause she cries a lot."

"No, I don't!" Susie responds as her face turns red.

"Well, I think you both have been very nice this year!" I say in hopes of defusing the ticking time bomb that is Susie's crying. Noah does make a good point. Susie does cry frequently and loudly. She feels things deeply, even the smallest of statements like this.

"I already know what I want from Santa!" shouts Noah. "I want the Elite Titan CS-50 Nerf blaster! And the new battleship Lego set . . . and a Nintendo."

"Isn't that a lot for Santa to get one person?" Rick asks as he looks at me with confusion.

"But Freddy always gets that much from Santa," Noah replies as he sways back and forth.

"Maybe some of those gifts are from his parents?" Rick suggests.

Noah pauses and then responds, "Not possible. His parents aren't cool enough to buy those things. It has to be Santa."

Rick and I look at each other and smile. I say, "Well, it's important not to get too greedy. Maybe just ask Santa for the thing you want the most."

"Fine. Just the Nerf gun then since Mom won't buy them for me."

I smirk at his response. If only he knew the truth about Christmas, maybe he wouldn't think I'm such a grouch. Noah continues, "But she also probably wouldn't buy me the Nintendo either." He pauses to think about his predicament. "I still want the Nerf gun."

After finishing dinner, we clean off the table and bring out the art supplies. We have a collection of colored paper and the sought-after sixty-four-pack of Crayola crayons *and* markers, stickers, and two envelopes that we will address to the North Pole.

Immediately, Noah picks up the red marker, his favorite color. He starts to run around with the marker as he screams random words with excitement.

Rick looks overwhelmed. I tell Noah, "Honey, you will need to sit down to write your letter." Finally, he settles down and returns to the table. Instead of sitting, he props himself on his feet as if a frog hovering over the table.

I look over to Susie. She struggles to get a sticker off the pad, so Rick takes the sheet and removes it for her.

"Hey, I was going to use that!" Susie shouts at him.

"I know I was just getting it for you," Rick responds, handing her the sticker. He looks at me with uncertainty, and I give him a thumbs-up, letting him know he is doing okay.

Rick leans over to me and whispers, "Why would she think I would want her sticker?"

I smile and whisper back, "We may never understand the minds of a child."

"Oh," Susie responds, swiping the sticker and placing it directly in the middle of her soon-to-be letter. "I'm going to ask Santa for a pony," she announces.

"A real pony?" Rick questions.

Susie's attention remains on placing the sticker on her letter. "Yep. I'll name her Cupcake cause I love cupcakes, and I will love my pony."

"Where is the pony going to live?" Rick implores.

Susie focuses on the letter. Her whole hand is wrapped around the marker as she writes her name in big, sloppy print. "In my room. I can share my bed with her."

"I don't think you and the pony will fit," I say.

"I can sleep in your bed then. I fit there."

"No," I quickly respond. "Big girls sleep in their own beds, remember, Susie? What about one of those new My Little Pony stuffed animals? They will be more comfortable to sleep with."

"But I can't ride a stuffed animal! I want to ride the pony!" she demands.

I try to find a counteroffer. "Unfortunately, Santa's elves can only make toys. They can't deliver live animals. He could get you a bright, sparkling pink stuffed animal pony. That sounds pretty good, right?"

Susie ponders the offer. "I want that!"

Luckily, Susie is still young and easy to convince. Plus, I know that the My Little Pony stuffed animals are on sale at Target, making it an even more satisfying purchase for me.

Noah announces, "I'm done! Can we send it now?"

I move next to him and look at the letter. "Let's see what you got."

*Deer Santa,*

*I hope you and the elves are good at the north pol. i been really nice to mi sister Susie witch is hard caus she likes to cry alot. Last year u got me a good nerf gun and this year i want the Elite Titan CS-50 nerf gun and i like the nitendo too but if i can not have it maybe bring it to my friens house so i can play. Thanks Santa! i will have the best cookies out four you.*

*Love, Noah*

"Can I read your letter?" Rick asks.

"NO! Only Mommy can read it," Noah says.

Unsure of where this spurt of anger came from, I tap Noah on the shoulder and look into his eyes. "Well, that's not very nice, Noah. Can Rick and I read it together?"

He crosses his arm and falls from his frog position into his chair. "Fine."

As I read over the letter, I notice the glaring mistakes. I want to use this time to improve his writing, but I also don't want to dampen his spirits during this fun activity.

"Very good, Noah!" I say. "I love what you wrote and that you will give the best cookie to Santa. That's very kind of you. Now, Santa only reads letters with no spelling mistakes, so can you read it over and see if you find any?"

Without checking, Noah says, "It looks perfect to me!"

"Oh, really, because I didn't see you even take a second look at the letter," I say back.

Noah giggles. "Fineee. I'll reread it."

"Remember when 'i' is alone? What do you need to do?" I ask.

"Draw it like this." Noah draws a capital 'I' shape.

"Yes! Perfect, can you make a new draft with that change and any others you might find? Just take it one word at a time."

Noah pulls out a new piece of paper, opens the cap of his red marker, and begins the process again. As Noah writes his letter, I give Susie more attention, leaving Rick to work with Noah. I told Rick beforehand just to nod and say, "Looks great." If he does that, then tonight will go perfectly. I just hope they can get along.

I hear Rick trying to help Noah. "Noah, wait. Before you continue, look at the intro. Do you see any errors?" I do appreciate Rick trying to get involved, but I'm worried he doesn't realize how sensitive Noah is about writing and reading. I told him before to stay positive and supportive.

"Everything is spelled fine," Noah snaps back.

"What about this word?" Rick asks as he points to the word 'deer.'

"Yeah, Deer Santa," Noah says, looking back at Rick.

"Could there be a different way to spell that?" Rick asks.

"I don't know, maybe." Noah begins to slouch in his chair. "I'm just not that smart."

This is my cue to step in. "That's not true, baby. You have made so much progress in spelling, and I'm very proud of the hard work you put into it."

"He thinks I'm dumb, though."

I glare at Rick. "Rick doesn't think that, do you, Rick?" He better not mess this up. All he needs to do is say no, and the crisis will be averted.

"No, buddy," Rick starts. Perfect, I hope he stops his sentence there. But, of course, he continues. "You just need to sit and focus more."

*Why would Rick say that? I told him to nod and smile. That's it!*

Noah begins to whimper. "But I already do work harder than everyone in my class."

I look back at Rick. "Why would you say that?"

"I'm sorry," Rick starts. He turns to me and lowers his voice. "I just think if he focused more, he'd be doing better. I just see him bouncing around and not focused."

I try to breathe in, but I feel too frustrated to deal with this. I try to take a breath. "Rick, can you step over here with me?"

"But . . . " he starts to defend himself.

I stare straight into his eyes and sternly say, "Rick." He gets up and walks away from the kids with me. "Rick, you know that Noah has dyslexia. This is really challenging for him, so your comments don't help. I told you not to focus on that."

Rick, as a steadfast man, continues and says, "Rachel, I'm sorry, but I think I'm right. Noah is just bouncing all around. Someone needs to get him under control."

I shake my head in disappointment. *Why is my adult boyfriend shaming my young child?* "Rick . . . Rick, I'm sorry, but I need to focus on my son right now."

"What do you mean?"

"I think this was too much too fast."

Rick reaches for my hands. "But Rachel, I—"

"Rick. Please," I interrupted. Let's just talk tomorrow about this, okay?"

I can see he wants to explain his reasoning, but he graciously nods his head, grabs his coat, and walks out. I didn't expect the night to turn out like this. This is the third time today I have managed to mess up a Christmas activity. *Why can't I do any of this right?*

## CHAPTER 8

# Sunday, December 11, 2016

*"Christmas is like candy;*
*it slowly melts in your mouth sweetening every taste bud,*
*making you wish it could last forever."*
— RICHELLE E. GOODRICH

### (14 DAYS UNTIL CHRISTMAS)

AS THE LIGHT PEAKS THROUGH THE CURTAIN, I roll onto my side until my alarm rings. I unlock my phone screen and read the message Rick sent last night that I ignored.

Hey, Rachel! I'm so sorry for what happened. I should have never questioned Noah like that. I feel like a jerk.

I know I should let it go, but my gut is nagging me that this is a bigger problem. I don't want to start trouble with Rick days before Christmas. I just want to focus on the good this season. I do believe that Rick meant well last night.

No worries. It was a crazy night.

I roll onto my back and stare at the ceiling. The surface is pure white. It's uncorrupted by the rainbow. Untouched by the painter. Unimportant to the designer. Its blankness allows my mind to become vacant. Desolate like a desert. I start to drift into the bleak sand when I hear Noah open my door. This alarm clock cannot be snoozed.

The Christmas activities continue today as we bake cookies with Grandma Sherry and Grandpa Bob. After Mason's death, I stopped visiting his parents. Perhaps it was too painful for both of us, but I noticed Susie and Noah referring to my parents as their only grandparents and never Mason's parents, so we made it a tradition to visit at least once a month. Noah and Susie deserve to know their grandparents, and Bob and Sherry deserve to be part of their grandchildren's lives.

When Noah and Susie reach the front door, Bob and Sherry kneel, allowing the kids to jump into their arms. Susie first goes to Grandpa Bob, who picks her up and twirls her around. Sherry gives each a long embrace.

Grandma Sherry looks like my childhood vision of Mrs. Claus. Her greyed hair is pulled back in a low bun, with small glasses propped on her button nose. While her stature seems small and frail, I know Bob makes her lift weights three times a week to ensure she is healthy for all their trips. Her internal pureness speaks through her docile presence. She was a nurse for forty years before retiring, yet she still volunteers at the same hospital helping families dealing with unexpected loss, something she knows too much about.

When she comes to me, she gives me a light hug with one hand around my shoulder and the other by her side. *When did she stop giving me the long embrace as she does for the kids? Was it after Mason's death, or has it been longer than that? Does she blame me?* I'm the one who asked him to pick up my prescription on that unusually sunny day in January. I know I feel that guilt every day. Perhaps she feels that judgment as well.

Next, I hug Bob. Bob's once thick black hair has transformed into a silvery crown. His piercing blue eyes remind me of Mason. Even in retirement, his body remains strong from all the adventures he takes with Sherry and the projects he finds around their ten-acre farm.

"And look at this Christmas tree! Who was in charge of picking this beauty out?" Sherry asks.

"ME ME ME!" Noah shouts as he bounces around the living room.

Grandma Sherry reaches for a homemade ornament. It's made with four large popsicle sticks that Noah decorated with Christmas stickers, feathers, glitter, and drawings. The eccentric frame outlines a black and white photo. Noah is on Mason's lap with a fishing pole, and Grandpa Bob is behind them, showing how to cast the fishing line to the center of the lake. As Sherry examines the ornament, a tear comes to her eye. "My three favorite boys," she says.

"Mine too." I wrap my arm around Sherry's shoulder as she continues to hold the ornament.

Noah squeezes between us to see what we are looking at. "I miss going fishing," he says.

"Me too," Sherry says.

"You never went fishing, Grandma," Noah says, leading us all to laugh.

"You make a good point, Noah. I mean, I loved seeing what you brought back from fishing."

"Oh yeah, I liked that too! Can we start making cookies now, since Grandma and Grandpa are here?" Noah asks.

"Yes! Let the Christmas baking begin!" I head into the kitchen as Noah and Susie drag Grandma and Grandpa behind them.

On the kitchen counter, I set out a broad collection of new and vintage cookie cutters. Some are related to Christmas, like gingerbread boys, snowmen, and reindeer. Others are more random, like a T-rex, an alien for Noah, and a pony for Susie. The kitchen table is covered with paper towels and a cooking tray in the middle to place the final product. There is a small ball of cookie dough at each seat.

Sherry picks up the T-rex cookie cutter. "I can't believe you still have this."

"Of course, it was Mason's favorite," I respond.

"Susie and Noah, can I tell you a story about your dad?" asks Sherry.

"YES, YES, YES!!" they shout.

"Your dad, right when he was about your age, Noah, used to ONLY make gingerbread T-rexes. He refused to make any gingerbread boys or women or kids, just a whole village of gingerbread T-rexes that he frosted with Christmas hats and sweaters."

"I want to do that!" Susie shouts as she grabs the cookie cutter from Sherry.

"Can the T-rex have some alien friends, too?" Noah asks.

"Of course. Whatever you dream up is possible," Bob replies.

Susie sets down the T-rex cookie cutter and picks up the pony. "Can they have a pet pony, too?"

"Definitely! T-rexes love having pet ponies," adds Bob, who is already rolling out his dough and getting into the Christmas spirit.

We cut out various shapes, bake them, frost them, and do lots of sampling at each step. Soon after Bob and Sherry pack up to leave, Noah and Susie are sprawled across the living room floor, grumbling that their stomachs hurt from eating too many cookies. I feel proud how well this event went, but I know we need to get ready for another week of school and work.

"I think it's time to get you two into bed," I announce.

Noah stomps up the stairs, with Susie following behind.

"Would you want to read a Christmas book before bed? Maybe *The Invasion of Aliens in the North Pole*? Or perhaps the classic *Christmas Elf Nerf Battle*?" I ask.

"Can we read the alien invasion? That's my favorite!" Noah says.

We cuddle together on Noah's bed, a custom rocket ship frame that Mason built. Noah is lying with his head propped up on the pillow and Susie next to him. I lay on my side with the book in one hand, and my other wraps around them. I hope this position will allow for a quick escape when they inevitably fall asleep before the book ends.

I hold up the book's front cover and read "The Invasion of Aliens in the North Pole, by Noah and Mason Taylor."

"Daddy was so good at writing stories with me," Noah says.

After Noah was diagnosed with dyslexia, he refused to read. I rented nearly every book from the library, trying to find something that he liked. Mason had a different strategy. Instead of getting him to read other people's books, he and Noah would write their own. I would then add illustrations and go to a local store to get the books bound. After Mason's death, we stopped creating stories and stopped reading the stories we already wrote. But I wanted to bring them back in memory of their father. Plus, their Christmas ones were always my favorite.

I hand him the book and help as he struggles to pronounce certain words. When I notice them drifting off, I finish reading. I gently remove my arm from below them, turn off the light, and head back downstairs to begin my work.

I open my laptop and click on my notes for the Myopic Therapy case. From the kitchen table, I see the lights from the Christmas tree highlight the picture Sherry was looking at earlier.

A strange urge begins to brew. I close my laptop and go upstairs to my closet to find my high-end acrylic paints that have remained unused for years. I pull down a box labeled *For Mom*. Inside are the paints and a fresh canvas. I take the box downstairs. I look at my watch. It's 10:25 PM. I know I should be heading to bed or working on the case. Instead, I cover the table with newspaper and place a canvas on top. I can't think of the last time I felt inspired to paint, but I decide to surrender myself to this urge. I paint freely for the first time since I lost Mason.

CHAPTER 9

# Monday, December 12, 2016

*"Christmas now surrounds us. Happiness is everywhere. Our hands are busy with many tasks as carols fill the air."*

— SHIRLEY SALLAY

## (13 DAYS UNTIL CHRISTMAS)

MY MORNING SIREN BLARES, causing my head to jerk up. *Why am I at the kitchen table? Oh God, what is that pain in my back? What was I doing last night?* Next to me is my phone, which has only five percent battery. Next to that is a palette of dried-up paint, and next to that, the reason I stayed up all night. I examine my work and smile, knowing my sleepless night will be worth it on Christmas Day.

I shuffle to my coffee machine with my hand on my lower back. I open the drawers searching for my mug that's three times the size of any standard cup. Perfect! It is right in the front. Probably because I use it often. The mug reads *Moms Need This Much Coffee*, something I purchased during one of my occasional therapeutic online shopping binges.

As the coffee heats, I wobble upstairs to wake Susie and Noah. I first knock on Noah's door and find Susie and Noah cuddled up next to each other just the way I left them last night. I lean on the doorframe and watch them. I wish I could pause life at this moment. There is no fighting. No crying. No growing older. No moving further apart from me. No empty home.

"Achoo!!" Susie releases a delicate sneeze that convulses her little body. Immediately, Noah wakes up and starts to bounce on his sister, causing Susie to break out into a hysterical cry. This is the morning I'm more used to. After some crying, fighting, and lunch packing, we get in the car and begin our typical Monday.

When I get to the office, I notice Stratford Junior's red Tesla parked in his assigned spot—the only place that has an electric charger. I'm disappointed that Stratford Senior's E-class Mercedes is not here because I want to ask him about the Christmas bonus. Usually, the Christmas bonus would be in my bank account by now, but I'm still waiting. *Did I do something wrong?*

I go to my desk and open my laptop. I cross one leg over the other and curl my back forward to look at my screen. My leg has a nervous tremble that hits my desk, causing my laptop screen to wobble. Unexpectedly I hear from Stratford Junior's office, "Rachel, can I see you in my office?"

My head whips back. Why would he want to talk to me? I rarely speak to Stratford Junior alone. *Is it about the Myopic case? Maybe he just wants to ask me a question about my dad for the GM case?*

"Are you coming?" he asks.

"Oh, right . . . Yeah," I respond. I force myself up and pull down the end of my skirt, a game I'm sick of playing with my wardrobe. I swallow the lump in the back of my throat and march towards Stratford Junior's office. I stop at the doorway.

"You said you want to see me?" I say with a meek smile.

He motions to the leather chair across from his ominous desk. "Yes, sit."

I sit down. My clammy hands stick to the leather handles, and my lower thighs become moist on the cushion. I debate how to position my legs. Should I cross my legs, or does that make me look unwelcoming? Maybe I should just swing them to the side as I learned from the *Princess Diaries*?

I try to get comfortable. His desk has only three items: a nameplate reading MICHAEL STRATFORD JUNIOR, J.D., his laptop, and a coffee mug embossed with the firm's logo. I know the office's chaos lives within the filing cabinets behind him, where I help organize all the legal briefs for him to review. Directly above Stratford's head, like a halo, is his J.D. degree from Wayne State University.

Mr. Stratford attempts a warm smile that feels misplaced on his typically stern face. He asks, "So, Rachel, how are things going for you?"

"Uhm. I think okay." My hands feel uncomfortable on the handles, so I fold and place them on my lap. "My latest client has been challenging, but nothing I can't handle."

One corner of his lip curves up. "Yes, the Clarks are a bit . . . eccentric. Please do let me know if I need to step in and help." He pauses and clears his throat. "As you know, I'm in charge of the performance reviews this year."
I simply nod. I had no idea that he was taking over this responsibility. Should I have prepared something?

Stratford Junior continues, "So, to start, I'm curious, from your perspective, how would you rate your performance over the past year?"

I feel caught off guard. The office is small enough with only twenty employees that he should know what I've worked on. Do I try to inflate my work and sound more impressive, or will he call me out for exaggerating? I begin to stammer, "I think I'm doing well, all things considered." I fiddle with my watch and unconsciously check the time. My gaze shifts back to his face. I try to gauge what he is thinking. I just see his blank stare. I decide I should continue. "My clients always mention my impressive response time . . . And . . . And I also closed the Emerson case, and I worked evenings and weekends to collect all the evidence . . . So overall, I'm proud of the direction I'm heading."

He says nothing, so I continue. "I'm actually glad you called me in because I wanted to discuss the Christmas bonus. See I—"

He cuts me off. "Interesting." His face remains unmoved.

My eyes widen. "Interesting" is not what I expect to hear. What does that even mean? I shift my weight to my other leg and lean closer to Stratford's desk, hoping he'll provide some explanation. Mr. Stratford's posture and face remain stoic. The attempt of a warm demeanor has vanished. He coughs to clear his throat and begins.

"My father and I both agree your performance is not where we want it to be. We do acknowledge that your past couple of years have had some . . . challenges, but at this point, we cannot extend the regular Christmas bonus to you. We hope that this action helps motivate you to improve so that we do not need to take more extreme measures. We appreciate you and hope to see you thriving at our company again soon."

I squeeze my crossed legs tighter and curl in my lips, holding back the swirl of questions I have, trying to find the right one to verbalize. My brain begins to scramble, wondering if I can make ends meet. And even if I can, what does this mean for my future at the company? Maybe they will fire me, and if that happens, no one will want to hire a struggling single mom who has a worthless degree in art and no formal paralegal training. I only have this job because of my dad. I can't lose it. I can't disappoint them. I can't let my dad find out about this. I should have worked harder. I should have stayed later. I should have been better. I should have been more focused. I should have done a million more things, but I didn't, and because of that,

I'm now in a position of disappointment and uncertainty of the future. The shoulds keep me in line, but I ignored them, and now I'm in uncharted territory.

As I search for the right words, I notice a warmth spread through my cheeks, heating my tear ducts. I know crying would be the worst response, but my brain no longer has control.

I manage to muffle, "But . . . I . . . I had no idea . . . What did I do wrong?" I feel just one tear drip onto my heated cheek.

"Rachel, we cannot have this conversation with you getting emotional. Let's find a different time to chat once the shock wears off. Clients are coming soon, so I hope you can stay composed."

I force my tears back. "Well . . . Mr. Stratford, I appreciate your time."

I walk out, moving straight towards the women's bathroom, my private sanctuary in the office. I place my hands on the cold porcelain sink and stare at my reflection in the mirror. Red rays radiate around my hazel eyes. My shallow wrinkles seem more profound, and the rings around my eyes appear darker.

I start my breathing techniques, hoping to reduce the negative thoughts zipping through my mind. *No surprise this is happening to you! You fail at everything! It's about time they figured out that you aren't that great!*

I look down at my watch. It's 8:55 AM. I have five minutes before my meeting. I take one final deep breath, in through my nose and out through my mouth. I pull down a paper towel and softly wipe my face with cold water. I rub around my eyes and straighten my posture in hopes of camouflaging my shrinking confidence. I must continue.

---

That afternoon, I go to Susie's school to help with the pageant practice. I was anxious about leaving after my talk with Stratford Junior, but, luckily, he left after lunch to meet with a client. I hope that making the sets today will be a nice stress reliever.

When I get to the classroom, I find Susie and her classmates sitting on soft puzzle-shaped mats while the teacher leads them in a song and dance. Karen is already here and seems to be equally interested in the music as the students.

I walk over to Karen and try to grab her attention. "Hey, Karen. I'm glad we can work on this together," I say.

"Oh definitely!" Karen responds with unprecedented enthusiasm. "These kiddos are just adorable!"

"Yes, they sure are." I look back at Susie and smile. "So, I was thinking, perhaps you can help the teacher run the practice, and I could start working on some sets for the stage. What do you think?"

"That sounds perfect! Your Halloween costume for Susie this year was absolutely amazing! My daughter is still raving about it."

I rub the back of my neck that's still sore from my night at the kitchen table. "Uh . . . Thanks. That's kind of you to say." I pause and turn my head over my shoulder, looking at the separated creative nook. "I'll just be back there if you need me."

Karen nods. I give one more wave to Susie, who is still looking my way, and then head back. Along the walls of this space are cubbies filled with the highest quality art supplies. We have crayons, pencils, glue sticks, finger paint, glitter—a bold decision on the teacher's part—and much more. Next to the cubbies are multiple spools of thick paper, which will be perfect for making the backdrop for the stage.

I look at the opposite wall filled with windows. Attached to the glass are hand cut snowflakes, each decorated by a student. I quickly identify Susie's because it has been colored with a bright pink highlighter and has her name printed largely in the middle. Each snowflake seems to be decorated with things the child finds unique about themselves. On Susie's snowflake, she has a stick-figure horse and our family. The image includes Susie, Noah, and me. Susie and Noah both have U-shaped smiles, but I have a straight line. *Why don't I have a big U-shaped smile like Susie and Noah? Does Susie see me as unhappy?* I feel a building pressure in my chest. I need to be better for my kids. I need to prove to them that I'm okay every day, even when I still feel broken inside.

My eyes shift to the last object on her star, a gravestone that reads 'Daddy.' My fingertips graze the snowflake. Susie is right to think that losing her father at such a young age will impact her in unique ways—ways I wish I could shield her from.

My thoughts are interrupted when I hear a collective high-pitch squeal from the class. I turn around and see Karen unveil the infamous Pixie Cupcake's box. Sugaring up the kids before trying to get them to sing together seems like a bad idea, but I'm glad I can hang in the back and paint.

I pull out my headphones and play a Christmas playlist to block out the squealing children. I look back at the wall of snowflakes. An ah-ha moment sparks in my brain, jolting my heart with what feels like a gallon of caffeine.

Immediately, I move into action. I rip off a long strip of paper from the dark blue spool and pull out the brown, yellow, orange, and red paint. I open the cubby of paintbrushes and dig for one with the thickest bristles. I pause for only a second as I feel the soft laminated wood of the brush diffusing the calmness of a summer breeze through my skin. I breathe deeply and begin to paint.

---

I feel a tap on my shoulder. My body jerks out of the abnormally small chair I managed to nestle myself into. My once-free chest tightens with anxiety. I turn around and see Karen behind me.

"I'm so sorry for interrupting you," Karen says, "but it's the end of the day, and the kids have all left." I look around and confirm what Karen is saying. The only two kids that are still here are Susie and Karen's daughter playing on the mats. I remove my headphones and look at my watch—4:30 PM. I'm late to pick up Noah!

"Oh, shoot! I need to get my son!" I scramble to clean the supplies and pack up.

"I can do that so you can head there?" Karen offers.

"You are a Godsend! Thank you!"

I start to rush out, and I hear Karen shout, "Rachel, I think you are forgetting something!"

I turn back around and see Karen pointing to Susie. Wow, I'm the worst mother in the world today.

"Mommy, do you want to hear the songs I learned today?" Susie asked.

"Let's wait till we get to your brother, okay?"

"You don't want to hear my song!" Susie whines.

I try to autocorrect. "You know what, Mommy would love to hear the songs right now."

"Okay!" Susie starts to belt out the song as she skips to her cubby to grab her things.

"Thanks, Karen, for cleaning up!" I shout as we shuffle out the door.

"Also, Rachel, these sets are already looking amazing! I cannot wait to see them complete."

I wave in acknowledgment.

As we shuffle through the building, I try my best to listen to Susie's songs, but my ears seem clogged with guilt for forgetting both of my children today as I painted. I check my phone. I have several missed calls from Noah's teacher. If she only knew I was in the building this whole time. How did I miss my phone vibrating in my pocket? Between Noah getting violent and now forgetting him, I can only imagine what this teacher thinks of me. I can only imagine what Noah is thinking. Having a parent forget to come is rightfully scary for a kid, but I remind myself that the last time a parent didn't show up for Noah, it was because they were dead.

I rush into Noah's classroom. "Mrs. Bushnell, I'm so sorry." I pause to catch my breath. "I just got super distracted helping with my daughter's pageant and somehow lost track of time." My hands are in a prayer position as if begging for her forgiveness.

Mrs. Bushnell remains calm. "It's okay, Ms. Taylor. I understand. But I know your son is worried about you. He and Marcus are with the principal."

*Shit, Marcus!* Not only did I forget about my child, but I also forgot that I need to pick up his best friend. I rush over to the principal's office. Inside, I see Noah anxiously pacing in the office hallway with his neck hanging low, staring at the ground for answers. Marcus is standing at a distance, clearly unsure how to help.

I shout, "Noah!" His head perks up, and he runs toward me.

I kneel, and Noah wraps his arms around my neck. His head nestles next to mine as he whispers, "I thought you weren't going to come."

"I know. I'm so sorry." I hold him tightly, placing one hand around his body and another on his warm cheek. *Why do I just keep disappointing people? Mason, are you up there? What am I supposed to do?* It's been almost four years since your death, and I still haven't figured out how to do this alone.

---

When we get home, I open the fridge and stare at the ingredients for the cauliflower tacos I planned to make tonight. It's a new recipe from a vegan blog. I don't have the energy to make it and then try to convince Noah and Susie to eat it.

I go to the pantry. The waffle mix is positioned right in the front. I decide to switch things up tonight and have breakfast for dinner. I feel this irresistible craving for sugar—an urge for freedom. I have already been a bad employee leaving work early to go to Susie's school and a bad mom for forgetting my kids. Why stop the train of bad-mom energy?

Several years ago, I found a recipe on Pinterest to make waffles shaped like Christmas trees. I said I would make this month special for them, so God damn it, let's do it. I open my phone and scroll through my thousands of pinned items that I have never had the energy or confidence to try. I follow the instructions, adding green food coloring to the waffle mix. The waffle maker creates one circle waffle that I then split evenly into four parts. I stagger them down the plate with their pointy side up to form a Christmas tree. At the top of the tree, I add a small swirl of whip cream as the star. I look at my finished product, feeling somewhat impressed by my 'mom skills' for the evening. I rarely have success with Pinterest recipes, but tonight I'm changing that around.

"Breakfast is ready," I announce. Noah and Susie immediately drop their toys and run to the kitchen table.

"Breakfast? Mommy, it's nighttime, though!" Noah proclaims.

"Well, today, we are switching it up."

After our breakfast dinner, I let Noah and Susie have an extra hour of screen time, so I can clean up the kitchen by myself, something they usually help with. I just want them to be happy; maybe if I can make them happy, I can also feel satisfied.

I collect the plates and take them to the sink. The maple syrup has already solidified, so I grab my extra rough squeegee. Each swirl of water and soap dissolves the sticky maple syrup revealing the simple white plate below, returning to the expected order of things.

CHAPTER 10

# Evening of December 12

*"Don't let the past steal your present.*
*This is the message of Christmas: We are never alone."*
— TAYLOR CALDWELL

AFTER THE KIDS ARE IN BED and the lights are out, I feel a void. My body screams for sleep, but my mind continues to wonder and question the events from today. I need to leave the confines of my room. I decide to go downstairs to the living room. The only light comes from the Christmas tree and the streetlights sneaking through the windows. Together they perfectly illuminate a small snow globe on the shelves that line either side of the fireplace. I pick up the globe and look inside at the miniature replica of our home. I see me holding baby Noah with Mason's arm wrapped around my waist. Mason made this right after Noah's birth.

I shake it, causing a violent storm inside the once stationary scene. As the flakes of chaos fall, I move the globe around delicately. I shift the globe left and right, adjusting where the flakes of chaos land. When the globe settles, I shake it again. The chaos feels more comfortable, more beautiful than the stillness of the scene—the constant downfall of responsibilities and expectations on what seems to be a perfect life.

When I painted today, though, those flurries disappeared. When I paint, the chaos settles. The world feels still, but the stillness is perhaps just a distraction from my responsibilities. It led to Noah feeling abandoned. My art, my selfish desire for stillness, caused them pain. I failed them.

In the darkness, I feel alone. I need to find something, anything, to fill me. I head upstairs and go into my closet that holds my past. On the left side of the closet are Mason's clothes, still unmoved since his death four years ago. Suits, blouses, and my occasional cocktail dress line the right side. Below, shoes for all occasions.

The bottom half of the walls are lined with dozens of various-sized canvases, each flipped so only the wall can know what they contain. I lean down and turn around the canvas nearest me. Even in the dimly lit closet, I notice the erratic colors, the life of the painting. In the bottom right corner, my signature. I sit on the ground and continue to stare at the portrait.

My attention moves to the racks above the clothes that hold moving boxes of various sizes. All the boxes are labeled with PENSKE MOVING COMPANY. Mason saved them after we moved into this house because of their 'sound structural integrity.' I notice the box that holds my paint set that I just used last night.

There is only one box that's not a Penske moving box. This box is labeled MEMORIAL EMERGENCY CENTER. Across the side is a sticker that reads:

MASON TAYLOR
JANUARY 6, 2013

I have looked at this box many times. I even took it down to feel that single strip of clear tape separating me from Mason's final set of items. Weeks after his death, I ripped this piece of tape and opened the flaps. Mason's smell mixed with asphalt and blood hit my nose. At the top of the box is the thick motorcycle jacket that was supposed to protect him if he ever got hit on the bike. I quickly closed it up, trying to capture his scent. I would save it for when I hit my lowest.

I look at the box now. *Am I at my lowest?* I might be losing my job. I let our kids down. I let Mason down by disregarding his favorite holiday. I was selfish enough today to forget about my children. Will it get worse than tonight? It has been worse before, but what about in the future?

I reach for the box and put it on the floor in front of me. I sit down with it. I place my fingers on the tape and rub it to the end. I delicately pull the tape away. I move each flap and breathe deeply. The original smells I remember have vanished. No asphalt. No blood. No Mason. As if it never happened. Trying to trap those memories in this box has failed too. My eyes well with tears, making it impossible to see the content within the box. I give myself time to weep, to feel the loss of the last objects that once held his smell. A reminder of the same pain I felt at his funeral.

## — 2013 —

I sit in the front pew with Susie on my lap, and Noah nestled at my side, his face hidden behind my arm. Susie wiggles in my lap and looks around. I assume she is unsure why we are here and who all these people are. Noah and Susie are both dressed in new black outfits that I hope they will never need to use again.

I move my head backward to see a church filled with hundreds, only really recognizing a handful of faces. While I don't recognize specific faces, I notice collections of people that represent different aspects of Mason's life. There was a group of men with wrinkled suits and dirtied hands from the mechanic shop and another similar group from his car racing events. I noticed families from Noah's school and Mason's old high school friends who still live in town. Hundreds of lives came today to acknowledge the loss of one.

From the back balcony, the depressed sirens of the organ begin to sound, alerting the start of the ceremony. In the back of the church is the casket being carried by six of Mason's cousins, who all work on the family farm. While the men are strong, they look weak, carrying the pure oak casket of their dearest friend. Slowly, they progress forward. I turn ahead and hold my eyes shut. I need to stay strong. I have cried every moment leading up to today. There can't be more tears to cry.

They place the casket in front of the altar. Everyone sits as the priest rises from his chair. He walks towards the crowd and begins. "Today, we are here to celebrate the life of Mason Gregory Taylor. Mason was a great, honorable man—"

With all the chaos of the five days leading up to Mason's funeral, I had mentally prepared myself to listen to people share stories about Mason and their love for him. But in just those first words from the priest, I realize I didn't prepare myself enough. My brain fixates on one phrase—Mason was. In this moment, I realize Mason will forever be a 'was,' referred to in the past—the language used in history books. No longer are we discussing Mason's plans for the future, but the memorial of his past. No one prepared me for this simple transition from 'Mason is' to 'Mason was.'

I feel the pressure building in my chest. The lack of air causes me to choke. I force myself to breathe as my eyes erupt with tears. On either side of me are Noah and Susie. Both look petrified to see me like this. I force myself to stop. I stop crying, but I also stop listening. I can't listen.

I look up to the crucifix of Jesus. A whole religion built off the suffering of one man to combat the suffering of all people. All I see in this church is pain and suffering. I vow never to enter a church again.

Time passes, and people begin to exit. I remain still in the pew.

"Rachel, I think we need to go to the reception," Bob says as he wraps his arm around me. I simply nod and stand up.

Noah and Susie are both restless. I think this has been enough for them, so I ask my parents to take them home. They willingly comply. I go with Bob and Sherry to the reception.

We are directed to stand next to Mason's dead body hidden below the closed casket. Person by person, the guests approach me to offer their condolences. Some offer flowers; others try to offer words. Some kneel and lean their hands on the casket, praying for an alternative, asking God how this could happen. Why did this happen?

With each person, regardless of my closeness to them, there was one phrase that everyone repeated, a phrase that still haunts me: *I can't imagine what you are going through.*

I couldn't imagine it either. I still can't imagine it. And yet, I have been forced to imagine what we all define as the unimaginable. I'm forced to not only imagine it but to eventually accept it and move on with my life like normal.

CHAPTER 11

# Tuesday, December 13, 2016

*"Christmas, my child, is love in action.*
*Every time we love, every time we give, it's Christmas."*

— DALE EVANS

## (12 DAYS UNTIL CHRISTMAS)

WITH A RATHER UNEVENTFUL MORNING, I go to the driveway anxious to get an early start to the day. I notice the rear door of Bonnie is slightly ajar, and when I try to start the car, I am met with silence. This can't be happening today. I need to get to work early and ask Stratford Junior about how I can get the Christmas bonus. I assume the battery is dead from the door light staying on all night—something a new car would prevent by automatically turning off the lights after several minutes.

I reach for my phone. I remember that my mom is at an all-day ladies' retreat at the country club. Who else can I call? I'm rarely in this situation. I open my recent messages. First is my mom, then Rick. I continue to scroll, seeing several chats related to work or commitments for Noah and Susie. No longer are there texts from my college art friends telling me about life in New York, or even random texts from Noah's school moms looping me in on the school drama. When did I stop getting those texts? I scroll past the work texts and mom-related texts and find texts from friends I haven't talked to in over a year. Sophia, my roommate in college, texted me over a year ago with Saw this video and thought of you. How you holding up? I never responded. And it was not the first message she sent that I didn't respond to. She isn't the only person either. I tell myself I should respond even if I'm a year late, but first, I need to fix this car. I scroll back to the top of the list and call Rick.

"Rick, it's Rachel," I say.

"What's up?" Rick sounds groggy, most likely woken up by the call.

"Hey, so, it's my car. The battery is dead. Do you think you can come over and help?"

"Uhhh . . . Okay. Can I come in an hour?"

I purse my lips and try to sound pleasant. "The sooner, the better, so Noah and Susie aren't late for school."

I hear a pause. "Oh, right. Okay, I guess I will come now."

"Thanks, Rick. I know this is an inconvenience."

"Yep." I hear him hang up on the other end. I head inside and explain to the kids that we need to wait for Rick to come to jumpstart the car. Noah shouts, "So we don't need to go to school today?"

"Oh no, mister, you're still going to school, but just a little late. Why don't you play with Susie until Rick comes?" Without hesitation, they scatter off to play, accepting this as a win. Rick's house is only a few minutes down the road. I start to pace through the kitchen. *When will Rick be able to get here? Will I still get to the office early enough to prepare for today's meetings on the Myopic case? Maybe this is my sign that it's time to replace Bonnie?* Bonnie has broken down many times before. I begin to reminisce on my memories with Bonnie. The adventures paired with the breakdowns. I think of the role this car has played in my life.

## — 2005 —

Shit! The check engine light is blinking! I just got this job, and Stratford has trusted me to meet with a client outside of the office. I mean, Brian will still be there for supervision as an associate, but still. I pick up my phone to call for help.

"Dad! The light started blinking. What do I do?"

"How far are you from the office?" I hear him respond on the other end.

I have the route memorized from studying MapQuest last night, but I look at my printout and see I have five turns and about three miles to my final destination.

"Like three miles? Should I pull over?"

"I think you will be okay, honey. Focus on getting to the client meeting. That comes first. Then call AAA to get it towed to the Honda dealership on Maple. You know the one near the gym your mom goes to."

"Yep, I know that one." But as I say this, a cloud of white smoke emerges from beneath Bonnie's hood. "Dad . . . "

Before I can finish, my dad cuts in. "Honey, I need to go. I have a big client meeting myself. Be safe. And make me proud!"

"But . . . " I hear nothing from the other end.

I decide to pull over. Perhaps Bonnie is like a computer. Maybe she just needs to be unplugged for a bit with her hood up, and she'll be back to normal in minutes.

I lift the hood. The smoke becomes thick and gloomy. I look at my watch. I have twenty-one minutes before my meeting starts.

From behind me, I hear a stranger. "Ma'am, do you need help?"

My heart seems to triple in speed. I jolt around to look in the direction of the stranger's voice. My eyes dart up and down, deciding if I can trust this random man. I'm drawn to his warm, piercing blue eyes. His uncombed black hair is peaking out of his ballcap. I'm shocked that he addressed me as "ma'am" since we look around the same age. Nothing seems out of the ordinary. That is until I look at his outfit. He is wearing a prison-like jumpsuit that seems blacker now than its original dark blue. Could he be an escaped prisoner? Are there even any prisons near here? And even if he did just escape from a jail, aren't the jumpsuits orange? I mean, sometimes they are blue on the countless *Prison Break* reruns I watch with my dad. It's not like we see a lot of that type in our patent law office.

I wave him away and stare back at the abyss of smoke. "Oh no, I'm good, sir!"

"Are you sure you don't want help?" the stranger calls back. "You know, I'm a mechanic at the shop just around the corner, so I might be able to help fix this for you."

This explains the jumpsuit. I look back down at my watch. I have eighteen minutes to get to my client's office.

I need to get to this meeting, but should I trust someone random to help me? "I'm sure the smoke will die down soon, and I'll be on my way . . . right?" I begin to question if his plan sounds better.

"Uhh . . . " he starts with an unrefined stutter. "I don't know if that's a good idea."

"Do you think my car will explode? I just need to go a couple more miles."

"It probably won't explode, but it's likely your engine is overheating, and if you keep driving, then it might be the end for this car."

"What do you mean? How long do I need to wait?"

"It's hard to say without taking a look, but probably like ten, maybe fifteen minutes. Even then, it isn't safe to drive."

I start to panic. This can't be happening to me. I don't want to disappoint Stratford on my first client-on-sight, and if I miss the meeting, I know Brian will tattle on me like a child. He already doesn't like me because he thinks I was just handed this job . . . which is not entirely false. Desperately, I say, "But I need to go to this meeting!"

I pace back and forth in front of Bonnie, and I stare at the asphalt road. I recite the MapQuest directions in my head, debating if I should just run there. Maybe I can cut through some buildings to trim off time. And if I take off my heels, then I might still be able to run my eight-minute mile pace from high school.

Unexpectedly, I bump into this stranger, who is now directly in my pacing path. "Excuse me!" I shout to him.

He leans down several inches attempting to get the attention of my eyes. His plan works. His eyes are calm. My breathing seems to sync with his. "You will get to your meeting. I could drive you. You said it was just a couple miles, right?"

I'm shocked by the man's forward offer. "Absolutely not! I don't know you!"

He pauses and looks around. "Okay . . . " His hand goes into his pocket to pull out a set of keys. "What if I just give you the keys to my car so that you can drive yourself then?"

I become even more shocked. "Why would you do that?"

"Well, it sounds like you need to get to this meeting, and I have a car that could get you there on time."

"But why? I could just steal your car."

He chuckles. "I don't think you will after you see it."

"Where is it?"

"Parked at my shop on the corner."

"Okay, but I could still just take it and never bring it back."

"I have faith that you won't."

"But why?"

He laughs. "I thought you had a meeting to get to?"

I look down at my watch. I have twelve minutes. I think through the route again. If I walk, I won't get there until the end of the meeting. I know I shouldn't take the risk of Bonnie exploding, nor should I get in a car with a stranger. But I guess I was never told not to take a car that a stranger freely offers. It will cause more trouble in my life if I don't show up for the meeting. "Okay, fine."

A soft smile appears upon his rugged face. I gaze back into his expressive blue eyes that reassure me that everything will be okay. He places the keys into my hand. I lock up Bonnie and place her keys into my bag. I'm not ready to hand over the keys to this stranger, even if he is a mechanic. We head to the mechanic shop that I can see on the corner. Behind the shop is a dirt lot with a row of about ten parked cars. I examine the lineup. Perhaps he drives the freshly polished black Audi with tinted windows? Maybe the Prius? I don't get an earthy vibe from him, though. We stop walking.

"Here it is."

He points to the car at the end of the lot. A pickup truck. A boxy, red, rusted pickup truck that seems to be decades old and is raised enough to fit another small car below it.

I point to the hunk of metal on wheels that we can loosely refer to as a car. "This is your car?"

"Yep," he says with a big grin.

"How can this car work but not mine?"

The stranger laughs. "So, do I still need to be afraid of you stealing it?"

"Hah, no! I don't even know if I can drive this."

"Sure, you can. You have to, right? If you want to get to this meeting?"

"Right." I look at my watch. Four minutes. I raise my left leg nearly knee height to reach the footrest. I swing the rest of my body into the driver's seat. The truck feels foreign yet safe. I fiddle with the keys to get the right one in the ignition. I clip my seat belt, adjust the mirrors, and place the car into drive. I begin to press the gas pedal but then stop. I need to know one more thing from this stranger.

"Excuse me, sorry, one more question for you," I say.

He pauses, nods, and looks up into the truck.

"I didn't catch your name?"

"It's Mason."

Got it. The stranger's name is Mason. I can remember that.

"It's nice to meet you, Mason . . . I'm Rachel."

CHAPTER 12

# Morning of December 13

*"Christmas, children, is not a date. It is a state of mind."*

— MARY ELLEN CHASE

IT HAS BEEN TWENTY MINUTES since I called Rick, but there is no sign he's on his way. No text. No car in the driveway. I distract myself by starting my morning work routine here. The first task is email. I find two emails from the Stratfords. The first is from Stratford Junior.

FYI, next week is the last week of trial for the GM case. We should get the verdict before Christmas.

I sigh in relief. I'm ready to end the GM case and hopefully hear fewer references to my dad at work. I wonder how my dad will react if he loses the case. Does he ever really lose, though?

The next email is from Stratford Senior, sent at 1:34 AM.

Hey, Rach, can you send me the paperwork from the Anderson case? Thanks.

I go to my document folders. Lost in the search, I hear the doorbell ring. I fling my laptop shut and run to the door. The first thing I notice is Rick's wet hair. "You showered?"

"Yeah, I just jumped in real fast before coming. Can you open the garage door for me? I need to leave soon for work."

It doesn't matter that he showered. What matters is that he showed up. "Right. Yes."

I go inside and open the garage. I grab the charging cables in the top drawer and hand them to Rick as I lean in for a hug. "I really appreciate you coming."

"Yeah, of course." He opens the hood of his new BMW. He pauses and looks back at me. "Any chance this will mess up my car?"

I shrug my shoulders. "Probably not." I'm used to Mason handling these things.

"Let me look up a video first," Rick says.

I look at my watch, seeing that the kids are both officially late to school. "I have a fun idea," I say. "What if I drop you off at your work, and then take the kids to school, and then pick everyone up this evening, and then we can all hang out tonight?"

He looks at me as if I suggested putting a puppy in the microwave. "You want to take my car for the day?"

"Yeah . . . " I stammer. "Just so that we can all get to work and school on time, and then we can spend the evening together. What do you think?"

Rick purses his lips. "I don't know, Rach . . . Let me just watch this video and try this first."

I wrap my arms around my chest and simply nod as I feel my body become tense. Thirty minutes later, Bonnie is running again. I give Rick a big hug and thank him for saving us this morning.

"So, I'll see you tonight?" Rick asks.

I notice my eyes wince a bit, and I try to cover it up. "Yep. See you tonight."

He kisses the top of my head. I collect the kids, and with a delayed start, we begin our day. I continue to think of the day I first met Mason.

## — 2005 —

When I reach the client's office, a young and beautiful receptionist greets me. "How can I help you?"

I try to pace my breath. "I'm here to see Martin."

"Are you Rachel?" ask the receptionist.

I provide a quick nod. I can only imagine what this stylish receptionist is thinking of me. My hair has melted from Bonnie's steam, and my suit is damp from my unattractive nervous sweats. I keep my arms glued to my side in fear of any foul smell that might escape.

The receptionist clicks around her computer and finally says, "It looks like Martin is still on his lunch break, so why don't you take a seat for now? I believe your colleague is already here."

I notice Brian sitting calmly and professionally in the lobby. "Cutting it close there," he says. "You look awful. What happened?"

"Long story." I turn back to the receptionist. "Actually, miss, is there a restroom nearby?"

Her perfectly manicured hand points to the left, where there are clear signs for the restroom.

"Thanks," I say. I attempt to walk away gracefully. I look back at my watch and see that I was only three minutes late. I guess that doesn't matter now.

In the restroom, I evaluate the damage done after this strange collection of events. A thin layer of sweat is battling the thick coat of hairspray I applied this morning to hold my curls. I pull it back into a ponytail.

I cautiously raise my arms and take a sniff. Yep. I'm glad I didn't open them out there. I take my jacket off, wet a paper towel, and wash my armpits with hand soap. Oh God, I should not be doing this. This is so unprofessional. But what is less professional: washing my armpits in the sink or possibly losing the client with my foul smells? I continue to clean when a new thought pops into my head. Oh God, did Mason notice this smell? I mean, he's a mechanic, so he must smell worse things than this. I take another whiff. But maybe not.

With my fresh armpits and new hairstyle, I return to the lobby. "Rachel?" Brian says. "I just got a call from Martin. It looks like his lunch meeting is running over. Let's just wait it out here."

"Okay." What else do I have to do? I need to prove to my boss and my dad that I can handle this job even though I lack official paralegal training and have questionable professional skills. Stratford took a risk on me, and I can't let him down.

Sitting here for the next thirty minutes, I review the main points for Martin's case. Martin is being sued over his copper wiring patent used in medical devices. The plaintiff claims that the patent infringes on the original distributor's formula, a typical lawsuit for new innovators in a more established space.

The front office door swings open. Martin announces, "So sorry I'm late, Brian. Let's get started." He quickly shakes Brian's hand and then mine. He leads us to a large glass conference room.

I follow close behind. "I hope your lunch meeting went well."

"Awh, yes. Very." Martin sits at the head of the table. "So, what do we have to review today? You guys gonna save my ass on this?"

"Well," Brain says, "we will certainly try our best. I have prepared a brief for us to review today. Essentially, it includes the position we plan to take when we enter litigation." I sit, stay quiet, and diligently take notes on the conversation.

"Great, has Stratford reviewed this as well?"

"Of course. No brief is sent without his final approval." We have been instructed to say this, but I still wonder how much Stratford Senior reads compared to his son, who is currently in his last year of law school. Usually, no one asks to clarify which Stratford was doing the review.

As the meeting comes to a close, all I want is to go home, peel off my business costume, and watch reruns of *Law & Order SVU* until I fall asleep on the couch. First, I need to find a way to get home.

I drive the truck back to the mechanic shop. I see Mason leaning over the front of a car. My attention is drawn to the greasy yellow towel stuffed in his back pocket. His dirty jumpsuit is cinching around his back, accentuating his peach-shaped bottom. I begin to bite my bottom lip.

"How'd it go?" asks Mason, forcing me to snap back to reality.

"Oh yeah . . . It was fine," I say. "Thanks again for letting me borrow your truck. My client ended up being late, so I guess I made too big of a deal getting there on time."

Mason continues to work on the car. "What a foolish guy to come late when he gets to meet with you."

I begin to blush. What's this stranger's deal? "Yeah, I'm not so sure about that," I say, hoping to change the subject. "Anyways, do you think Bonnie is safe to drive back?"

He turns to me. His eyes glisten with curiosity. "Bonnie?"

I wince and then force a smile. "I mean my car. Do you think my car is okay?"

Mason smirks. He takes one step closer to me as I stand outside of his truck. "You call your car Bonnie?"

"A lot of people give their cars a name," I protest. "Your big ol' truck over here doesn't have a name?"

"Unfortunately, no."

I take one step closer to him and point to his car. "Okay, well, let's give him a name now."

"So, my truck is a man, then?" he questions.

"I mean, it would be one hell of an ugly woman, don't you think?" I smile, impressed by my friendly banter.

"You make a good point."

I take another step closer to Mason. "So, what will it be?"

"Hmmm . . . I like the name Clyde."

"Clyde? Interesting choice. Why Clyde?"

"Well, your car is Bonnie, right?"

I nod in affirmation.

"Bonnie and Clyde seem to be a pretty good duo in history."

"Weren't they criminals?"

"Sure, they were known for causing trouble, but a little trouble is good. Don't you think?"

"So, you are a troublemaker, then?"

"Only the good kind of trouble."

"There is no such thing as good trouble."

"That's because you probably have never experienced it," he says with a smile.

I take one final step closer to him, leaving a ruler's distance between us. My heart races, but my soul rests at his beachy blue eyes. Pearls of sweat intermix with the grease spots on his cheeks. His lips are dry yet desirable. "What do you mean?" I ask.

"Let me show you what good trouble looks like. On a date. Unless there's someone else in the picture?"

My heart races faster than at any moment from this day. I don't know what to say. I haven't dated someone since college, and even then, I never felt this nervous. I try to avoid his eyes in fear that I might fall for his charm. "I probably need to go home," I respond.

"How about this? I drive you home tonight, and in exchange, I'll meet you back at your house tomorrow with a fixed car and a planned date."

What is going on?! He is not even my type, and I'm not the kind of girl that wants to cause trouble. I just want to watch the timeless and sexy Elliot Stabler solve countless crimes on *Law & Order* while I eat a pint of Ben & Jerry's ice cream. This Mason guy has been so kind to me, though. For goodness sake, he let me take his car.

As my anxiety continues to process the million and one ways this will play out horribly, I hear myself vocalize a response.

It's just one word: "Sure."

CHAPTER 13

# Later on December 13

*"Christmas is a season not only of rejoicing, but of reflection."*
— WINSTON CHURCHILL

I ENTER THE OFFICE AN HOUR LATER than usual, and my eyes are immediately drawn to the mountain of paperwork that has fallen on my desk. I did leave work early yesterday for the pageant practice, but how could there be this much paperwork since then? I don't think there was even enough time for our printer to print all of this. I start to flip through the documents and notice that it's the evidence for the GM case. All ten thousand-plus pages of it that I had neatly organized in Stratford Junior's requested fashion. The pages are now mixed and scattered on top of the folders that used to contain them.

My body becomes tense. I take a breath and slowly walk over to Stratford Junior's door. I knock. "Hey, I just wanted to ask about the GM evidence on my desk?"

"Oh yes, come in." I open the door but continue to stand in the doorway with my arms folded as I lean on the doorframe. "I needed to find something for the closing remarks today. It wasn't in the spot I expected, so I had to open all the files. Can you reorganize them this morning? I sent you the new filing structure I would like."

I pull in my lips, biting down my anger. "Of course. I'll do that first thing."

His eyes never leave his screen. "Thanks. And then the review for the Myopic case you are working on will also be ready for today? I want to take a look at it tonight."

I force a smile. "Of course."

Refiling the GM evidence will set me back at least half a day, maybe more, depending on the new filing method. Why even bother with a new filing system if the case will be closed this week? I want to stomp back into Junior's office and say, *Hell no. You made this mess. You clean it up!* I take a breath, though. I remember the bonus.

I turn back to him. "Actually, I wanted to ask you about the bonus."

His eyes remain on the screen. "Yes?"

"I want to understand why I'm not getting it this year."

"Well, Rachel, you are a good paralegal. Arguably one of the best. But—"

I try to interject.

"Let me finish. You leave before everyone else on the team, and you have these unexpected demands during the day. Example A was last week. You just left during a critical meeting. This might have been acceptable under my father, but we cannot allow this kind of haphazard work."

I know I need to stand up for myself. God, wherever you are, is this when you grant me the courage so I can make some changes? Or is this my moment of serenity? Should I accept that I have a job and work harder to keep it?

I breathe in courage and respond, "Yes, but I do come into the office before everyone else. And I continue to work every evening. I just need to shift my working hours . . . " I pause in fear of referencing my family at work, but I do anyway, "to accommodate my family."

His face is unmoved. "Right. But we need you in the physical office. Research shows that having the team in the same physical space is key for building synergy. With you always leaving unexpectedly or early or running around trying to chase down your son—well, that hurts our team's synergy. I just need you to be here and stay focused like the rest of us."

I feel my courage draining, but I make another plea. "But I get my assigned work done each week? And you even said I'm one of the best paralegals on the team."

"Yes, but part of the job is being a member of this team and being here with your colleagues. Look, Rachel, I know you are a good worker. As I take more of a leadership role in running the office, I want to emphasize the importance of team collaboration. Does that make sense?"

My neck muscles restrain from shaking no and instead move up and down. I accept defeat on this, but I still want to find a way to get that bonus so that I can afford the best Christmas possible for my kids. "Stratford, is there anything I can do before the end of the year to show you I deserve the Christmas bonus, at least? I can do some extra work on the Myopic case. In fact, I already started reviewing some related cases."

He pauses and stares out the window. "I'm not sure. I need to see a commitment to change."

"What can I do before Christmas?" I give one more desperate plea, "Please, Mr. Stratford. I need this bonus for my family."

His eyes finally peel away from the screen and towards me. His head is motionless, but his eyes dart up and down, examining my desperation. "Fine. No more excuses until we file the Myopic case, and I can see about the bonus. Deal?"

My heart thumps against my chest. There is still a chance I can afford Christmas. I can get every gift on their Christmas list rather than just a couple of the smaller ones. They finally won't need to feel bad when they go to school and hear all the amazing things Santa brought for everyone else in their class. I won't need to explain to them why Santa brought them less. All I need is to put in more work until Christmas, and I can make this a reality. Instead of my usual eight to four, I will need to be here seven to seven like Stratford Junior. That is what my kids need from me.

I take a deep breath in and close my eyes. I remind myself it goes beyond just this Christmas too. I am their only parent, their only source of protection. This job gives me that ability to protect them. If I don't show Stratford Junior that I will show up, I might lose this bonus and this job completely. I dramatically nod my head up and down, and say, "Deal."

I leave his office and head to the restroom. I use speed dial and press one as my clammy hands stick to my phone.

"Hey, Mom? Sorry to bother you at your fundraising event," I say quietly.

"Are you okay?"

"Yeah . . . It's just that . . . I have some work that has a tight deadline. I need to stay late tonight and probably the rest of the week."

"Well, that's great news for the firm! I'm sure your father will be excited to learn all about it."

It doesn't feel like great news for me. "I feel bad for asking this, but can you pick up the kids tonight and have them sleep at your place for the next couple of days? Just until I can get this work stuff under control."

"Of course. I'm always happy to take my grandbabies for a couple of days."

I already feel swarmed with guilt for not giving the world to my children. I'm a parent, yet I still rely on my mother as if I were a child myself. I hate asking for more, but I also know I can't cover the pageant practice and get this all done. "Also, I'm supposed to help with the pageant practice for Susie today and tomorrow at 2:30. Can you cover for me? I'm helping with the sets and can email you what I was planning to do."

"Honey, don't you worry! I can do it."

"What about your event today at the country club?"

"My grandbabies take priority. You take priority."

I sigh in relief but am filled with guilt. "Thank you, Mom. I'm sorry that I'm putting this all on you so last minute."

"My job as your mother is to support you."

I just wish I could do the same for my kids. "I appreciate it."

"No problem. Anywho, it sounds like Betsy is finally about to finish her hour-long rant and will allow us to get in line for the buffet. Good luck today!"

I hang up and look in the mirror. I lock eyes with my reflection. *I have made my decision, and I won't let you down.* I march back to my desk and begin my sprint to impress Stratford. To save my job. To do right for my family. To get the money for the best Christmas ever.

CHAPTER 14

# Saturday, December 17, 2016

*"Santa Claus has the right idea – visit people only once a year."*

— VICTOR BORGE

## (8 DAYS UNTIL CHRISTMAS)

I ROLL OVER TO UNPLUG MY PHONE, but instead, I meet Rick's warm and inviting body. I asked Rick over last night since the kids are still staying with my mom. The house seemed too quiet. I needed someone here.

I nuzzle my way into the crevice between his shoulder and chest that seems perfectly shaped to support my head. I wrap my arm around his body, caressing his skin. It feels good to wake up with him. To not be alone.

"Good morning, beautiful," Rick's voice is rusty. He rolls over and wraps me in his arms. I gladly accept, appreciating being the one held by another.

"Are you excited to meet the family today?" I ask. Today is my mom's Christmas party, and I have invited Rick for the first time. I rarely see my extended family outside of this annual event, so I hope he doesn't feel any pressure. It's mainly to appease my mother, who wants to show him off.

He rolls on top and pulls me under the covers. "Or we can stay right here all day," he says.

The idea feels so tempting. Blissful. Even freeing. I start to breathe in his spiced wood cologne and feel more guilt than bliss. I haven't seen my kids now for several days, yet I'm feeling blissful? I throw off the sheets and jump from the bed. "I wish, but we need to get to my parents early to help set up for the party," I say. I pick up our clothes that are now scattered across the floor. I feel Rick's arms around my waist. "Just ten more minutes?" he asks.

Of course, I want ten more minutes, but we simply can't do it. I have a list. Obligations. "Rick, we should get ready. I still need to get my aunt a gift, and then I need to pick up the cake."

"Fine," he responds. He starts to put on his clothes from last night. "I'll get ready at my place and meet you at your parents in an hour?"

"Yes, see you there," I respond. Typically, my mom mandates a business formal dress code for her sophisticated Christmas soiree, but this year she loosened up and noted on the invitations that business casual will now be accepted. I pick out a green velvet sweater with a black flowing skirt and pair it with black tights and flats.

I also still need to get something for the gift exchange. Each year, we are assigned one person to give a gift which is great for cutting down costs. This year I was assigned

Aunt Roxanne, my mom's sister. Aunt Roxanne is everything my mother stands against. For starters, Roxanne never got married or had any children. She lives on the outskirts of Nova. Her clothes never seem to fit because she is more interested in comfort than style. My mother struggles to even look at her sister, between her ragged clothes and her greyed hair that Roxanne refuses to dye.

Roxanne has a mysterious nature to her. She is pleasantly quiet in a way I don't see in most people. She never seems anxious enough to be in a rush or depressed enough to not be in a hurry. Just perfectly still. No one is sure how she makes money, but she never comes around asking for anything, so she must somehow get by. My mom's conspiracy theory is that she has a marijuana business in her home. She believes when Roxanne dies and we get the house, we will find stashes of pot and cash.

I have yet to buy her a gift because of my extended hours at work. Instead, I go to my closet and pull out a clear bin filled with random objects labeled THE LAND OF MISFIT GIFTS. Each year I add gifts I receive and don't plan to use to the box. When I need to give someone a gift, my first stop is always to see if I can transform any of these random objects into a thoughtful present simply by wrapping it in shiny paper and adding a bow.

I pop off the lid. A grenade of uncomplimentary smells assaults my nose. I smell lighter hints of a peach bath bomb mixing with wild fig wall scents and a dash of birthday cake from a flavored candle. I continue to sift through, finding nothing that matches the little I know about Roxanne. She doesn't strike me as a woman who would waste a tub of water on a bath nor light a candle—especially a birthday cake scented candle. I try to think about what I do know about Roxanne. I know she loves her dogs and walking in the woods. I look in the box for anything dog-related. It's unclear why someone would get me dog-related items since I have never owned a dog or am interested in it.

I also know the only thing Roxanne and my mom have in common is reading murder mystery novels. My mom gives me books, but I always fall asleep within five minutes of reading them. I leave the closet and instead go to my nightstand to rummage through my collection of books. I see some famous authors like James Patterson and Mary Higgens Clark, which I assume Roxanne has already read. At the top of the stack is a book by Margaret Madison, a lesser-known mystery novelist. My mom believes she's superior to all other mystery authors. Perhaps this will be a new read for Roxanne. I pick out the two latest books by Margaret, pop them in a festive box, and add a bow. Perfect. One thing off the list, and I saved a couple of bucks with a re-gift.

---

"Mom! I'm here!" I shout as I open their front door with a cake for the party in one hand and the gift for Roxanne in my purse.

"Mommy!" I hear Susie shout as she runs in my direction. When she reaches the front door, she wraps herself around my legs. It has only been a couple of days, but I swear Susie seems an inch taller. "I missed you, Mommy! Why were you gone for so long?" She pulls back from my legs to look into my eyes. My heart feels torn. *How do I support my children? Did I do the right thing in prioritizing my job? What moments did I miss in their life that I will never get back?*

"I'm sorry, Susie. Mommy had to work more than usual this week, but you will have my attention all weekend. Where is your brother?"

"He's with Grandpa in his office," Susie replies.

I head down the main hall that's lined with family photos. The frames are uniform, but the images are all so different. They include many people—some with Mason and some without. There are different clothes, different styles, and different poses. Even in the smallest detail of my smile, I notice changes. Besides my outdated hairstyles, the biggest change is my smile that is transforming to look more and more like my mother's.

When I get to the office, I find Noah on my dad's lap at the desk. Behind the desk are floor-to-ceiling bookshelves containing primarily law books and a complete collection of Britannica Encyclopedias. One set of books look out of place. As I focus on them, I see the Harry Potter series, one childhood interest I remember enjoying with my dad.

I look at Noah and say, "Are you helping Grandpa with his work?"

He pops off my dad's lap and runs over to me. "Mommy! I missed you!" He hugs my legs and then pulls away. "Grandpa was showing me patents of Nerf guns."

That sounds like my dad. He stands up and says, "Just preparing our next generation of lawyers," winking at me. "How are things going at work for you, Rachel? I heard the Stratford firm got the Myopic case. Sounds interesting."

The case is the last thing I want to talk about. I simply nod. "Yeah, I'm glad we have some new workload outside the GM case."

"Agreed," he responds. "It's been a long case. I'm ready for a change myself. I sure would have enjoyed the case more if you were the lawyer I was arguing against in court."

"Well, you were arguing against some of my logic. The Stratfords just presented it."

"It might be time for you to go to law school."

I think back to the many years I considered applying to law school. I simply respond, "Perhaps. I'll think about it."

"That's my girl."

I leave the office and head into the kitchen, where I find my mother fussing over each dish the caterers are preparing. She is wearing a bright red A-line dress that pulls in at her waist. Her face looks like porcelain, and her hair is pinned up in an elaborate bun, her ears adorned with pearls. I remember last Christmas she demanded that my dad buy them for her. Around her neck is the matching necklace.

"There you are, honey!" She comes to hug me and adds, "Why such a casual outfit?"

I look down to reevaluate my outfit. "You said business casual. I would argue this is business casual."

"Yes, for the guests, but not for you! You are part of the family. We need to look our best for them. Come. Let's look upstairs to see if we have anything for you to change into."

"Fine." I drag my feet as I follow her upstairs to my childhood closet, where she still stores clothes for me.

"And your makeup," my mom continues, "let me do a little spot check. I wouldn't want anyone thinking anything with that bright-colored eyeshadow."

---

By the time Rick comes, about fifty of the hundred guests have already arrived. Rick is dressed in his typical business suit with a festive yet tasteful tie decorated with mistletoe. My mom greets him. "See, honey," she directs to me, "Rick must have gotten the memo to keep it business professional. I can always count on Rick." Before I can even greet him, she grabs his arm and begins to parade him around. "Rick, you must come meet my dear friend, Sheryl."

I simply wave and mouth to him, "Good luck."

The next guest to arrive is my Aunt Roxanne. My eyes drift to her oversized, brightly colored Christmas sweater that she has paired with somewhat fitted sweatpants. She clearly missed or just completely disregarded the memo about the dress code. She slinks through the crowd, awkwardly nodding and apologizing to anyone she bumps into as she navigates to the kitchen. I decide to follow her. I touch her shoulder, and Roxanne reacts with a soft "sorry," assuming she was in the way.

"Hey, Aunt Roxanne," I say, "I just wanted to come over and say hi."

Roxanne slightly bows and then comes in for a hug. "Oh, Rachel. Yes. How are you doing?"

"Oh, I'm good. Happy for the holidays but ready for this brutal winter to end."

"Awh, yes, the snow is particularly bad this year. More time to spend inside, though. Are you still painting? Mother like daughter, I guess."

My one eyelid squints. "What do you mean 'mother like daughter'?"

She looks around and seems to get nervous. "Oh, never mind. How are you faring with the loss of Mason?" she asks nonchalantly.

No one ever asks about Mason anymore. For the first couple of months after his death, people would try to ask. Rarely did they offer an open ear. Instead, they offered pity, casseroles, or unsolicited advice on loss based on their elderly parents' or childhood cat's death, leaving me to listen to their grief. But then, one day, it stopped. Perhaps, everyone felt it had been long enough for me to get over his death. Or, perhaps, they feared mentioning his name would trigger me into a spiral of tears. The questions faded, and I was expected to move on, regardless of how I felt.

"Uh . . . yeah, it still hurts, but I'm good." My throat becomes dry. I look for water and notice Rick near the sink. "In fact, my boyfriend is here with me." I point in his direction. "He's right over there with Mom. Do you want to say hi?"

"Okay," she responds sheepishly.

I introduce my aunt to Rick, who gives her a firm hug. Roxanne then turns to my mom.

"Merry Christmas, Barbara!" Roxanne announces.

My mom stands motionless, trying to take in and accept Roxanne even though she did not follow the dress code. In fairness to Roxanne, she is consistent and never follows the dress code, yet each year my mom is shocked by her sister's attire. She leans in for a hug. "Little Roxanne! How are you?"

"Things are well! Lots of snow out in the woods, but it's beautiful to watch fall. I'm so happy to see you!" Roxanne responds with a sincere and calm cadence.

"Yes, and you too." My mom pauses and looks around awkwardly. "I think we are running out of cocktail sauce for the shrimp. Let me replace that and come back."

My mom vanishes, leaving Rick and me with Roxanne. I remember the gift in my bag and get it out for her. "I actually have something for you."

"Oh, that's very sweet." She opens the lid and reveals the two books I packed inside. She smiles wide. "Oh, thank you, Rachel. You know how I love a good book."

"Yes. Have you read any books by Margaret Madison before?" I ask. "My mom claims she's the best mystery author."

She grins. "Well, that's quite a compliment. I'm excited to give her a try." She pauses and adds, "I didn't know she still reads mysteries."

"Oh yeah, she finishes a mystery novel basically once a week."

A faint smile appears on her face. "I didn't realize that. That's good to hear."

The conversation ends there, and we stand together. Usually, the silence would make me feel awkward, but it feels natural and unpressured with Aunt Roxanne. It seems okay to just exist with her, to breathe without a forced smile or conversation.

CHAPTER 15

# Thursday, December 22, 2016

*"Your children need your presence more than your presents."*

— JESSE JACKSON

## (3 DAYS UNTIL CHRISTMAS)

ON MONDAY, we learned that we lost the GM case. It was simply stated in an email from Stratford Senior. No one dares to mention it. We have all been too busy preparing the Myopic case. Only minutes after getting news of the GM loss, Senior sends another email saying that we should file for Myopic by the end of the week.

The clock in the conference room reads 12:35 PM, but no one is moving to get their lunch. Sam's posture seems pulled up by a set of strings as his fingers fervently prance across his keyboard. John, with a more slouched posture, smacks his keys at an equally fast rate. Both Sam's and John's necks seem to have a form of paralysis, preventing them from looking anywhere besides their screens. I can no longer concentrate with the knocking from my stomach, but I don't dare move.

This continues until 5:30 PM. My legs shake under the table, and my eyes forcefully strain open. I hear pings from my stomach for food, my eyes for sleep, and my back for movement, but I respond to none of these. I only respond to one demand. I need to finish this submission.

Tonight is Susie's pageant. I already told her that I won't be able to come, and she was devastated. I question if I'm doing the right thing. How do I best support my children? I need to make money, but I also should physically be there for them. Susie needs me to get back into good graces at work and earn that Christmas bonus to support her. Maybe there is still a way to do both. "How late are we planning to stay tonight?" I ask.

Stratford's eyes don't move. "Until it's submitted."

I breathe in deeply. I look at the picture on my desk. Susie, Noah, me, and Mason. A seemingly perfect family. One decision. One moment. One well-intended choice changed that, though. We never know when our last moment will be. I need to be with Susie. I need to be with my family. I have given more than enough to this firm, not just these last two weeks but for the last decade. As Stratford Junior said, I am one of the best paralegals here. That should be enough. Perhaps it's the photo of Mason or the delirium from the lack of food today, but I stand up, placing my hands on my desk for support, and look at Stratford Junior. "I need to leave at 6:15 today."

John, Sam, Brian, and Stratford all regain mobility and turn towards me. They then look at Stratford Junior, who continues to stare at me. All I hear, feel, and concentrate on is my beating heart.

"Fine. We will finish without you." His eyes return to his screen, and the pounds on his keyboard seem to match the thump of my heart.

My throat dryly swallows the reaction, and my eyes return to my screen. "I'll be online in the evening." No one responds. This won't help my case for the bonus. It was just a matter of days before he would decide, but Susie needs me at her play. She already has one parent that can't come. Perhaps I can't give them all the gifts in the world, but I can provide them with love from their one surviving parent.

---

I enter the backdoor of the small auditorium. The whispers of the hundred or so people in the audience slowly dissipate as the lights dim. I navigate the central aisle with my phone light. I bob my head looking down each row, trying to spot my mom and Noah. Noah spots me first and shouts, "Mommy!" My mom provides a stern "Shush." I delicately manipulate my body over the people in the row as if in a live version of the game *Operation*.

"I didn't think you could make it," my mom says.

"I need to be here for Susie." I give a big squeeze to Noah. I missed him. I miss Susie.

"Do you think that's such a good idea? I thought this case was really important for the firm. Your father told me about your firm losing to GM."

"Yes, but Susie is more important," I respond confidently, trying not to second guess my choices.

My mom looks at me skeptically with one eyebrow raised. "Alright."

I squeeze Noah one more time and then turn my attention to the stage. The backdrop sparkles with Christmas lights, creating a starry night against the dark blue sky. The brightest light is above the barn where baby Jesus lays in a manger. Painted in the distance are the three kings traveling on camels bearing their gifts for the new child while sheep graze in the pasture nearby. The scene invokes the magic of the season. That the birth of one child can change the world. As a nonbeliever, the scene still invokes magic and reminds one of the potential for change and love during this season. It reminds me that every child's birth is a miracle and each Christmas I get to spend with my children is a gift.

How did my mom do this? The set is even better than I envisioned. I notice she even incorporated the idea I mentioned in my email. Highlighted by each light is a star decorated by every student.

"Mom." I stop in shock. "This is beautiful. Did you make this?"

She simply nods. “Of course. You said you needed help.”

“I didn’t realize that you were so good at painting,” I add.

She smiles. “There is a lot you don’t know about me.”

My head shakes left to right. “Why didn’t I know this about you?” I ask. She knows I love to paint. She knows I went to college for it, yet she always minimized it. She made painting seem pointless. Frivolous. Yet here she is, a better painter than me—more than just natural skills. I look at the shadow work around the manger, the craftsmanship that could only come from training. “It looks so professional, Mom.”

“Well, thank you. Let’s focus on the show, though.”

My attention shifts from the stage to my mother, who keeps her gaze forward. Maybe she just paid someone to paint these sets? She does love to throw money at problems. But then I remember the small comment from Roxanne. Maybe she has been painting her whole life and has never told me. She has always gone to the country club for her female-only outings. Maybe she is secretly painting, indulging in the frivolousness of an unsatisfied passion that burns inside. Perhaps I have inherited that fire from her. Is there a whole other side of my mother that she has hidden from us?

The kids come on stage, but my eyes are still focused on my mother. What else do I not know about the woman who raised me? What was her life like before me? She never would answer me as a kid, so I stopped asking.

I shake all the questions from my head and focus on Susie. She's in the front left corner, intermixed with the other thirty students. I can see her sparkling slippers shining with her matching bow that's nearly the size of her head. Her skin glows beneath the stage lights like an angel of innocence.

Together they attempt to sing "Away in a Manger" as they sway and perform simple gestures with their hands. Luckily for the parents, we are built with the ability to autotune their singing and instead hear a choir of synchronized angels—our angels that were gifted to us on this Earth. Innocent and free. Yet someday, our angels will grow up, they will make mistakes, some will commit crimes, and most will lie to the ones they love the most. When does that change happen?

I look back to Susie. Unlike the other kids, she is not scanning the audience trying to find her family. Instead, she focuses on the girl to her right, replicating her moves with a slight delay. Susie stumbles through the dance and forgets to keep singing. She looks frazzled and frustrated to be out of sync with the rest of her peers. *Don't worry, Susie, I'll protect you.*

CHAPTER 16

# Friday, December 23

*"Christmas waves a magic wand over this world, and behold, everything is softer and more beautiful."*

— NORMAN VINCENT PEALE

## (2 DAYS UNTIL CHRISTMAS)

BEFORE HEADING INTO WORK, I agreed to meet Karen for a coffee since I ditched her with my mom for the pageant. She was so kind when I told her I needed to stop helping. Plus, I secretly want to know if my mom paid someone to make the sets or if she really did come in and work on them.

At the cafe, I splurge and get the full-fat eggnog latte *with* the gingerbread scone on the side. It is the day before Christmas Eve, so it's time for the holiday treats that I rationalize as mandatory calories during the season.

I cozy up in the corner booth looking out on the bustling downtown avenue. The subzero weather and pounding snow don't stop the Michiganders from continuing their day. My attention drifts to one couple. The woman is running ahead while her partner trudges behind. I assume she is rushing to find those last couple of perfect gifts. Perhaps she is still trying to find a gift for him. Based on his wind-burned face, I assume the one gift he wants more than anything is to stop shopping and return home.

"Rachel!" My head turns to see Karen. "So happy to see you!" I had become so distracted by the world beyond the window, I forgot that I came for more than just the delicious scone and latte.

"Oh, yes!" I respond. "Glad we could find time to meet. And thanks again for covering for me at the pageant and dealing with my mom. I'm still so embarrassed about it all."

"Oh, no worries! It was nice of you to ask your mom to step in and help. I mean, those sets! They were beautiful. I didn't realize that you and your mom were artists."

"So, my mom really did come in and do the sets, huh?"

Karen giggles. "Of course, Rachel, you and your mom are very talented! Between the costumes I see you make for Susie and those sets, you two could start a business. Do you have other projects you work on together?"

"My mom and I?" I say dumbfoundedly. "I mean, not really. I didn't even know my mom painted, and I just doodle sometimes with the kids, but it's not art."

"If it's anything like those sets, I would beg to differ."

I cough to clear my throat. "Well, that's kind, Karen," I respond, feeling awkward that this has become the focus of our conversation.

"I'm serious," she continues, "you both could be professional artists!"

I try to accept the kind words with grace. "How about you and Pixie Cupcakes?"

"Oh, it's lovely! I'm doing part-time right now, so I can spend more time with the kiddos and husband, but that doesn't stop me from sneaking in a cupcake every day." She provides a big smirk as she raises the oversized mug to her lips.

"You must be expecting a break in business after the holidays with everyone's New Year's resolutions and all?" I ask.

"Just a couple of weeks, which is a nice break before we are in full production for Valentine's Day. And by then, we can't hit the demand."

"Sounds like a lot of fun."

"Oh, yes! It's truly magical. I mean . . . " She pauses and looks out the window. "It's my dream." Karen looks back at me. "Anywho, how 'bout you? You're a paralegal, right? That must be fascinating."

"Um . . . " I pause to think. Fascinating? My dad certainly finds it fascinating. And so does Stratford Junior. But do I?

Karen leans closer to me. I realize I never responded. "Yeah, it's fine," I reply. "It pays the bills, and I'm good at it." I look at my watch and see I have been here for thirty minutes. "I might actually need to head into work soon."

"Oh . . . " she says with hesitation.

I wonder what she means with her unusually short response. I ask, "What's wrong?"

She fidgets in her chair and looks into her cup as if she is reading my fate through the remaining tea leaves. "Oh . . . I just . . . I guess it's just strange to me."

What part does she find strange? That I have to pay the bills and go to work, or that I need to show up to my job to make money? I ask, "Strange that I need to go to work today?"

"No, just that . . . " She begins to stammer, pauses, and then looks at me. "Rachel, you are so talented. Why work a job you don't love? Your art. It could be a business, you know?"

I grasp onto my mug as if a shield to protect me from what feels like unwarranted compliments. "Karen, I appreciate the support, but I have two kids to raise. I don't have the time or money to start a business."

"I understand . . . I just—I just wonder . . . For Susie, I'm sure she wants you to be happy."

My breath thickens, taken aback that she would even mention my daughter and question my ability to keep her happy.

"Would you want Susie to work a job that's just fine?" Karen frowns. "I'm just saying that because I know I felt that way before my cupcake store, but I can help you. Let me help you."

Now I remember why I don't like Karen. She judges just like the rest of them.

I push up from the booth. My internal flames consume me. I begin to release my breath, but instead, I release anger. "You know what, Karen? I'm sorry I don't have a husband who can sponsor my existence to live my dreams. I have no husband and two children that rely on me every day, so no, Karen, it's not an option for everyone to live their dreams like you." I pick up my bag and leave, not even finishing the last sips of the eggnog latte.

As I drive to the office, shame starts to bank the angry flames. Why couldn't I stay calm? No one wants to hear those ugly thoughts. No one wants to spend time with the sad, angry woman. I have never said anything like that to someone, but then again, no one has ever said anything so direct to me. I'm used to people tiptoeing around me in fear that they might mention something about my dead husband, so instead, they say nothing.

Reflecting on the conversation, I realize I admitted something in the heated moment that I have never disclosed to anyone. Being a paralegal was never my dream. Perhaps somewhere in me, I already knew this, but I have never verbalized it.

I pull my car into the parking lot and look at the office building. This is the only career I have ever had. And I'm good at it. What other choice do I have? I park Bonnie in my spot and notice Stratford Junior's red Tesla in its usual place. The least I can do today is get that bonus.

Inside, Stratford Junior's door is closed. I set my bag down and pull out my laptop to check my email. I have five new messages. The first message is from my dad. Inside it says:

I got some good news today. I will share it with you at Christmas.

My dad has yet to enter the mobile age and still sends messages via email instead of text. I assume he found some evidence I can use for the Myopic case. He likes to get involved in any new case as if he doesn't have enough to work on at GM.

Next in my mailbox is an email from Stratford Senior.

Rachel - I talked to my son and was confused to hear you didn't get the yearly Christmas bonus. It's a gift from the company. He should have given it to you in the first place. You will see it on your paycheck in two weeks. –SS

Does this mean that all my extra hours and missing my kids was for nothing? I purse my lips. I got what I wanted, yet I feel so dissatisfied with how I got it. Junior told me that he and Senior agreed not to give me the bonus, but now Senior is saying the opposite. Why would Stratford Junior do that?

I look at his door. The once ominous door looks small. I envision bursting into his office and yelling so fiercely that Stratford Junior's posture begins to curve in fear of my wrath. But I don't. Instead, I breathe. I remain in my chair and return my gaze to the screen. I got the bonus, and I still have time to get every gift on Noah and Susie's long Christmas lists and more. This will be the largest pile of gifts they will have ever gotten. A Christmas they will never forget. I made that happen for them. I can make up for the last two weeks on Christmas day.

I breeze over the rest of my emails and try to get through the day. Christmas is finally about to begin.

CHAPTER 17

# Christmas Eve

*"T'was the night before Christmas, when all through the house, not a creature was stirring, not even a mouse."*

— CLEMENT CLARKE MOORE

## (1 DAY UNTIL CHRISTMAS)

TODAY ALREADY FEELS LIKE CHRISTMAS. Snow is falling beyond the frosted bay window. Three stockings are hung on the fireplace, and presents circle the decorated tree. Christmas songs whisper from the speakers. The smell of pine dances with the freshly made cinnamon rolls in the kitchen.

"Grandpa and Grandma are here!" Noah shouts as he dashes to open the front door.

Grandma Sherry is wearing a black button-up cardigan that's decorated with hand stitched snowflakes. Grandpa Bob has a simple green half-zip sweater and a Santa hat on top. "Ho ho ho," he bellows as he walks in with a bursting bag of presents. I assume most of the gifts aren't things Noah and Susie need. But the concept of what a child needs versus what a child wants has never stopped grandparents from spoiling their grandbabies on Christmas.

"It smells so lovely in here," Grandma Sherry says as she uses one arm to hug me. Every Christmas Eve since meeting Mason, we would make Sherry's homemade cinnamon rolls. Mine still never taste quite as good as hers.

Grandpa Bob arranges the presents below the tree. Noah is right behind him, questioning, "Is this for me? It's so biggggg!!"

"You'll have to wait and see, mister," Bob responds.

"I really hope I get the big one!"

"I bet it's for me!" Susie demands.

We collect around the kitchen table, each with a cinnamon roll the size of our face. Within seconds, Susie and Noah have found a way to get frosting all over their face, fingers, clothes, and up their noses. I would probably get upset for any other meal, but at this moment, I feel joy to just be with them for another Christmas. I want them to feel the Christmas magic, even if that comes at an extra cost for me later when I need to clean them up. I have done everything in my power to make this the most magical Christmas, and I won't ruin it now over some icing. Instead, I live vigorously through their boundless joy.

"So, kids, what do you think Santa will be bringing you this year?" Sherry asks.

"A pony!" Susie shouts.

"A My Little Pony, though, since the elves can only make toys, right?" I chime in, ensuring that she won't be let down tomorrow when there is, in fact, no live pony under the Christmas tree.

"Yes! Bright pink!"

Check. She should be happy then.

"I want the Elite Titan CS-50 Nerf gun!" shouts Noah.

"That's very specific! What if Santa's elves don't make that type of Nerf gun?" Sherry asks.

"Santa elves can make anything. They have magic!"

Grandma Sherry chuckles. "Oh, right! Good point."

"Kids, do you want to open the presents from your grandparents?" I ask.

Both Susie and Noah bounce up, screaming yes.

Noah runs to the tree and starts shaking boxes, trying to guess what is inside each package.

"Noah, be careful! Let's not break any of the gifts," I say.

"No worries, we know not to get these rascals anything breakable," Bob jokes.

Gift after gift, Susie and Noah squeal with excitement. They shout and run around, parading their new toys until the ground is covered with a pile of ripped wrapping paper. The beauty quickly transformed into a pile of chaos.

"I have one more gift for you guys," I say. I head to the side closet and pull out a large flat package and hand it to Sherry.

"What's this?" Sherry asks.

"Just a little something that I made for you."

Sherry delicately pulls away the wrapping paper to unveil an image that Sherry holds dear to her heart. Inside the frame, decorated with a feather on top, is an acrylic painting of the same image Sherry found on the Christmas tree; the one of Bob, Mason, and Noah going fishing. Sherry embraces the artwork just like she embraces Noah and Susie.

Sherry pulls in her quivering bottom lip. "Rachel, this is beautiful. I don't have words." She sets the painting on the coffee table, stands up, and approaches me. She wraps both her arms tightly around me—how I have missed these hugs. I know at this moment that my sleepless night of painting was worth it. My body is reminded of the impact art can have on the world around me.

We sit in the living room and watch the kids play on the carpet with their new toys. Outside, a white mist of snow begins to fall. I grasp my mug of sweetened coffee and look towards Sherry. We lock eyes, and I notice a soft stream of tears. We have seen each other cry many times, but I recognize these tears as joyous ones. Sherry mouths "thank you" with pure sincerity. Neither of us wants to do anything to change this perfect Christmas scene. I listen more closely to the Christmas song playing on the radio.

*Let there be peace on earth,*
*And let it begin with me.*

*Let there be peace on earth,*
*The peace that was meant to be.*

At this moment, I feel that peace in my little world sprawled across the living room floor. I feel the Christmas magic myself.

---

After Bob and Sherry leave, we have one more Christmas Eve tradition to complete. Noah, Susie, and I are dressed in our matching flannel PJs decorated with penguins playing in the snow. All the lights are dimmed, leaving only the glow of the Christmas tree and the television to compete for our attention. Together, we cuddle on the couch to watch *Elf*.

Near the end of the movie, I hear the infamous line that I know Noah is waiting for:

*The best way to spread Christmas cheer is by singing loud for all to hear.*

Noah jumps up and starts dancing around the room, singing, or, more accurately, shouting along with the Christmas carols in the scene.

Noah enters a state of pure euphoric joy—carefree singing, dancing, and complete presence in the now. I take in this beautiful moment, the embodiment of Christmas magic. My focus is interrupted by a vibrate in my pocket—a text from Stratford Junior.

Can you submit all final expenses for the year? Thanks!

I wonder if he even realizes it's Christmas Eve. Does he have anyone to celebrate with? I respond to his text.

I will submit them first thing when I'm back at work next week. Merry Christmas!

As I put down my phone, I realize I completely missed Susie also getting up to dance with Noah. Their small hands are connected as they swing back and forth. I hold down the power button on my phone. I'm unwilling to sacrifice one more of these moments for a job that doesn't satisfy me. This flash in time will not be taken away from me. I toss the phone under a throw pillow, and I get up to also jump around the room. I breathe in this miraculously joyous moment, never wanting to exhale and lose one gasp of the Christmas magic dancing through my living room.

---

It has been hours since I tucked Noah and Susie into bed. Delivering the gifts from Santa is the last thing I need to do to ensure a perfect Christmas. I decided to wait longer than usual just in case Noah's plans I saw in the car are true. I sneak back into Noah's room to ensure he's still in bed. With one peek, I see the lump of his body curled up in a blanket. I do the same with Susie.

I head to my closet and grab the two suitcases containing Santa's presents. I grip each bag, open the door delicately, and tiptoe down the stairs. When I look upstairs, Noah's and Susie's doors remain closed. So far, so good.

I unzip one suitcase and take out the first beautifully wrapped present with a tag reading To Susie, From Santa. I place the gift nimbly under the tree.

"Mom?"

I turn around. "I thought you were in bed!" I say.

Behind the coach, Noah is crouching with an arsenal of Nerf guns. His face, still and confused. His body is motionless.

"I thought *you* were in bed," he responds. "Santa will be here any minute. I don't want you to spook him off."

Noah doesn't seem to suspect anything. Maybe there is still a chance I can save this. "Oh, okay, I'll head back up."

"Why do you have suitcases?" he asks.

Noah approaches the bags, and I quickly try to cover up what is inside. He picks up the gift I just placed under the tree. "From Santa? Why does it say 'From Santa'?"

Busted. Do I try to cover up this lie further? Maybe I can say Santa was sick this year, so I needed to help him? Noah continues to stare at me as I search for my answer. "Oh, honey, I'm so sorry. I don't know what to say." Well, that was the worst thing I could say. I have officially ruined Christmas for Noah.

"Mommy, is Santa not real?" Noah's eyes start to water. "But . . . But I was going to catch him and show everyone at school pro-proof," he says through his whimpers. He can no longer hold the tears back.

"Oh, honey, oh no, please don't cry. I'm so sorry!" At this point, I don't care if his tears wake Susie because I'm paralyzed by the pain I have created for Noah. On the holiday that he associates with his father. Did I just ruin his memory of his dad? Will he ever have faith again or believe in the magic of stories? Will he lose his childish curiosity? Of course, I know that Santa is fictional, but he was so real to Noah. I stay silent, knowing he needs some time to mourn the loss of his reality that he held onto so tightly. Just like mourning the loss of his dad, I know that Noah is mourning the loss of Santa right now. The gravity of loss is different, but both are still losses.

I cradle Noah as he cries into the corner of my penguin PJs that we are both still wearing. Finally, Noah lifts his face. "So Gus was right? There's no Santa?"

"I'm so sorry, sweetie, but yes, the Santa you see in the movies and books is not real." I know I need to come up with something to save the moment. And I need to find it fast. "But, Noah, the essence of Santa is alive in our home, in our family, in our community, and all over the world. There is no man with a white beard and a red suit that delivers presents, but I deliver them for you, and so do the parents at your school. We are like a team of Santas that work together to create that magic of the season we all love so much. And *that* magic is real! It's just that the source is a little closer to home than the North Pole."

Noah lifts his head. Tears continue to roll down his face. He locks eyes with me, searching for hope. "So, you buy us gifts every year?"

I nod.

"And you eat the cookies we leave?"

I nod.

"And you just keep the letters we write?"

I nod.

Tears begin to well up again. "How am I going to face everyone at school?"

"You'll be brave, just like your daddy taught you. And you won't be like Gus and make fun of anyone who doesn't know who the true Santa is yet."

"So, I just lie to them?"

He makes a good point. "If they ask you, then you should be honest, but you don't need to do what Gus did and announce it to the class."

He takes a moment to think. "So you buy me all my Nerf guns?"

I laugh that this is the point Noah is struggling with the most. "Yes, honey. I guess your mom is cool enough to buy some Nerf guns."

Noah hugs me tightly. "So my mom is Santa? I guess that's kinda cool."

"Yeah, it's kinda cool, isn't it? What makes Mom being Santa cool to you?"

"Because that means we can have Christmas every day if you are the one making it."

Noah nuzzles himself into my chest. I can feel his little heartbeat beneath his PJs that are damp from his tears.

"So, the tooth fairy is still real, right?"

I giggle. "I'm the tooth fairy too, and the Easter bunny, and the leprechaun for St. Patrick's Day . . . they're all me."

"That's a lot!"

"Yep. But it's worth it. Let's get you back to bed. What do you say?"

He nods, hugs me tightly, and says, "I love you, Mommy."

"I love you too, Noah. Do you want to set up the presents with me? Be my little elf?"

"Can I open my gifts now?"

"That wouldn't be fair to Susie, *but* you can eat Santa's cookies with me."

Noah smiles, and his small hands wipe the tears from his cheeks. He then wraps his arms around me and whispers, "You're the best Santa, Mommy."

My heart warms. *Perhaps I'm not such a bad mom after all.*

CHAPTER 18

# Christmas Day

*"One of the most glorious messes in the world is the mess created in the living room on Christmas day. Don't clean it up too quickly."*

— ANDY ROONEY

"SANTA CAME, SANTA CAME!!" Susie and Noah shout as they jump on my bed.

I roll out of my bed, rub my eyes, and fumble to find my robe and slippers. I'm still exhausted. I couldn't sleep after ruining it for Noah last night. Mason would never let that happen. I force a smile. "Let's go down and see what he brought."

Susie runs ahead while Noah stays behind.

Noah's index finger directs me to come closer to him. I lean down, and he whispers into my ear, "I decided not to tell Susie that you're Santa. So you better not tell her either. Deal?" He holds out his pinky finger.

I smile. Maybe today will still be special. I interlock my pinky with his. "Deal!"

"COME ONNNNNNNNN!" Susie shouts from below.

Beneath the tree are two large piles of presents for Noah and Susie, each gift wrapped in various shades of red and green patterns. "Santa" splurged and only used wrapping paper because he knows half the fun is ripping off the decorative paper to reveal the object within.

"Wow! These are all for me?" Susie shouts as she digs through her assigned pile of presents.

"Can we open them, Mommy?" Noah asks.

"PLEASEEEE?" Susie adds.

"Let's wait for your grandparents to come. I need my two helpers to prepare breakfast with me."

Soon after, we hear the doorbell, alerting Noah and Susie that they're one step closer to opening presents. Without even hugging her grandparents, Susie shouts, "Okay, it's time to open gifts!!"

"Hold your horses, honey. Let's give your grandparents a proper welcome and then eat breakfast."

My parents arrive in their Sunday best, while the rest of us are still in our matching PJs. I offered to get my parents each a set, but they said no. I'm sure they have already attended the earliest Christmas service at church, something the kids and I stopped doing after Mason's death. My dad is holding a large reusable bag of professionally wrapped presents.

"Merry Christmas, everyone!" my mom announces as she moves through her first round of hugs for the day.

I turn to hug my dad. "Feeling that burn to get back to work yet?" he asks. "I know I'm starting to feel it."

I don't know the feeling he's describing. Perhaps it's just the opposite of the pure torture I feel every year when I need to go back. "Not yet," I respond.

"I think you might feel it later today," he says with a wink. Why is he acting so weird?

I collect their coats, serve breakfast, and then head to the tree to open the gifts. I let Noah start. He examines and shakes each box.

"Oh, be careful!" my mom declares. "You wouldn't want to break anything we brought."

He opens the biggest one first. He violently rips off the paper and jumps up when he sees the toy below.

"Oh, boy! It is the Elite Titan CS-50 Nerf Blaster from Santa," Noah shouts. He looks back at me and attempts to wink one eye when, in reality, he just gives a long hard blink with both eyes.

"Santa is always listening," I say, smiling back at Noah.

Noah opens the Nerf gun's box while Susie plays with the wrapping paper spread across the floor. She seems more enthralled with that than any of the actual gifts under the tree. Next year, I'll just wrap empty boxes with the shiniest paper and bows for her enjoyment.

Once we complete Santa's gifts, we move onto the gifts from Grandma and Grandpa. First up is Susie. Her present is wrapped in an elegant shimmering gold paper with a thick red velvet bow. Distracted by the soft bow, Susie seems to forget that the toy is *inside* the box, not the box itself. I attempt to rip a corner of the paper, causing Susie to cry.

"Okay, perhaps Noah can open his first," I say.

Noah has no problem. With just one rip, he reveals a PlayStation logo on the box. He jumps up and squeals, parading the box around the room.

Anger forms in red blotches on my cheeks. My parents know I don't want game consoles in the house. I just talked to my mom about this! I don't know why I'm even getting mad, though. They never listen to me and my opinions.

"Well, that's very generous," I respond with a forced smile. "Noah, what do we do when someone does something nice for us?"

"Thank youuuuuuuu, Grandma and Grandpa." He runs to them. He stops to consider if he needs to put down his new prize before hugging them both.

"Of course, sweetie!" my mom says. "You deserve the world! Now, Rachel, open your gifts."

My eyes are still fixed on the PlayStation that Noah is parading around the room. I shake my head and decide it's best just to move on. I can always return it and put the money in a college fund for Noah, instead.

I look at the two presents in front of me. Since I was a kid, my parents would give me two separately wrapped Christmas gifts. The first would be an ornament that's supposed to hint at what the main gift will be. Last year, my ornament was a lilac, my favorite flower, and the main gift was an expensive collection of lilac body wash products. Perhaps it was my mom's secret way of saying I needed to shower more.

I pick up the smaller gift that seems the right size for an ornament. The package reads *To Our Dearest Daughter, From Mom and Dad*. I delicately remove the paper. Inside is an ornament that reads WAYNE STATE LAW SCHOOL, my dad's alma mater.

My head tilts, and I look at my parents, sitting together next to me on the couch. "What does this mean?"

Even my dad looks excited. "Open the next box, honey," he says.

The next box is long and flat, wrapped to match the first one. Inside is a sweater and an envelope positioned carefully so that I can still read the print on the sweater—WAYNE STATE LAW SCHOOL. "I don't understand?" I say to them.

"Open the envelope, and it'll make sense," my mom says.

I follow their instructions.

*Dear Rachel,*

*It is time for you to become a lawyer. In the GM case against your firm, it became apparent that your talents should not be squandered simply as a paralegal. When I was doing my IP lectures at Wayne State this semester, I also met with the dean of the law school. I showed him your magnificent work, and he was impressed. He asked if you would want to join the program. You can start this semester.*

*This Christmas, your mother and I have decided to pay the cost of law school so that you can grow in your career. We are excited to have another J.D. in the family. I'm so proud of you and your ambitions.*

*Love, Your Father, and Mother*

I read through the letter once, not fully understanding the meaning behind the words. I start reading from the beginning, still unable to make sense of it. "Wha . . . What does . . . What does this mean?"

"Honey," my dad starts, "you're going to law school. Your dream is coming true."

My head shifts right to left uncontrollably. "But . . . The LSAT? Don't they need a new score? And an essay, don't they need that?"

"I gave them the score and essay that you planned to submit a couple of years ago. I handled it for you."

I can feel sweat forming below my pajamas. "Is it warm in here?" I rush over to the thermostat to make it cooler.

My mom asks, "So, what do you think, darling? You are going to law school! Isn't that your dream?"

I study her cheerful yet timid grin. How do I respond? I pull at my clothes, which are starting to stick to my stomach. Is this my dream? Maybe she's right. Perhaps my dream is law school. I just never thought it was an option after Mason's death. But even before his death, did I ever really want to go to law school? I put my hand to my chest.

I look at Noah and Susie. Both are consumed with their toys; they don't see how this decision might impact their lives. My eyes focus on the PlayStation. I could never get that for Noah on my current salary with the cost of this house, Noah's support for his classes, and their private schools. Going to law school will provide me with more options and more money. I can support Susie and Noah better. I force half my lips upwards into a smile. "This is extremely generous, Mom and Dad. Thank you!"

"Oh, do you like it?!" my mom implores. "Try on the sweater! I want to take a picture and send it out to people."

I slip the sweater over my head even though I'm already too warm. "When do I need to decide?" I ask.

"What is there to decide?" my dad responds.

"Well, I could choose not to go?"

My dad lowers his eyebrows and tilts his head. "Why would you not go?"

"I mean, law school is a lot of work, and I would be making no money, so how will I support the kids?"

"We can subsidize all of that, and you know your mom is always available to help."

I feel internally conflicted. This gift is beyond generous, but do I want to go to law school? I hug my mom tightly and then my dad, hoping they aren't bothered by my sweat and apparent discomfort. I love that my parents support me in taking bold moves in my career; I just don't know if this is the step I want to take.

I shake the thoughts and try to refocus on today. On Christmas. I hand over the last present to my parents. "Noah, Susie, and I have been working on this little gift for you."

"Oh, how sweet," my mom says with a wide grin.

The box is wrapped in thin paper with no shimmer and is decorated with Santa faces and candy canes. Inside the box is a book titled *Adventures with Grandma and Grandpa*. My mom begins to flip the pages, seeing pictures with the kids and barely legible notes from Susie and Noah.

"Do you like it, Grandma?" Noah asks.

"Oh yes, it's charming, honey!" She places it down almost immediately.

---

Later that day, I dress Susie in a velvet red dress and Noah in his suit. We get in the car to honor one more family tradition. A tradition we never hoped to have—visiting the grave of their father on Christmas Day.

The ground is covered in a concoction of mud and snow, coating gravestone after gravestone. Loss after loss. Each stone represents a life, but the land feels so lifeless. As I look around, I notice we are the only family here. We approach Mason's grave. I grip Noah's hand on my left and Susie's on my right. I brush away the mud covering his stone, revealing the inscription.

MASON TAYLOR
NOVEMBER 1, 1983 – JANUARY 6, 2013
A HUSBAND, FATHER, AND SON
A MAN THAT BELIEVED IN COMPASSION OVER FEAR

My heart wails with pain, and the crisp air has dried my eyes. Noah clings to my leg. All we can do is stare at the resting place of the man we all loved so deeply. The man that taught us to love Christmas and each other so tenderly. I place a mistletoe on his grave, lean down, and press my lips on the engraving of his name in remembrance of the Christmas promise we made many years ago.

## — *2005* —

Cuddled by a fire pit on Christmas night, my legs are swung across Mason's lap, our hands intertwined under the wool blanket. It's been three months since Bonnie's fateful breakdown. I have never been more thankful for that car.

Mason turns to me. "Promise me this," he starts. "Even when we are old, wrinkly, and being pushed around in wheelchairs, we always share a Christmas kiss like tonight? Even if you can't stand me or if you are annoyed at some crazy thing I did over the last year, promise me one kiss under the mistletoe?"

"What if we aren't together anymore?" I ask.

"I have a feeling we will be," he says with a wink.

"Well, assuming we are still together . . . I think I can do that," I respond. "But we don't have any mistletoe."

From his pocket, he pulls one out, holding it above us. He slowly leans closer to me, grabbing the side of my neck for one more kiss . . . and another . . . and another as he whispers, "Rachel, I'm madly and deeply in love with you."

I pull back just slightly, staring into his incredibly blue eyes. "I'm madly in love with you too, Mason."

# CHAPTER 19

# Christmas Night

*"And so this is Christmas . . . what have you done?"*

— JOHN LENNON

AFTER TUCKING SUSIE AND NOAH INTO BED, I return to my room feeling like I could have done more to make this Christmas special. Sure I got all the gifts on their lists, and we did all the customs that we used to do with Mason, but did I help them feel the magic Mason would make every Christmas? For God's sake, I was too lazy to lift the sheets off Noah's bed to check if it was him and ended up ruining his Christmas. Now that I'm alone in my room, I cry, holding a pillow to my face, muffling the noises of my grieving. The pain of loss is as fresh today as the day the cops came to our door.

I head to the closet, desperate to find something of Mason's to hold. To remind me of his touch. His smell. His kiss.

His clothes still hang on the racks, untouched since the accident. On the top shelf, I look at the box labeled

JANUARY 6, 2013. I see the corner of the tape peeling off. I know his smell has escaped the box, but at least I can touch something that was with him in those final moments. It is time for me to actually open the box and look at these items for the first time since the accident.

I pull the box down and slowly peel back the stickless piece of tape. I open each flap cautiously. On the top are the clothes he wore on the night of the accident. The thick motorcycle jacket was supposed to protect him if he ever got hit on the bike. His favorite light-washed jeans and a shirt that was once white but now darkened with stains. I hold each item tightly, missing the man that once wore these clothes.

Below his clothes is his backpack. He always brought this bag when he was on the bike. The bag contained tools in case his old bike ever broke down. I notice some of the tools are missing. He must have used them when fixing the girl's car.

My hands shake, but I manage to unzip the bag for the first time since the accident. On the top is my prescription addressed to me. After the accident, I completely forgot about taking the prescription. I guess I never really needed it in the first place. This was all my fault. It was my request. It was my prescription. It will always be my fault.

In the back of the bag, I notice a thick manila envelope. Handwritten on the front, it says *To My Love, Rachel*. I stroke the letters gently as more tears stream down my face. It's Mason's handwriting. My eyes rapidly blink as I try to process what this letter could possibly contain. We used to write letters to each other during the holidays, but we stopped doing that many years before he died. Was it just one that he found from the past, or did he write more recently? Are these my husband's unintended last words to me?

My shaky hands try to delicately open the envelope. I pull out the thick stack of papers, and the first thing is a letter from Mason. I close my eyes and force a breath. I open my eyes, holding back tears as I read the letter.

*Dear Rachel,*

*First, I want to start by saying you are the most amazing wife, mother, best friend, and conspirator for our crazy adventures. Life without you would be unimaginable. As your husband and number one fan, I need to make sure I'm always doing what I can to help you grow and become the woman you envision in your dreams, no matter where that leads us as a family. This Christmas, I hope I can provide just that.*

*For many years I have sat by your side, watching you going in and out of the office for a job that we both know you don't love. While we talk about you leaving when our heads lie next to each other at night, I know you are afraid to act on it, unsure how it will impact our family. I do not want to sit by watching you lose time on a pursuit that is not bringing you daily joy, as you provide for me. Life is too short for you to spend one day not living out a dream.*

*Rachel, you bring pure magic to this home; the world deserves to see and experience the magic like Noah, Susie, and I are so lucky to experience.*

*This Christmas, my gift for you is hope. I hope to show you that your dreams, passions, and talents are viewed as amazing beyond just my biased eyes. You create beautiful images seen only by the eyes of this home and thought-provoking art that you hide in our closet; I want you to see what I see and know that others want to experience it too.*

*Attached in this envelope are three things that you can choose to use or choose to ignore as some typical trouble-making mischief from your loving husband.*

*First, I attached banking information for an account that I have created in your name. Inside is $10,000. This money can ONLY be used by you AND for you! No spending this on the kids like you usually do. I have been collecting this money over time to give you the resources to expand into any creative expression of your choosing. You can leave it sitting there, but I do hope you will spend it on your heart's desires. I hope this can provide some comfort, knowing you can rely on me to support the family as well.*

*Second, every story we write with Noah makes me grow even closer to you and our family. I know you joke about quitting your job and working full-time illustrating stories, and I need to ask why not? So, I wanted to ask others: Should my wife do this full time? Of course, my answer is yes, but I wanted to see what publishers thought. I contacted one publishing firm in Detroit with some copies of our favorite stories that we created with Noah. Within a couple of weeks, they got back to me with a resounding yes: They are interested! Attached is the letter from them with their contact information. It is your choice if you want to reach out to learn more or not, but the option is there for you if you want to illustrate.*

*And lastly, for your paintings. Attached is an email correspondence with a gallery in Ann Arbor that is very excited by your portfolio and is looking forward to showcasing your work. Again, the contact information is there for you if you want to pursue this.*

*Rachel, you have made me a better man. You support me in every dream I have dreamt of. This Christmas, my gift to you is the time, resources, contacts, and, most importantly, hope that you will find and live out any dream you create. I love you, Rachel. Merry Christmas!*

*With all my love, Mason*

*Ps. Sorry for delaying your Christmas gift until after the holidays. It took a bit longer than expected to get this account set up.*

Behind the letter is a statement from Bank of America containing the account information for the money Mason set aside. The account is in my name, which is probably why I was not notified about it after Mason died. The letter is dated January 6, 2013. This was why he was at the store for so long. This was why he went to get my prescription.

As I flip through the pages, my eyes become waterfalls. I keep returning to the last words Mason wrote:

*This Christmas, my gift to you is the time, resources, contacts, and, most importantly, hope that you will find and live out any dream you have. I love you, Rachel. Merry Christmas!*

No amount of breathing techniques can create an external calm for my internal chaos of emotions. My guilt for causing Mason's death is replaced with the guilt of failing him with not living the life he wanted for me. I have failed him yet again.

"Mommy . . . " I hear from outside the closet door.

I attempt to stop my tears by rubbing my eyes with my shirt. I open the door and find Noah standing in his PJs. His face filled with concern.

"Mommy, are you okay?"

What do I say? Should I be honest? *No, I have not been okay since your daddy died. That each day, I feel like a show horse with an audience observing my every step waiting to see if I'll soar or fall over every obstacle. That I feel alone every day. That I feel like a horrible mom to you, an ungrateful child to my parents, and a fraud everywhere I go.* Or do I lie? Do I take a breath and show him I'm strong while my internal soul continues to crumble like an imploding building?

"I'm okay, honey. You don't need to worry about me," I say, hoping to delay the tears welling in my eyes. I stretch out my arms to him. Noah approaches and falls into my lap, squeezing me tightly. His head snuggles into my chest.

He looks up to my damp eyes and says, "Mommy, it's okay if you're not okay."

I look into Noah's soft blue eyes. Noah looks more like Mason tonight than ever before. My face tightens. I need to stay strong for Noah. I must show him I'm okay. But even with these thoughts, the dam that protects me from my grief deconstructs. I dig my face next to Noah as I weep. "You're right. I'm not okay. I'm really missing Daddy."

"Me too." He holds out his arms to either side. "Do you miss him this much?"

I choke a bit on my laugh and squeeze Noah closer. "I miss him that much and a million times more."

"I miss him that much too."

I feel embarrassed to have my son comforting me on Christmas night. I did a horrible job. If Mason were here, I never would have been caught with the gifts from Santa. Noah wouldn't be missing any of the traditions. Christmas would have been magical, but instead, Noah finds his mother sobbing on the floor of her closet. I feel so pathetic as more tears pour out of my eyes. "I'm sorry I ruined your Christmas again this year."

He places his small hand on my cheek, wiping the tears from my eyes. "You didn't ruin it, Mommy. I loved everything about this Christmas, especially figuring out Santa lives right in this house." He wraps his body around me, and I squeeze tighter. I still feel like I have failed him.

"I'm sorry I didn't protect your daddy better for you."

"Mrs. Bushnell says God just needed Daddy to help him in heaven, and we will see him again when we go to heaven."

For so long, I have carried the blame for Mason's death, but perhaps Mrs. Bushnell is right that there is a bigger reason for his death. I just wish that this mysterious God figure would make the reason clearer. I look down at the handwritten letter from Mason. I notice that the letter seemed unimpacted by the accident. No rips. No stains. The letter is in perfect condition, as if Mason just walked into the home and handed it to me. Perhaps this is God's sign.

"Yes, honey, perhaps that's true."

"Can I help you feel better?"

"You already have, my sweet boy . . . You already have."

CHAPTER 20

# Monday, December 26, 2016

*"Every time a bell rings an angel gets his wings."*

— IT'S A WONDERFUL LIFE

BETWEEN THE POSSIBILITY of law school and Mason's letter, my body is shaking with indecision. Maybe I can do both. Maybe I can go to law school and do more art. Other people have done it before me. I can live out both of these identities, the one constructed by my parents and the one I was creating with Mason. I roll over to see Noah next to me in the bed. He is on his back, sprawled out like a starfish—just like Mason would sleep. His breaths are long, rhythmically pulling his round tummy up and down.

I look at my watch. It is 9:17, an acceptable time to wake Noah from his slumbers. I tickle his sides lightly, howling like a monster. "The tickle monster is here!!" The room fills with joyous giggles. "Should the tickle monster go visit Susie?" Noah gleefully nods his head up and down, jumps from the bed, and scampers over to Susie's room.

Once we collect downstairs and make breakfast, I inform the kids that we need to put away the Christmas decorations. Noah shouts, "I don't want Christmas to be over!!" He leaps onto the couch, folds his arms, and tightens his face to pout.

Immediately, Susie joins him. "Me neither!!"

And to be honest, I don't want to pack away Christmas either. I take a look around the room. Splashes of red and green mark every corner. The tree, a growing memorial for our family and our experiences. Stockings above the fireplace. A wreath to welcome guests at the front door. The house feels barren without these holiday gestures. Like Noah and Susie, I'm also not ready for the magic to be packed away until it's allowed to come out again next year. I don't want to collect the Christmas gifts we have scattered around the first floor and take them back upstairs to possibly never be seen again. Never played with. Never explored. If it is still Christmas time, then I don't need to make a decision on my two Christmas proposals. I can just let them sit with us.

"How about this: you both get to keep one thing out, and we pack up the rest?"

Noah and Susie scan the living room. Will they pick the Santa that climbs up and down the plastic ladder? Or perhaps the mitten-shaped bowl that holds candy? The box of Christmas books?

Susie squeezes her latest gift from Santa. "I want to keep my pony!"

"Susie, you already get to keep that! I want to keep the tree!" Noah proclaims.

"Noah, we can't keep the tree because it'll die, and all the bristles will fall on the floor."

Noah folds his arms. "It looks pretty alive to me. I want the tree!"

"Well, we can't keep the tree, but perhaps there is an ornament on the tree that we can keep out. What do you think of that?"

"Fineeeeeee." Noah gets up from the couch and slowly circles the tree. Occasionally, his small hand reaches out to examine a specific ornament. He focuses on the angel on top. We bought the angel the first Christmas without Mason. Unlike many angel tree toppers, this angel is male, symbolizing Mason looking over the home during the Christmas season—our Christmas guardian angel. He tries to jump up and grab it. "Can you help get it for me, Mommy?"

"Of course. I love that choice."

"Now Daddy will always be watching us."

"Yes, Noah, he will," I say with a smile.

"And I want to keep the snow globe!" Susie shouts, and I nod to let her know that's okay.

I look back at the angel, and my mind returns to Mason's letter. I decide to text Sherry and Bob. They deserve to know I opened the box. I wonder if they knew about this bank account.

Can you come over tonight? I need to show you something that I found . . . It's from Mason.

Immediately, Sherry texts back:

We can be there at 6.

---

"Grandma and Grandpa, do you want to see my new Nerf gun?" Noah asks as he holds up his gift to them.

"It looks very nice!" Sherry cordially responds.

"Actually, Noah," I say, "Can you take your sister up to your room to play?"

"But I don't want to." He pouts.

My eyes widen, and I stare directly at Noah. "It's not a question, mister."

"Fineeeeeeee." He motions to Susie to come upstairs. With each step, he makes a more dramatic thudding noise. "I'll just be up here if you need meeee," he adds longingly.

Sherry and Bob sit on the couch. "So, is everything okay? Your text worried me," Sherry says.

I grab the folder and sit next to Sherry with our legs only inches apart. I hand the folder to her. I notice how frail her hands have become. Almost immediately, she recognizes the handwriting on the envelope. One of her hands grips the folder, and the other goes to her mouth, hoping to mute her trembling lip. Bob notices as well and pulls Sherry closer, wrapping his arm around her. "Breathe, honey. We can do this . . . together."

I inch closer to Sherry and rest my hand on her knee. "I thought you needed to see this. Last night, I decided to open the box . . . from the accident . . . And inside his bookbag was this letter addressed to me."

"What is it?" Sherry asks, looking up to me, her wounded heart exposed through her eyes. A wound no mother should need to bear. A wound too deep to ever suitably repair.

"It's the final Christmas gift Mason was planning to give to me. I remember now that during our last Christmas together, he said my gift was delayed in the mail, and I didn't think twice about it . . . until I found this. He was on that bike to finish the last part of the gift. He was bringing it home . . . but . . . he never made it home . . . I just let this sit up there for years, too afraid to open the box." My cloud of guilt for the cause of Mason's death is starting to fade, but a new storm is forming in my heart—regret for not living the life Mason hoped for me.

"What was the gift? He never told us about it," Sherry says.

"It is probably better for you to read it."

Sherry looks up at Bob. He gives a small nod, letting her know he's ready for whatever is inside.

She pulls out the packet of papers. On the top, she sees the handwritten letter from Mason. She quickly wipes away the few tears that escape her eyes before they can hit the letter. Sherry reads each word out loud.

"I had no idea," Sherry whispers.

"It certainly sounds like a thing Mason would do, though," Bob adds.

Sherry nods with a gentle smile. "Yes, it does."

Bob turns to me. "So, what are you going to do? Have you told your parents or Rick about it?"

I pause. Should I tell them about starting law school in a couple of weeks? Mason supported my thoughts about law school but always asked if it was my real desire. I was never able to give him an answer. It was a big fight for us, and I'm sure he talked about it with Bob and Sherry. I decide it's best to wait to tell them about my parents' offer.

"I'm going over to Rick's tomorrow, so I plan to tell him in person. But I honestly don't know what I want to do with the money . . . things are so different now than when he wrote this letter. I feel like I'm barely supporting this family. I'm barely surviving, let alone attempting to live out some unestablished dream."

I'm embarrassed by sharing all of this with Mason's parents. After Mason's death, I have felt this pressure to be strong. I needed to be strong for Sherry and Bob, who lost their only son. For my children, who lost their father. I was sick of people looking at me with pity, offering casserole after casserole. I made a conscious choice many years ago that I would act strong, even if I'm feeling weak. Right now, I do not feel strong.

"Rachel, I want you to know that we will support you regardless of what you choose to do. Our boy would do anything to make you happy, and we will do the same," Bob says with a voice that echoes the same tone as Mason.

"Thank you, Bob . . . I really do appreciate all you have done for me. I don't have the words to thank you."

"I think it's because you speak through painting, honey. I think Mason was right about that. You are gifted," Sherry says.

"I just don't know if that's practical. I have kids . . . I have to support them alone now."

"You're not alone." Sherry reaches for my hand. "We're here for you, and Mason continues to find ways to speak to you . . . like this letter. You don't need to quit your job, move to the mountains, and forget about all your responsibilities. But, day by day, look for those signals from Mason. He is out there giving them to you," Sherry says as she holds up the letter from Mason.

I wrap my arms around both Sherry and Bob. "I miss him every day," I whisper.

"I miss him too, Rachel. He was such a good man," Sherry says.

I pull back from the hug and look at Sherry. "That's because you were a good mom."

"And you, a good wife. He was so lucky to find you."

I always felt that I was the lucky one to be with Mason. I never knew Sherry felt that Mason was lucky to have me.

## CHAPTER 21

# Tuesday, December 27, 2016

*"I'm dreaming of a white Christmas, just like the ones I used to know. Where the treetops glisten and children listen, to hear sleigh bells in the snow."*

— WHITE CHRISTMAS

I ARRIVE AT RICK'S HOUSE, aware of the extra weight in my bag. Inside are both letters—the one from my parents and the one from Mason. I remind myself there is no reason to be nervous. I slowly raise my hand and knock on the door.

Rick quickly opens the door as if he was waiting there for my arrival. I unwrap my scarf as he helps to take off my coat to hang in the side closet. With the logistics out of the way, Rick gives a quick kiss on my lips. "Merry Christmas, Rachel!"

As he draws me in for a hug, I get a waft of his pinewood and cider cologne that he only uses on fancy date nights. I notice that his shirt is crisper than usual and tucked into a pair of dress pants that I have never seen before. I provide a warm smile as I harbor my anxiety over my news. "You smell good!" I say.

"Look around," he says as he spins me around the room.

So distracted by my worries, I didn't even notice the transformation of his empty bachelor pad into a romantic paradise. The fluorescent ceiling lights are off, and instead, the room glows with Christmas lights. The typically bare white walls are adorned with photos of us.

"Rick, this is beautiful!" As I turn back to him, he kneels down. In his hands is a black velvet box. Carefully, one hand holds the base, and the other lifts the top, revealing a ring that is only appropriate for an engagement.

"Rachel, I love you so much, and I want to spend every day with you. Will you marry me?"

I can't seem to catch my breath. Just breathe!

"I . . . I . . . don't know what to say! It's all so beautiful."

"Say yes. Say yes to being my wife!"

He attempts to slide the ring onto my finger.

I take a step back. "But the kids! What about Noah and Susie?" Why would he propose when he has barely gotten to know them?

"I know I need to work on my relationship with them, but I will be there for them as their . . . Dad."

I reactively jerk back. "But they have a dad."

"Well, yes, of course. I mean, I can be a father figure . . . a stepdad."

"Are you ready to be a stepdad?" I ask. We have never talked about this before. Rick rushed into his first marriage as well. Why would he try to do that again?

"Yes . . . I'm ready to be your husband."

Husband? My husband is Mason . . . was Mason . . . I guess I just have never imagined someone else filling that role. I love Rick. I do . . . I mean, I think I do . . . I know I don't want to hurt him . . . I also know I don't want to lose him. I can't handle more loss.

I look back at the ring and cannot help thinking about the last time I was proposed to . . . by Mason.

## — 2006 —

Mason looks directly into my fear-filled eyes. "Hold my hand."

"I can't do this," I whimper.

"You can do anything, Rachel. I'm here with you. Look at me." My eyes remain focused on the thousands of feet between us and the bottom of the mountain. I look at the path ahead that's only large enough to put one foot in front of the other. This narrow strip only lasts ten feet, but it's ten feet of pure risk. My eyes shift from the bottom of the canyon back to the narrow path.

"Hey, Rach, look at me? You're going to be okay."

I raise my eyes to meet him. Together we breathe.

"I know you can do this, Rachel. But also know we can always turn around. If you want to take this challenge, I'm here with you every step, but I'm also happy turning back."

"I . . . I . . . just don't know!" Tears begin to form, and my breathing becomes thick. I tremble in fear.

"Let's take a step back and just enjoy this moment. The view is already spectacular."

I nod in agreement. Carefully, we back away from the edge and move to more stable ground below. My hands shake as Mason holds me tightly. We simply stop, breathe, and observe the world around us. I breathe in, noticing the thinness of the air. I fear the air is too scarce to continue. I breathe out, noticing the infinite continuation of mountains, reminding me that I'm only a small dot in this scene. The rocks merge into the eternal sky—all surrounded by the same air that I breathe. I breathe in again and notice how fresh the air tastes in my lungs. I hold the air in longer, savoring it like a decadent meal. I breathe out, feeling the strength of the mountains. My fears feel as small as the ants running up the trail next to us. I smile and turn to Mason.

"Thank you, Mason," I whisper, as if not to disturb the creatures around us.

"For what?"

"Giving me time . . . this time to just think about what I want to do. Time to just breathe at this moment."

"Take all the time you need, Rachel. If it means camping out here for the night, I will do it."

I smile wide. "I can't imagine my life without you, Mason. You push me to new limits and new places. You got me to this mountain top. To this moment. To this life that I love more deeply each day."

Mason lovingly grips my hand. "Why imagine a life without each other then? Let's be together until we grow old. Until one of us needs to roll the other up this mountain in their wheelchair."

My gaze turns to him to see if he's serious or not. "What are you saying, Mason?"

He lets go of my hand and begins to spin around, staring at the ground. He picks up one of the pebbles on our path. He turns back to me and gets down on one knee. "Rachel, this may not be the rock you deserve, but I can promise you that I will always be the husband you need me to be. Will you marry me, Rachel?"

My eyes well with tears yet again, but this time tears of pure joy envisioning the life I will spend with Mason.

"Yes! Yes, a million times! Yes!" I throw my arms around Mason's neck. Squealing with joy, Mason lifts me. My body becomes weightless.

"So, are you ready to take me to the top of this mountain, future husband?"

"Are you sure you want to go? We don't need to. I think the view is pretty good from here," Mason says with a wink.

"I want to go. I want to go with you. I want to go everywhere with you." I grab Mason's hand and head back to the ledge. I breathe in again and go.

---

"So, what do you say? Will you marry me, Rachel?"

I snap out of my head and look back at Rick. I bite my lower lip and look around the room. I touch his warm cheek. I move my hand down to his heart, feeling its elevated beat. Rick is here. He is alive. And he wants me. I can't lose Rick too.

"Yes. Yes, I will."

CHAPTER 22

# Wednesday, December 28, 2016

*"What is Christmas? It is tenderness for the past, courage for the present, hope for the future."*

— AGNES M. PAHRO

THAT MORNING, I WAKE UP AT RICK'S HOUSE. His legs are wrapped around my side as I lay flat on the bed. I stare past the expressionless ceiling. I hardly slept, yet my eyes are wired open. This Christmas was supposed to be about the kids. It was about making them see the magic of the season. Connecting with their father. Yet somehow, it has become about me. I think of the three paths that I have received this Christmas. My eyes shift down to the engagement ring, weighing my left hand onto the sheets.

The ring is simple and elegant—a white gold band with a single prong setting holding up a sizable brilliant-cut diamond. I tilt my hand down, and the ring gets stuck around my knuckles. I shake it a few times and watch it land onto the sheets as if it was never meant to be on my hand in the first place. Like it doesn't belong to me.

I bring the ring closer to my eyes. On the band's inside, opposite the diamond, it reads TIFFANY & CO. This ring is more glamorous than me, even on my finest days.

Rick unlocks his leg from my side and pulls himself up to kiss me on the cheek. "Good morning, fiancé. I see you're examining the ring. What do you think?"

It's the classic ring that so many girls dream of when they play house with their friends and envision their future. It's the style of ring that I can wear to a cycling class, and several bikes over, a girl would be staring at it with jealousy, causing her to spin the wheel even more frantically. It's the ring that would make the PTA moms, like Marie, question if maybe I could be one of them—the elite, powerful, perfectly put-together moms. I slip the ring back onto my finger. "Rick . . . It's stunning . . . I just . . . I'm still so shocked."

"You didn't see it coming?"

"Not even in the slightest."

"I mean a little bit, though, right?" He pauses, but I don't have an answer. "You know, since I met the kids and your family for the Christmas party, the timing just felt right. I figured this would be a good way to end the year."

For me, the timing feels . . . It feels rushed. I remind myself that Mason is gone, and Rick is here. He is good to me. And he wants to be with me. He accepts me for where I'm at in life. Rick won't lead me to the top of the mountain, but he'll hold my hands at the foothills, which I need right now. I think about the letter from Mason and the possibility of law school. How will our engagement fit in? Can I make them all work together? Can these different versions of myself coexist?

"Rick, I wanted to talk to you about some stuff that happened at Christmas."

"Sure thing, babe." He picks up his phone on the side table to check the time. "Shit. I need to run into work today. There's a lot of loose ends before the close of the year. Can we talk tomorrow? You have all week off?"

"Yeah, I do . . . Sure, we can talk later."

"Thanks, babe." He throws his body out of bed and grabs clothes from his closet. "We should do dinner with your parents and mine this week to share the news." He comes back to kiss me, adding more pressure than usual. "I love you, Rachel."

I raise my lips ever so slightly. "You, too." And with that, I'm alone again with my thoughts. Alone with three proposals that seem unable to exist together. I close my eyes and breathe in. I look at the time and decide I need to go home anyways and relieve my mom from the children.

I pull on my thick sweater and jeans from last night and enter the cold winter morning outside. I open Bonnie's trunk first to get a snowbrush, so I can remove the mist of snow that is now covering her. When I attempt to put the key into Bonnie's door, I notice that my hands are shaking, not because of the cold, but nerves. I shake my head to remove my fears of the future and focus on the now. I need to go home to my kids. I finally get in the car, throw my bag on the passenger seat, and grip the steering wheel. The haze of white continues to inhibit my view even as I sit stationary in Rick's driveway.

I take a deep breath. My hands steady, I turn the key in the ignition and drive home. When I get home, I pause and look down at my left hand. The diamond of the ring has twisted to face towards my palm. I wiggle it past my knuckle and slip it into the side pocket of my bag. No one needs to know yet.

"I'm home," I announce as I walk inside. I don't have time to take off my coat or set down my bag before both Susie and Noah attempt to wrap themselves around me as if I'm the park's newest attraction. My mom is in her usual position on the couch with a book resting on her lap as she looks towards me.

"We missed you, Mommy," Susie proclaims.

"I missed you, too! Did you have fun with Grandma?"

Noah starts to bounce around the room. "We had a Nerf battle, but she wasn't that good."

"That's not very nice, Noah," I say.

"But it's trueee," he demands.

Luckily, my mom doesn't look offended. She responds, "Fighting is just not in my blood, I guess."

"I can teach you," Noah shouts.

She smirks and asks me, "How was your night with Rick? Anything exciting?" She adds a wink at the end, which feels out of place on her usually perfectly ordered face. She must know about the proposal. Did Rick ask for my parents' blessing? Retrospectively, this makes sense, but why would he tell them before even talking with me? My mom still hasn't gotten over that Mason never asked for their blessing before our spontaneous engagement, so I wouldn't be surprised if she told Rick directly that he needs to talk to her first.

I tilt my head. "Did Rick tell you?"

"Of course, Rick told me! You know I have always liked that man. He's a true gentleman."

Susie and Noah have lost interest in the conversation and are back to playing with their toys. "Susie and Noah, do you remember Rick?"

Susie looks to her brother, who continues with his Legos. "Yeah," he responds.

"Rick wanted to know if you would play with him again?" I ask.

"I don't want to," Noah responds.

"Why not?"

"Cause he thinks I'm stupid."

I sit on the floor with him. "No, he doesn't, honey. He just picked the wrong words that night. Sometimes grown-ups do that."

My mom butts in. "Noah, give the man another chance."

Noah doesn't shift his focus away from the Legos. "Fine."

"Would Rick take us pony riding?" Susie asks.

"Honey, I think you're still too small to do that."

Susie begins to pout. "But that's why the pony is small so that I can ride it."

"I'll talk to Rick to find something for us all to enjoy. Can you both go upstairs for now so I can talk to your grandma alone?"

"Why can't we stay down here with you?" Susie asks.

"Because it's just for adults."

Susie and Noah collect the Legos from the floor, put them in their box, and carry them upstairs. I sit down on the couch opposite my mother. "They will come around with Rick, don't worry. I'm just so excited for you. Between law school and now your future with Rick, it's all turning around for you."

For me, it feels like things are turning upside down instead of around. "There's actually another thing that might impact my future."

Her eyes widen as if getting to the suspenseful chapter in one of her novels. "My God, are you pregnant?"

"No, Mom! Why would you think that?" She shakes her head as if it's the only other shocking thing that could happen in my simple life. "No, it's . . . I opened the box I got from the hospital with Mason's items from the accident."

"Rachel, why go turning up those painful memories? You have so much to look forward to. There is no need to look back on that."

I pull back a bit. "Mom, let's remember he is the father of Susie and Noah. I can't just forget about him."

She reaches out to touch my leg. "That's not what I'm saying. I'm sorry. What were you going to say?"

I walk over to my bag and grab the envelope from Mason. I hand the packet to her. She reviews each document, shaking her head back and forth in disbelief. When she's done, she looks back at me. "Oh, honey, this is from years ago. You aren't the same person anymore."

My mom is right about that. I'm no longer the woman that takes adventurous hikes with her family, that rides pregnant on a motorcycle clutching the back of her husband, or simply breathes the air around her without the anxiety of what happens next. I'm now the woman that constantly fears what I will lose, making it impossible to think of what I could gain if I did take those risks again. "I know, but with Susie's pageant and everything, I realized I really miss painting."

"That's okay. You can still paint a little here and there, especially with all the help the school needs. That could be a perfect fit for you."

"No, Mom. I mean, I want to really paint again. I want to paint for *me*. Like I did before. I want to *be* a painter."

"Oh, honey. Have you forgotten what life was like after your stint in art school? You couldn't survive. If it wasn't for your father stepping in and getting you that job with the Stratfords, God only knows what would have happened to you."

Within three months of graduating, I hadn't been able to sell a single piece or get featured in a gallery. After years of telling my parents that I could make a living out of art, it took only three months in the real world for me to realize that my parents were right. Now, I question it. I jumped ship before I even had the time to truly fail. And as my mom noted, I'm not the same person anymore.

"And I do appreciate that and all that you and Dad have done for me. But I love painting . . . And Mom, I think you know what that feels like. I mean, those sets . . . They were amazing. Roxanne was saying—"

Suddenly my mom's tone changes from an overly concerned mother to a woman on defense. "When were you talking to Roxanne about me?"

"Just at the Christmas party . . . She said you used to paint growing up."

"Why would she tell you that? She has no place to tell you that." My mom gets up. She nervously folds the blanket back on the couch and collects her book and reading glasses.

"Mom, why are you getting so upset? She didn't say anything except that you used to paint, which I already assumed after seeing the sets you made for the pageant."

She tries to collect herself by brushing back her hair and straightening her blouse. "I'm not upset. I'm just surprised she would talk about that. It was ages ago. It doesn't matter anymore. Anyways, I should be heading home to make your father lunch." She takes her coat from the closet and wraps her scarf around her neck. She looks back at me. "Rachel, you are so lucky to have Rick . . . and law school. These are opportunities so many people can only dream of. I know you will make the right decision." She gives me a hug and leaves.

When the door closes, I continue to question her sudden exit. Even as a child, I have never seen my mother act so abruptly. What is she hiding from me?

CHAPTER 23

# Thursday, December 29, 2016

*"Christmas is not a story of hope. It is hope."*

— KEVIN ALAN MILNE

"MOMMY, ARE WE THERE YET?" Susie asks from the backseat. We have been driving for forty minutes on gravel backroads covered in a snowy mush. I look at my phone and notice I no longer have service.

"We should be there soon," I reply.

"Why are we going to see Aunt Roxanne, anyways?" asks Noah.

"Well, because she misses you guys."

"But we never visit her," Susie notes.

I look back at them and smile. "Well, perhaps it's time to change that."

After talking to my mom, I decided to reach out to Roxanne. I feel like there's so much my mom is holding back. Aunt Roxanne is the only person who might have answers. I wonder if I can better understand what my mom was like before having me. Maybe it can help me know who I am and what to do with these three decisions.

As we get closer, I notice steam coming from a brick chimney attached to a modest A-frame dark wood cabin. The first floor of the house is a plain rectangle. A large set of wooden stairs leads to the top triangle-shaped second floor, treated with large windows overlooking the surrounding forest of pine and oak trees. We pull into the makeshift driveway and are greeted by a four-foot statue of Buddha emerging from the snow.

I get out and then unclip Susie and Noah from their seats. "Now, be nice to her. She doesn't have many visitors, so I want her to feel comfortable with us there. Okay?"

"I'm always nice," Noah responds.

I pull Susie into my arms and hold Noah's hand. We walk up the flight of stairs, avoiding the scattered patches of ice. When we ring the doorbell, we hear howling and scampering dogs inside.

"Calm down, Lily and Bailey, calm down. I'm coming." Roxanne opens the doors, and the dogs run outside, down the stairs, and into the woods. We do the opposite and run inside the warm house.

"Do you want me to try to get them to come back inside?" I ask Roxanne.

"Oh no, there's a dog door, so they can come and go as they please."

I can only imagine how much dirt that tracks in. Regardless, when I look inside, the house is ordered and tidied. The lofted ceilings produce a reverence about the space that continues into even the most minor details in the home, like the bonsai tree at the entrance table surrounded by various crystals. It's as if we have entered a Buddhist temple that's nestled away in a rustic log cabin. I look to Noah and Susie, who both have their noses scrunched.

"What's that smell?" Noah asks.

"It's incense," Roxanne responds. "It helps with relaxation."

"It smells gross!"

"That's not very nice, Noah," I say.

Roxanne smiles. "That's okay. It's certainly not for everyone." She looks back at me. "Is there anything I can offer you guys? I'm not used to having guests, but I can throw some snacks together for the kids. I think I have some cookies."

"I like cookies!" Noah shouts.

"Okay, there we have it! Let me get that ready for you." Roxanne leads us to the kitchen. The kids settle in with their cookies and the activity books I packed so that Roxanne and I can talk in the living room.

Roxanne cozies herself into her couch, and I sit on the other end. "It's nice to hear from you, Rachel."

I smile warmly. It does feel nice to see her too. "Thanks for having us on such short notice."

"Is everything okay?" Roxanne asks with genuine concern in her eyes.

"Yeah . . . I just . . . I feel like my mom is hiding something from me about her past. I was wondering if you could help fill in the blanks for me?"

"What makes you think that?"

"I mentioned to her that you told me she used to paint, and she got really upset and left. I don't understand why she won't talk about it with me."

Roxanne's face curves to show a curious perplexity. "Oh, really? I thought she would have told you since you went to art school and all. I didn't mean to cause trouble."

"No, you're fine. I was just hoping you could explain to me why she won't talk about it."

She pauses. "Well, I don't think it's my story to tell. She clearly has some reason why she wants to keep it private."

I ignore Roxanne's politically correct answer and try another direction. "What was she like, when you were kids?"

Roxanne releases a modest laugh. "She was . . . " She looks up to the lofty ceiling. "She was brilliant. She was my role model. She was my best friend."

It's hard to believe Roxanne and my mom could ever have been friends, let alone best friends. "What happened?" I ask.

"I don't know . . . just life. We made different decisions and took different paths."

"Why won't she tell me about the time she painted?"

"I can't answer that for you. I wish I could. You need to find a way to talk to her."

"But how?"

Again Roxanne pauses to think. She looks around the room. "You said Barbara still reads novels?"

"Of course. She always has a book in her purse."

"She likes Margaret Madison, right?"

"Yeah, she's her favorite."

Roxanne gets up and goes to the bookshelves that line either side of the fireplace. She probably has over one thousand books, but Roxanne narrows in on one section and pulls a book from the shelf. "Could you get her to read this?"

I look at the cover of the book. *A Mother's Haunting*, by Margaret Madison. "I feel like my mom has already read all her books."

"I don't think she has read this one. It had a very limited release, so not many people have it."

"What's it about?"

"I think it's exactly what she might need to hear."

I smile and take the book from Roxanne, unsure how a book could change her fixed mind, "Thank you. I appreciate it."

She looks at me, her eyes warm like a fire on a winter night. "I'm always here when you need to chat."

---

That night, the lamp on my nightstand illuminates my room. When I lean over to turn it off, I notice the book Roxanne gave me sitting below the light. I examine the cover. It's black with a haunted-looking mansion on the front. In *Goosebumps*-esque lettering, it reads *The Mother's Haunting by Margaret Madison*. How could this three-hundred-page mystery novel change my mother's mind about anything?

I put the book back down on the nightstand and get my laptop to search for the title. I can't find the book online. In fact, there is little information about Margaret Madison in general, her identity as mysterious as her novels. There are no photos, no recordings, no trace to her true identity.

*The Mother's Haunting* is mentioned only once in a transcript of a phone interview with Margaret Madison. The interviewer asked whether the order in which she writes her novels is the same order they're published. Margaret replies, "No, in fact, some novels I don't publish, or I do a very small invite-only release. Some of the truths I try to expose in my novels are not ready when I complete the text. I need to wait for the right moment for certain books to release. I guess I'm waiting for the right reader. Hopefully, that day will come soon for all my books." The interviewer continues to press for hints on how many more unpublished novels she has and what they are about until she finally discloses the name of *Mother's Haunting*.

I notice my eye twitching, so I put my laptop back and decide to go to bed. I will give my mom the book at her New Year's Eve party on Saturday.

CHAPTER 24

# Friday, December 30, 2016

*"Snowflakes, my Christmas memories gather and dance — each beautiful, unique, and gone too soon."*

— DEBORAH WHIPP LIKE

"I DON'T WANNA GO OUTSIDE!" Noah shouts.

"But I want to make snow angels!" Susie shouts back.

Rick stares at me, hoping I can find the solution. He has only been here for a minute, and the two of them are having a meltdown. I need today to go well. I need to see that he can be a father to Noah and Susie. I reach for Rick's hand and squeeze it to reassure him that everything will be okay. "What about this, Noah? After we make snow angels, then we can have a snowball fight. You love snowball fights."

"I don't want to," Noah insists.

"I'm going outside!" Susie says as she runs out the front door.

I signal to Rick to follow her so that I can handle Noah. I simply glare at him. "Noah . . . Please go put on your snow pants. We're going outside, and you can choose to sit on the deck alone, but you need to at least come outside."

He folds his arms. "I'll go outside, but I refuse to play."

"Okay, that's fine."

Outside, I see Susie running around and tumbling in the snow. Rick is watching from the porch. "Don't you want to join her?" I ask Rick.

"Oh no." He looks down. "I wore the wrong clothes for playing *in* the snow. I thought we would just watch." Rick is wearing what looks to be an expensive tan peacoat with dark-washed jeans and stylish leather boots.

I explicitly told Rick that the kids wanted to play *in* the snow *with* him. "Do you want to borrow some sweatpants? I might actually still have Mason's old snow pants."

He raises an eyebrow. "Uhh . . . I think I'm good. I can still do stuff with my hands." He waves his expensive black leather gloves. "I did remember these, at least."

I smile and remind myself he is trying. Playing with kids is still new to him.

Noah throws himself onto a porch chair with his arms still crossed. "Are you sure you don't want to play?" Rick asks.

Noah's face remains scrunched up. "I'm sure."

I nod to Rick. "Can you go ahead with Susie? I need to talk to Noah."

Rick kisses me on the cheek and goes down to Susie. I sit next to Noah, placing my hand on his knee. "Okay, Noah, what's going on? Something is bothering you."

He crunches his face into his knees. "No, there isn't."

"I know when you're lying. Come on, tell me. Is it Rick? He didn't mean what he said last time."

He shakes his head. "It's not that."

"What is it?"

He looks up. His blue eyes meet mine. "I don't want a new dad."

I shake my head. "What makes you say that?"

"I overheard you talking to Grandma." I should have known that I never really have privacy when he is lurking nearby.

I place my index finger on his chin and look into his spiraling eyes of pain. "Let me be clear. No one could ever replace your father."

"Mommy, I don't want you to marry him."

"Well, *if* we do get married, it'll be something we all will discuss beforehand, but I want you and Susie to at least try spending time with him. And even if we do get married, you don't need to call him dad. He will never replace your father."

"I don't like spending time with him."

"You have only met him a couple of times! You can't possibly make that judgment yet."

"Yes, I can!"

I pause. "Think of it like trying your veggies. You have to give it multiple tries over multiple meals. Let's give him a fair shot today and go hang out?"

Noah looks back at me. "I won't call him dad."

"That's okay. Come play with your sister and me, though."

He unfolds his legs and lets them swing down. His mitten-covered hand reaches for mine, and we run down the porch to the front yard. Rick is pushing together a small snowball to add as the next layer of a snowman. Susie is adding more snow to the base. *Maybe this can work*, I tell myself.

Soon after, we start a snowball fight. Rick and Noah compete against Susie and me—I figured this was a good way to get the two boys to bond, and I'll mostly follow Susie, making sure she has snowballs to throw and blocking any unexpected shots coming her way. After only a couple of minutes, I hear Noah yelling at Rick and Rick getting agitated. He throws a snowball targeted at Susie, but I jump in front. Either I'm getting brittle, or that actually really hurt.

"Hun, be careful, okay? Your shots kinda hurt," I say. It seems that comment only makes Rick more unsettled.

"Okay, I got Susie, so don't throw, Rick!" Noah demands.

Rick doesn't listen and throws his hardest one yet. The force of the two snowballs knocks Susie to the ground and leads to a storm of tears.

"I told you not to throw!" Noah screams and runs inside the house.

I go to pick up Susie. "Are you okay?"

"I didn't even want to play this in the first place! I just wanted to make snow angels," she moans.

"I know. They shouldn't have done that." I should have been there to protect her from the hit anyway. "Can you go inside with your brother? I'll be right there, okay?" Susie nods and slinks up the stairs into the house.

Next, I turn to Rick, who is standing frozen in the same spot. "What happened there, Rick?" I say compassionately.

"I don't know. I guess I didn't hear him."

"Not just that. Why were you throwing so hard? I told you to stop doing that."

"In fairness, I was being told a lot of things by you and your children."

I feel my eyelids widen. "Really, Rick? *Your children.* You do realize if we get married, it'll be the four of us. They will be your children too. You need to be able to enjoy spending time with them."

"Running around in the snow, even if it was just you and me, is not my idea of a good time."

I fold my arms and demand, "Okay, then what is a good weekend to you, Rick? What's a good weekend look like that involves Susie and Noah?"

"There are plenty of things I would want to do with them. Just not this."

I feel myself becoming angry, a furnish among the snow. "Then what, Rick? Tell me what you would want to do with them."

"I don't know . . . We could do a family golf outing."

My internal temperature increases. "You have met Noah, correct? You think he would have the patience to stand still and swing a club for hours?"

"Okay, what about the beach?"

"Right, the many beaches we have access to in the middle of Michigan." I realize I'm being snarky, but I feel like I need to defend my children.

"Why are you attacking me, Rachel? I will be a good role model for them, and I will provide for you and the kids. Sure, I might not be their best friend rolling around in the snow, but I will be a good father."

I pause and look down at my boots. "I'm just not so sure, Rick." I need to do what's best for my children, and Rick doesn't feel like the right answer for them.

I look up at his red face. He rushes off the lawn and to his car. "I will not be insulted like that."

I turn back to my children, back to my responsibilities.

CHAPTER 25

# New Year's Eve

*"A Christmas miracle is when your family doesn't get into a single argument all day."*

— MELANIE WHITE

TODAY WE ARE CELEBRATING the New Year with my parents. When we arrive at their house, they already have everything out and ready. The large mahogany dining table is covered in a bright white tablecloth. All eight settings, even Susie's and Noah's, have a stack of four plates with various shades and designs of silver that's then topped with a cloth napkin wrapped in a circle holder that reads NYE.

Across the marble counter is a banquet of food that could feed a whole soccer team of teenage boys or a hundred reasonable adults. The spread includes every color of the rainbow. Pink shrimp with red cocktail sauce. Orange carrots and green bell peppers with tan hummus and pita. Blue tortilla chips with an array of dips. The kids run to the food but realize it's all healthy. My mom chimes in,

"No worries, I have some mac and cheese in the oven for the kids." They squeal in excitement.

"Wow, Mom, this is quite the spread of food for only us."

"There's just so much to celebrate in this New Year." She wraps her arms around me. "I'm so proud of your decisions. Being with Rick and going to law school."

"I haven't decided on either of those, Mom."

My mom starts to walk around the counter, making adjustments so that each detail is perfect. "You will come around. I know you, honey. You're like me. You always come around." She smiles wide.

"Mom—" I look at my bulging purse, and I grab the book from Roxanne. "Mom, I got this book for you. It's a limited release book from the author you're always reading."

She reaches out for the book. "I never knew she did limited releases. That was very thoughtful of you, Rachel. Where did you get it?"

"Oh, just online," I say. I know the credit should go to Roxanne, but I fear she won't read it if I tell her it's from Roxanne. She will question why I'm spending time with her.

"Well, thank you, Rachel. You are such a good daughter." She places the book on the coffee table and is then startled by the doorbell. She nearly runs towards the door. "I got it!"

I hear the door swing open. "Marsha! Donald! So happy to see you tonight. And Rick, you look more dashing than ever. Come in."

My eyes widen, and I turn around to see Rick and his parents in what seems like matching Ted Baker peacoats and cashmere scarves. My mom takes their coats and hangs them in the closet. "Rachel! Big congratulations to my future daughter-in-law," Marsha announces.

I look around, making sure Susie and Noah aren't in the room. They will be unhappy to see him after yesterday. I'm unsure if I'm happy to see him either since we haven't talked since then. I guess, for a part of me, it felt like the end last night.

"I wasn't expecting you guys," I say. I'm sure my face reveals my shock. I fear that I look more like a deer in the headlights than a child coming home to a surprise birthday party.

Rick wraps his arm around my waist and presses his lips against my forehead, and whispers, "I'm sorry for yesterday."

My eyes meet his. I don't want to fight here, so I nod and smile.

My mom says, "I hope you like the surprise! I thought it would be fun to celebrate your engagement and law school."

Rick holds my waist even tighter. "And why haven't you told me about law school, honey? That's fantastic!" He pulls back and holds my hands, then whispers, "Why aren't you wearing the ring?"

I wince. "Rick, I didn't know you were coming tonight." I turn to everyone. "Is it possible to be careful mentioning the engagement in front of Noah and Susie? I still need to explain it all to them, and with their father's anniversary coming up . . . I just want to make sure to be sensitive to how they feel."

My mom's eyes dart to me, communicating how embarrassed she is for me saying that in front of Marsha and Donald. I try to autocorrect. "But I'm so thankful we are able to gather today to celebrate. I really appreciate you coming."

My mom then says, "How about we head to the dining room? We have prepared a spread of appetizers to start the night, and I believe Jeff has some Cuban cigars for the gentlemen later."

Rick wraps his arm around my waist and applies slight pressure to my back as if he is a cattleman maneuvering his flock. The pressure causes my muscles to tense, and I jerk away. "I need to go to the bathroom."

I sprint down the hall and quickly close the door. *I can't do this.* My breath thickens as my eyes seal shut, too afraid to look at my reflection in the mirror. Perhaps they won't notice if I hide in here for the rest of the night? And what about Noah and Susie? How will they react when they see him?

Instead of looking at my reflection, I look up at the ceiling, envious of its blankness and its simplicity—no one asks it to be a fresco one day then become blank again the next. Free to just exist without the attention of anyone.

I flush the toilet to make it seem like I really did need to go to the bathroom. I call for Noah and Susie and find them alone in the living room building new worlds with their Legos. I go to them and wrap them both into my arms.

"Is everything okay?" Noah asks.

"Of course. But I want to let you know that Grandma invited Rick and his parents for the party tonight."

"Why?" Noah demands.

"Because." I pause, searching for an explanation. "I honestly don't know why, but they did."

Susie pitches in, "I don't like him."

"I know. I know. Yesterday was rough, but I need you both to be nice to him."

Susie begins to pout. "I don't want to."

"Susie, you need to. This is Grandma's party, and she wants everyone to get along."

Noah declares, "I won't talk to him."

I need to find a new solution that will work fast. "How about this, if you are nice to Rick and his family, I'll let you both get a new toy when we go to Target next week-end. Does that sound fair?"

"I want a pony!" Susie demands.

"They might have one of the stuffed ponies you like."

"No, I want to ride a pony."

I counteroffer, "How about a new pony figurine?"

She persists, "No, I want to ride a pony."

"Me too!" Noah demands. I never realized he wanted to go as well. It's dangerous when they pair together and outnumber me.

I can't believe I have stooped so low to be negotiating with my children to be nice, but I'm exhausted, and I feel like I'm out of options. I can't deal with my mother's wrath if Susie and Noah are misbehaved. My eyes shift between Noah and Susie, who have the seriousness of a lawyer in court. I guess being a lawyer is in our blood. "Fine. I'll try to find a place, okay? But just one time, and if the pony is too big, then we will need to find a different place."

Susie launches her small, well-dressed body into my arms as she squeals with excitement. "Thank you! Thank you! Thank you!"

"But you both need to be on your best behavior. Otherwise, no horse riding, understood?"

Both violently shake their heads. "Let's go join everyone. I expect to see smiles and politeness all night." They run to the kitchen to greet the adults, both with their mouths wide with fraudulent smiles. They both lock onto one of Rick's legs and say, "We missed you!" I make a small gesture to suggest they calm down the acting. They need to at least seem believable.

Rick looks at me. "See, I knew they would move on from yesterday." He says this as if he knows them better than their mother, unaware that their sweetness is only thanks to my bribery.

The night continues with discussions of this, exceptionally cold winter, the success Donald and Rick have had in the markets this year, and other topics that bring a heaviness to my eyes. It seems nearly impossible to stay awake till midnight with this crowd. Susie and Noah passed out on the couches around 8:30, before their regular bedtimes, making me question if they deserve their prize given they were asleep most of the night.

I move the kids to the guestroom so that they can sleep more peacefully. Part of me wishes I could join them, but instead, I return to the couch in the living room next to Rick.

My mom gets up. "Now that the kids are in bed, it's time for champagne."

She walks to the wine cart that has a chilled bottle of Dom Perignon and six crystal champagne flutes. She hands them out, and Rick stands to give a toast. "A toast to my soon-to-be wife—"

My dad stands and chimes in, "And to my daughter, a soon-to-be lawyer." My heart races. Have I committed to these things already? Everyone acts like this is all set in stone, but they both feel negotiable to me. Everyone stands and clinks their flutes, but I remain seated, staring into the abyss, searching for my reaction.

"What's wrong, honey?" my mom asks.

I shake my head out of its trance and stand up. "Nothing." My arm resists lifting the champagne flute, fearing that accepting this toast is accepting this future that has been decided for me. Rick lowers his flute to mine and makes a clink. I close my eyes holding back tears, feeling like that one forced clink has sealed my fate. That the contract has been signed now in the eternal skies. That my future is no longer in my hands.

CHAPTER 26

# New Year's Day

*"Peace on earth will come to stay,*
*when we live Christmas every day."*

— HELEN STEINER RICE

FOR NEW YEAR'S DAY, we agree to go to Bob and Sherry's house for dinner. While the drive is only about an hour, it's hard to stay focused because it's a perfectly straight road. Every inch is lined with dry and shriveled corn husks that meet the horizon with an occasional rundown barn or a rusted tractor sitting in the field waiting for the spring to raise the crops and allow them to get back to work. After my restless night, I can feel my weighted eyes tempted to shut briefly, thinking, *the road doesn't change for the next forty miles. I can close my eyes for just a little bit.* I keep shaking my head and looking back at Noah and Susie, who are both fast asleep in the back. I need to protect them. *Stay awake, Rachel.*

When we pull into their drive, we see Bob sitting on the porch's wooden rocker. He jumps up and goes to the car to help them out. He then leans down onto one knee, allowing each of them to jump onto one of his shoulders. He pulls them up and twirls them around as they giggle. "How are my favorite grandbabies?"

"We missed you, Grandpa!" Noah says.

Bob smiles wide and sets them back down. "Well, that's good news cause I'm missing you all the time!"

"Grandpa, guess what?" Susie shouts.

"Hmmm . . . You love your grandpa?" he responds with a smile.

"Well, duh!! Guess again?"

He rubs his chin. "You love your grandma Sherry?"

Susie giggles. "Stop it! Mommy agreed to let me ride a pony!"

Noah jumps up, trying to get his eyes to reach Bob's. "And me!"

Bob's eyes widen, and he turns towards me. "Oh really!" He looks back to Susie. "I thought your mom said you were too small to ride."

Susie says, "She changed her mind."

"I'm glad!" He turns to me. "I know a guy down the road with some horses. I can give you his name and number?"

Begrudgingly, I reply, "That would be great."

"Grandpa, why don't you have any ponies on your farm?" Susie asks.

"Well, I mainly focus on crops like corn."

"Why?"

"Huh . . . " He rubs the top of his head as if genuinely perplexed. "I guess cause that's what my dad did, and then that's what his dad did . . . and we just have always been growing corn here."

"So will I play with cars like Daddy then?" Noah asks.

"Son, you can be anything you dream of. Mechanic, farmer, doctor, lawyer, Nerf gun maker"—he looks to me—"painter . . . Just keep dreaming for now—no need for you to worry more about that today. Anyways, let's head inside. Sherry has prepared a feast for us."

The house remains unchanged since the first time I visited the farm with Mason. The first thing anyone will notice when they enter is the sheer amount of wood. Wood floors, wood paneling on the walls, and wood furniture. The only non-wood items are the La-Z-Boy chairs and sofa originally from the '70s and the occasional outdated rug. Even with all this familiarity, something feels different. Above the wooden fireplace mantel, I notice one change to the room. The photo I painted—the centerpiece of the home.

"You hung it up?" I ask.

"Of course!" Sherry says as she goes around the room, embracing each one of us. "We love it! You know, Betty and Jerry next door came and just loved it. They were asking all about it. When we told them it was you, they asked if you could paint their grandbabies. I gave them your number. I hope that's okay."

Still processing that someone would want my art, I say, "Yeah, that's . . . that's great!"

"Perfect! I hoped so. And you know they would pay and all too. Absolutely no pressure, though. I let them know you are very busy and in demand."

"I wasn't even expecting money."

"Well, you ought to, hun. You're very talented. Anywho, all for you to decide. For now, it's time to eat."

We gather around the table filled with large serving dishes of mashed potatoes, caramelized carrots, sauerkraut, homemade biscuits, and macaroni and cheese. In the center is a plate of juicy pork chops. At each of our seats, there is a simple porcelain plate.

We all take our places and pass around each dish. Before we eat, Bob asks to hold hands in prayer before starting his usual New Year's Day speech that I have heard for many years.

"So, do the kids remember why we eat pork on New Year's Day?" Bob asks, looking at Susie and Noah.

Susie and Noah violently shake their heads no, leading Bob into his yearly speech about pigs.

"We eat pork on New Year's Day as good luck for the new year. Unlike other animals, the pig's snout will only move forward to find food and never backward. We eat pork today to remember to look forward to the new year instead of looking back to the past year. Does everyone want to go around and say what they are looking forward to this year?"

"I'm excited to play more and go to school less," shouts Noah.

I hope he won't be disappointed when he realizes that he'll be going to school the same amount this year as every year. If anything, he will do more because of the extra tutoring sessions he needs. Next is Susie. Her legs are crossed, and her elbows are far from the table. Her hands instead are folded and placed delicately in her lap. She looks fragile, like a glass doll.

"Being a horseback rider!"

"Remember, we agreed to just one ride," I add.

She nods. "That's enough for me to be a horseback rider!"

The conversation turns to me. "What do you look forward to Rachel?" Bob asks.

What do I want next year? Of course, I want to be a better parent for Susie and Noah. That's always true. But how do I do that? I consider the ring from Rick still hidden in my bag, the offer for law school, and the letter from Mason. I look to Sherry, who fills me with warmth and acceptance. I look at the painting above their fireplace. I can't predict my future, but I do know one thing that must become true in the new year for me to be happy, and I will make decisions that move me towards it.

"I want to paint. I want to be a painter."

After dinner, I text Rick. We need to talk about all these changes.

---

Once the kids are in bed, I get a text from Rick that he's here. I know we need to address everything that has happened over the last week. I grab Mason's letter and a blanket before heading outside. I wrap the blanket around us as we sit together on the porch.

Rick leans in for a kiss, but I pull back. "Rick, we need to talk."

His mouth tightens, and he pulls back from me. "Is it about the snow thing? I thought we were over that."

"Well, I do want to talk about that. But there is also something else. On Christmas, I found something from Mason." I hand him the letter. I need to see if Rick can support me in my desire to paint. Maybe we can figure out the kid stuff, but I also need him to see this side of me that I have kept hidden.

He looks perplexed. "Where did you find this?"

I look down at my hands on my lap, my fingers intertwined and clenched. "In a box of his belongings, from the hospital after his accident."

"And you hadn't noticed it before?"

I feel too embarrassed to tell him I have never actually gone through the box. That I have opened it, but I never got the courage to go through it until this Christmas. "I guess not. Go ahead and read it."

He skims through the documents with no changes in his facial expressions. Is he shocked? Mad? Surprised?

Does he even know I went to art school? It isn't something I typically advertise to people. Finally, he asks, "So, what does this mean?"

"Rick, I want to paint. You know, in college, I studied art, and soon after, I gave it up because I felt like I would never be able to make a living. And those paintings you found in the closet? Those are all mine."

"Okay. But then you found the paralegal gig, and I thought you loved that."

In fairness, that's the story I have told him. It's the story I try to convince myself of, but it no longer rings true. "Yeah, and being a paralegal was good for me . . . but I don't enjoy it anymore, Rick."

"Okay, but you are about to go to law school."

I hesitate. "I don't think I want to do that either."

"But your dad . . . He worked so hard to get you in . . . And yesterday. We celebrated you starting law school."

"I know. I just haven't had the courage to tell them yet."

"I'm shocked. This is not the Rachel I know."

I pull my lips in as my eyes look at him. I reach to hold his hands, hoping he doesn't mind how clammy they have become during this conversation. "But I guess it's the Rachel I want to become, and I hope you can support me in that."

He pulls his hands away to rub his exhausted face. "I mean, of course, I can support you. Once we are married, you really won't need to work. You can just focus on being a mom and a wife."

I guess I have never thought about that. The idea of having Rick financially support me. That certainly would solve some logistical problems, but something about that just feels wrong. "Rick, that's kind. I don't expect you to 'provide' for me in that way. I plan to have a job. Maybe I can stay with the Stratfords and then paint on the side. What I meant is that I want you to believe in me and push me to paint."

"Okay," he says with confusion and already setting a mood of skepticism for this plan.

"I might need you to support me and watch the kids so I can paint," I add, hesitating to see his reaction.

"I could do that."

"And what about the kids? We still need to talk about what happened last week."

"Look, I was stressed, and I messed up. It's not a big deal."

"But Rick, it is a big deal. To be frank, I can't marry you if they are unhappy."

"They will come around."

"I'm not so sure." I look up at him. "When you were married to Patty . . . why didn't you have kids?"

"I don't know. We just didn't want kids."

"Rick, are you sure you are ready to have kids now?"

"I'm ready to be married to you, Rachel. What else do you want from me?"

"But Rick, you don't want kids."

"That doesn't matter, Rachel. I want you."

"You can't just have me."

"I know that."

I look down at my hands. I look at the ring that would stir envy for many women. I think of Rick's proposal. His ability to protect me and support me. With Rick, I would have the freedom to paint every day. I wiggle the ring off my finger and place it in his palm. "Rick, I do love you. And I don't think I'll ever find a man as generous as you. But I need a partner that *wants* kids, not just me. I'm so sorry."

"Rachel, you can't be serious. You realize that in a matter of years, they will grow up and do their own thing. They won't need you anymore. They'll move on, but you will just be here waiting for them to need you just like your mother does for you."

I have never heard one statement filled with more insults than that. I want to shout back. I want to tell him he's wrong. He knows nothing about what it means to be a parent. Instead, I take a breath. "Rick . . . I'm sorry, I just can't marry you."

Sternly, he says, "I won't come back this time, Rachel."

Without any doubt looming in my mind, I nod and say, "I know." I lean in to hug him, but he walks away.

"You'll regret this, Rachel."

And perhaps I will. But for now, I plan only to look forward. I look at the letter that Rick threw back onto the chair as he rushed off. I reread the future Mason described for me. I want this future. I just don't know how to make this future possible without Mason.

CHAPTER 27

# Monday, January 2, 2017

*"Seeing is believing, but sometimes the most real things in the world are the things we can't see."*

— THE POLAR EXPRESS

WHEN MY ALARM RINGS, my eyes are already pulled open. I keep thinking about last night. This is not Rick's and my first fight, but I feel confident it will be our last. I can't stay with Rick. It's not what is best for Noah and Susie. It wasn't what was best for me. I decide to look forward. There must be some way for me to do more art and continue law. I can find a way to juggle both and keep everyone happy. Maybe I can put off law school until I figure out if I really have a future in painting and just keep working with the Stratfords on the side. Then I won't completely disappoint my family.

My attention is interrupted by Susie running into the room. "Mommy, why aren't you up yet?" I return to my reality. Motion must persist. Decisions must be made.

She jumps on the bed, and Noah follows close behind. "Mommy, you look sad," Noah says as if a fact rather than a question.

"Mommy always looks like that," Susie says.

I reach for Susie and place her on my lap. "What do you mean, Susie?"

Susie unintentionally avoids meeting my eyes. "You just look like that a lot."

I think back to the star she decorated for school. Noah and Susie both have broad U-shaped smiles, but I had just a straight line. She must have been feeling this way for a while. Why does she think I am so sad? "Like what? Can you show me?"

She pushes her pursed lips out as if an angry Bratz doll. Wow, I pray I don't look like that ever, for any situation or reason.

I try to keep my tone neutral. "Do you think I look like that, Noah?"

"Nooo . . . more like this." He makes his eyes wide and his lips as straight as possible as if a possessed clown. I don't know which interpretation of my face is worse. Noah continues, "But sometimes you look like this." He makes a huge fakely happy grin showing all his teeth. "We like when you do that."

I intentionally force my lips from curving down, self-conscious now of how my face moves. "I had no idea you both thought I looked so . . . " I searched for the right word. Tragic? Sad? Pathetic? Disturbing? "So . . . unhappy most days."

"It's okay. We still love you," Susie says as she lunges her body around my chest for a hug.

"How long have you felt this?" I ask.

Immediately, Susie answers, "Basically, forever."

Damn. I don't love this morning roast from my children. "Noah?" I ask

He won't look at me, and I notice him fidgeting. "Noah?" I ask again.

He jumps off the bed. "We should get ready for school."

My eyes widen. Noah never willingly gets ready for school, let alone encourages it. Why is he avoiding the question?

I get out of the bed too and get down on the ground with him. "Noah, wait, do you think I have been looking sad for a long time?"

"I don't know, maybe."

"Honey, you can tell me."

"I don't know, since Dad died, maybe."

Wow. My heart pauses. I have tried hard to put on a good show, but somehow Noah and Susie have read through it. I thought I was strong from them, but I guess I failed at that too. My face returns into a frown. "I still miss your daddy, but I am happy, guys. I don't want you to question that." I think of the last four years. Am I happy, though? Maybe they are right. I notice my face. Motionless. Sagging. Exhausted. I notice my heartbeat. Slow, predictable. Unwilling to spare an extra beat for passion. I know it's time for a change, but first, my responsibilities. "Okay, but let's get ready for school."

---

When I pull into work, I feel drained. I want to break my routine and go home. I want to be alone. To pause time. To take a moment to think. Instead, I feel as if I'm under a curse that keeps me in this never-ending loop of nothingness, this loop of existence that I have sunk into. Where is the happily ever after that they advertise in the stories? Where's my guardian, my protector, my fairy godmother? The curse of reality seems to have no escape, just continuation.

I sit at my desk, pull out my laptop, and stare at the black screen. My arms hang next to me, too heavy to operate as if a puppet whose strings have snapped. I lean back in my chair and stare at the ceiling, tormented by its blankness. Nothing can be that white. That pure. That unstained. I feel an urge to get my brushes and splash colors to correct it. To make it less free to be anything and, instead, make it something. My body, though, is motionless. Too scared to pick an existing color. Or to take my current colors and create a new one. What design would I give to this canvas that can't say for itself what it needs? It just stares blankly, asking me, "What do you want to paint me? I will not resist." My body, though, continues to resist. Motionless by indecision.

"Rachel, are you coming?" I hear from Brian. I notice everyone collecting in the conference room. I get up and return to my reality. There are still seats at the glass conference table, but I opt for the couch that surrounds the outside of the room, hoping to go unnoticed during the meeting. I pull out my legal pad and flip through the pages filled with a mixture of notes and doodles. My eyes are drawn only to the details of the doodles.

"Before we start," I hear Stratford Senior begin his speech seated at the front of the conference table, "I want to give a congrats to Rachel. She will be leaving us in two weeks to begin law school at Wayne State." When I hear my name, my shoulders become tense, and I try to lower my head like a turtle shrinking back into its shell as Stratford Senior continues. "You'll be missed, but we'll be happy to have you in the summers unless your father tries to snatch you up for himself." I should have known my dad would have told them already. I'm not ready for this.

Everyone's eyes become laser focused on my face. Jerry, a paralegal who has applied to law school five times and has been rejected every time, is sitting next to me. He whispers to me, "I didn't know you applied."

Unsure what to say, I reply, "It's a long story."

"I guess with a dad as well-known as yours, you don't need to apply anyways."

I want to be mad, but he's right. It's my connections that got me into law school. Not my skill. Not my passion. Not my ability. I'm undeserving of law school. And maybe I could have earned law school for myself, but why does that matter now. It was never my dream.

After the meeting, I go to my secret hideaway in the women's bathroom. I need to tell my dad. I dial his number and nervously pace back and forth. After a couple of rings, he picks up.

"Dad?" I choke out like a desperate girl running into her parent's room to protect her from the scary monsters in the closet.

"Yes, sweetie. Why are you calling during work?"

I can't hold back the words, so I try to release them as fast as possible so that I don't wimp out. "Dad, I can't go to law school."

I hear him cough to clear his throat. He becomes quiet. "Why not? It's all set up for you."

"That's the problem. I didn't earn it."

"Sure you did. The dean was impressed by your work with the Stratfords."

I should have known my dad would debate each point I make. He couldn't argue against only one point: I just don't love law like he does. Sure he would try to fight it because it's a truth I have been hiding in a place that even I couldn't fully access since Mason's death. But now that I have seen it, I can't unsee it. I just need to say it. He needs to know. But I become mute.

"Rachel, you still there?"

I force out, "Yep."

"Here, let me set up a time for you to meet with Dean Longhorn, okay?"

I want to shout no, but I remain silent, my default, instead of speaking up for myself. I try to choke out no, but silence is all I can produce.

"I need to go, but I will text you with the details."

The call ends. I look at myself in the mirror. *Why can't I be stronger than this? All you had to say was no, and you failed at that too.* I push those feelings down like overflowing garbage in the trash bin and go back to the desk. I must continue.

---

After the kids are in bed, I try to fall asleep, but I can't turn my mind off even in the darkness. I say I don't want to go to law school because I want to paint, yet I'm not painting. I haven't painted full-time since I was in school. Even with Mason, I worked as a paralegal. I occasionally painted, and he supported me in taking it further, but I enjoyed spending time with him. With our family. I wanted the life we were building together. That was enough for me.

I go to my closet and look at the higher shelves. I notice the box where I found Mason's letter. I reach for a box next to it that has my paint supplies and take it downstairs. I line the kitchen table with old newspapers and pull out a new 16"×20" canvas. I examine my collection of over sixty acrylic paints. I feel nothing.

All I can do is stare, my mind as blank as the canvas in front of me. How did I decide what to paint when I was in school? Typically, I had an assignment. Instructions on what was expected of me. But without that guidance, I see nothing in my mind. I feel nothing in my soul. Maybe I have lost that urge to paint. Maybe this is no longer 'my thing'. Maybe there is no 'thing' for me except existing.

I get up from my chair and pace. I search for inspiration. Somewhere, anywhere. I find nothing. I feel trapped again, but this time in a cage of my own making. I go to the front door and take out the manila folder from my purse. The lettering on the front brings me comfort and familiarity. I pull out the letter and review each word Mason chose. Each a prayer for my dreams.

I move past the letter and look at the business cards Mason provided for the publisher and the art gallery. In my hands are two concrete avenues of hope. I want to call, but I stop. What if they say no? My small flame of hope would be extinguished. I pack away the letter and the paint set. I'm not ready tonight.

CHAPTER 28

# Tuesday, January 3

*"God never gives someone a gift they are not capable of receiving. If he gives us the gift of Christmas, it is because we all have the ability to understand and receive it."*

— POPE FRANCIS

THIS MORNING, I'm greeted by a new collection of paperwork on my desk. Stratford Junior has gotten into a bad habit of leaving a pile of papers on my desk without instructions, expecting me to decode what the task might be based on the stack.

I flip through the papers and notice it's a big part of the evidence we have collected for the Myopic case. I notice Stratford Junior's door is cracked open. I ask him directly what this means instead of trying to decipher it on my own. I don't have the time for these games.

I knock and start to talk. "Hey, Stratford, what's with the paperwork on my desk?"

"Oh, right," he starts, "I figured since you are on your path to becoming a lawyer that you can try to write up the discovery document?"

My mind is shouting. *Are you kidding me?! NO! Absolutely not!* I stop and breathe and instead say, "But you need to be a lawyer to submit the discovery document."

His attention stays on his computer. My blood boils with anger. "Right, I can submit it, but it's good practice for you to write it."

"But I have over five hundred pages of new documents I need to read today."

"Yes, we need you to do both."

"Well, when do you expect this discovery document to be done?"

He continues to type. "End of the week."

The end of the week is Friday. Friday, January 6. The anniversary of Mason's death. I begin to stammer, "But . . . But . . . Friday . . . I need to take Friday off. You know that."

He finally looks at me with a smile like the Grinch with his diabolical plan to steal Christmas. "Welcome to being an associate. You need to start making sacrifices."

Without thinking, I shout, "Start? You want me to *start* making sacrifices. Stratford, I have made so many sacrifices for this company. You must see that, right?"

"Well, prepare to start making more if you want to be an associate and even more as a partner."

I think about the hours of pageant practice I missed. The rehearsed scenes I will never get back. The nights I didn't tuck my kids into bed because I needed to stay here late. I have already made too many sacrifices for this job. Hell, I might be an awful artist, but I will never be able to give it a fair shot with a job like this that continues to demand more from me but never gives back to me. It never renews me.

I breathe out heavily and begin to shake my head. I feel lightheaded. Stratford Junior continues to act unfazed by this conversation. My heartbeat finally starts to rise. To beat with more purpose than this morning. I straighten my posture and finally say the word I have feared most. "No."

And that got his attention. "What did you say?"

"I said no. I'm done making sacrifices for you. For this job. Not anymore. I'm sorry, but I'm done acting like this is okay."

"But—" I hear from him as I walk out of his office. I collect my belongings at my desk, and I walk to my car. In the safety of Bonnie, I collapse. *What did I just do?*

As much as I tried, I had no more tears to cry. Just rage. Pure, firey, hell-bent rage. With my eyes wide, I blast music from the stereos and drive home. I'm not cautious. I'm not trapped. I feel free. And with that freedom, when I arrive home, I finally start to paint.

---

My paint session is interrupted by my need to go to Susie's school for a semester parent's meeting. On this rare occasion, I'm one of the first parents there. As I walk the halls, I notice myself becoming more observant. The hallway sparkles with artwork from each child and religious posters reminding everyone of God's greatness—the mysterious man in the sky. I notice a poster with an eagle soaring through a pristine blue sky with the same prayer I remember seeing in the principal's office. *God, grant me the serenity to accept the things I cannot change, the courage to change the things I can, and the wisdom to know the difference.* I smile, knowing today I turned towards courage.

I look down the hall and notice Karen and her husband entering the building. I lower my gaze. I hope she doesn't see me. I haven't talked to Karen since our failed attempt at a friendly coffee date. I feel awkward about the whole thing. But part of me feels justified. It wasn't fair for her to pass judgment on my situation.

I lift my head again in her direction to see if she notices that I'm here. I notice her husband is with her and is wearing a casual half zip and jeans instead of his usual form-fitted suit. His chiseled face seems different. The left half appears to slope down more than the right. He no longer looks like the Disney prince, I remember.

"Hey, Rachel, how are you doing?" Karen asks with a wide smile. Her tone is doused in warmth and cheer as if our last conversation never happened. I look back at her husband. Only half his face allows him to smile while the other remains stagnant. I shake my head, knowing I shouldn't stare at him.

"Uh . . . " My body becomes still. I don't know how to respond. I close my eyes. "Yeah . . . I'm . . . I'm trying to figure some things out . . . but I'm good." I respond weakly. "How are both of you?"

Karen lovingly embraces her husband's hand and looks deep into his eyes. "We are really good." She looks back at me. "Happy to be here. And Rachel, I'm always happy to help if you need anything."

How can she offer *me* help? I was rude, but I feel desperate for help right now. "Do you think we can get coffee tomorrow?" I ask.

"Of course, same place and time?" she asks.

I realize I am jobless and now free indefinitely. "That sounds great."

CHAPTER 29

# Wednesday, January 4, 2017

*"Christmas is doing a little something extra for someone."*

— CHARLES M. SCHULZ

I LOOK OUT THE SAME WINDOW at the coffee shop as I wait for Karen. The cold persists, but the Christmas lights that wrapped the light poles have vanished. Snow falls, but the joy has evaporated. The winter season no longer charms the town members but has become a nuisance to their productivity.

I grasp my mug, warming my tingling fingers as I scroll through my phone. I look at the email my dad sent this morning.

I set it up so that you can meet Dean Longhorn at his office tomorrow at 8 AM. He's a great guy. He will make you feel more secure about starting law school, I promise. –Dad

All I need to do is text him back with one word, no. Or an elongated version of no like Thanks, but I can't or literally any string of words with a negative sentiment. But my fingers just hover above my phone motionless. Maybe I just need to meet the man out of respect for the effort my dad put into this. When I look back down, I see I have an incoming call. It's my mom. I breathe deeply. I do need to talk to her about everything that has happened, and I don't see Karen here yet, so I decide to answer it.

"Hey, Mom. I should have called you sooner, I—"

My mom cuts me off. "What is this about you and Rick? I just got off the phone with Marsha. And your dad said you are having doubts about law school. What's going on, Rachel?"

My nerves return and transform me into an awkward, wet clam. Perhaps I have avoided calling my mom because she is the person I know will judge me the most.

"Rachel, are you still there?"

She deserves an explanation, though. She has sacrificed so much for me. "Yes. Sorry, I should have told you sooner. I just—"

"How did you let this happen?" she demands.

"Why do you mean?"

"Come on, Rachel. Rick has always adored you, and you never gave the same amount back. He wouldn't have left you unless you did something."

I was shocked to hear my mom in attack mode. Sure, my mom is opinionated. She frequently oversteps with her opinions and her gifts, but rarely does she attack me with those opinions. "Mom, I know you think Rick was perfect, but he wasn't. He doesn't want kids, and the kids didn't get along with him."

"They seemed perfectly happy to spend time with him at the New Year's Eve party."

"That's because I bribed them to be nice to him." I notice others in the coffee shop turn and look at me. I try to lower my voice.

"That doesn't sound like you." As she says this, I see Karen at the front counter ordering her coffee. I have limited time to try to calm my mom down.

"Look, I just wanted everyone to get along for the evening, but the kids were upset with Rick because he came over the day before, and it got to be a little too much for everyone."

"Well, why did you let that happen?"

"Mom." I take a breath, realizing this downward spiral will cause more harm than good. "I'm sorry, Mom. It just wasn't meant to be. I can't change that now."

"Marsha begs to differ. She says that Rick is torn to pieces. Just call him, sweetie. I'm sure you can make it work."

I breathe in deeply. I know I made the right decision on this. "No, Mom. Rick and I are over. I'm sorry, but you need to accept that."

"Rachel, this is a big mistake. Your kids deserve a male role model in their life. It's your duty as their mother."

"Stop. I know what's best for my children, and they didn't want Rick . . . And frankly, nor do I."

"Is this about Mason's letter? Rachel, I'm sorry, but you need to move forward with your life. You have all the pieces right in front of you with Rick and law school."

"I don't want those things. You want those things for me, but I have always wanted to paint." I notice Karen approaching the table with her latte. "I'm sorry, but I need to go."

"Don't you hang up on me! We need to finish this discussion."

"We can talk later, Mom. I'm sorry." I hang up and wave to Karen.

"Hey, Rachel!" Karen says. Her wool coat is not closed, revealing her joyous pink dress underneath. As always, her boldest accessory is her smile.

"Sorry about that. I was just talking to my mom." I slide out of the booth to hug her. "Thanks for meeting with me today."

"No worries! And I wanted to apologize for —"

"Don't! It was my fault! I shouldn't have gotten so upset about what you said. You were just offering to help, and I appreciate that," I say.

"Well, I overstepped. I shouldn't have tried to force my opinion like that on you."

"No, no, you were just trying to be kind. If I'm being honest, I think a part of me has been jealous of your life. It seemed so perfect to me."

"Seemed perfect?" Karen inquires.

I blush, regretting my word choice but also feeling an itching curiosity after seeing her husband yesterday. "I . . . I feel silly for asking this. Did something happen to Ben?"

She smiles with grace as she wraps her perfectly manicured hands around her dramatically large mug. "Yes, Ben had a stroke about six months ago. He ended up leaving his company to focus on his recovery. He's just starting to get back out into the world."

I pull my lips in, wishing I could take back the poor word choice I made earlier. "I'm so sorry, Karen."

"No need. It's nothing you did."

Her face is still dressed with a wide smile. "Karen, I don't understand. How do you come off so happy when you must be dealing with so much?"

"Well, I guess there is always good to be found. I wake up each day with a husband that's still breathing, and that's enough for me. I know you can understand that blessing I have received from God."

I close my eyes and nod. "Yeah, you're right. Still, I'm so sorry. Is there anything I can do to help you?"

Her already wide smile moves up an extra inch. "I did have an idea that I wanted to run by you."

"Okay, yes, anything."

"Have you been to the bakery?"

"Yeah, on Hudson. Who hasn't in this town?"

She chuckles. "So, as you know, the inside has all the crazy paintings, but the outside is just white and bland. It's time for us to get a paint refresh anyway, and since murals are becoming so popular, I was wondering if I could commission you to design and paint the outside."

My eyes widen as my neck jerks my head back. "Are you serious?"

"Yes. I will pay and everything. I like your style, and I think you will be able to bring the whimsical theme inside to the outside, but with a new, updated energy. What do you think?"

"Wow, Karen . . . Are you sure you want me?"

"Of course!"

I pause. "I mean . . . Let me think about it." I don't know exactly what I need to think about. I don't have a job. I want to paint for a living. She offered me that. Yet, I'm still hesitating.

"Totally understand. No rush. Just an idea."

"I really appreciate that you thought of me. And you are right. I want to paint. I just need to figure some stuff out." *What do you need to figure out?* I hear my inner critic voice, but it seems like Karen is in no rush, so I can take the time to think about how this might change things for me.

"Well, hopefully, this project can be your first step in that direction?"

I smile wide. "Yes, definitely!"

Karen looks down at her bright pink Kate Spade watch. "Anywho, I need to get into the bakery. But call me soon." She leans in for a hug and heads out.

CHAPTER 30

# Thursday, January 5, 2017

*"Christmas magic is silent. You don't hear it — you feel it. You know it. You believe it."*

— KEVIN ALAN MILNE

WHEN I PARK ON WAYNE STATE'S CAMPUS, I expect to feel . . . something. I feel no excitement, no nerves, no fear. Instead, it feels like another chore on my checklist. I kept going back and forth about whether I should cancel the meeting, but a part of me is still curious to know what Dean Longhorn saw in my application. Was I accepted just because of my dad? I navigate the campus and find my way to Dean Longhorn's office. His door is open, so I peek my head in.

"Hey, Dean Longhorn, I'm Rachel. Is this still a good time to talk?"

"Yes, come in." He gestures to the two chairs in the corner of the room. He gets up and moves to the chairs as well. I delicately fold my legs, wishing I wore a pantsuit instead of my skirt that's digging into my stomach.

I hope I can make this quick, so I don't waste too much of his time. "Thank you, Dean Longhorn, for meeting with me so last minute."

"Of course, Miss Taylor," he replies. His long Spidery legs are folded over each other. He leans back in the leather chair as if ready to puff on a cigar. "Your father speaks so highly of you. We are honored to have you as part of our spring term class. He mentioned you have some hesitations, though?"

I smile, honored by his compliment. I have dedicated a decade of my life to being a paralegal. Could I make it as a lawyer? Did someone else see potential in me? "Yes, Dean Longhorn, I'm so grateful for this opportunity . . . It's just that . . . I wanted to understand what you saw in my application."

"Miss Taylor, you are a good candidate for the program. It's that simple."

I want to ask point-blank: Was it because of my father? I know I need to have more sophistication with my questioning. He is a dean of a law school, for goodness sakes. "But, I guess I'm curious if there was something on my resume that stood out to you?"

He says nothing, pauses, and finally gets up to open a drawer in his desk. He pulls out a file and brings it over to me. "Here is your file with notes from our admission team." He hands me the file, but before he releases it, he says, "Just because I'm giving this to you doesn't mean I find it wise for you to review. Miss Taylor, the anxiety you harbor about your abilities will not be good for you long term. May I suggest that instead, you gain confidence in your skills rather than question your path?"

I hold the folder in my hand, tempted to open it, but after Dean Longhorn's speech, I feel like I can't in front of him. I look at the tab in the upper right-hand corner with my name. Inside are the reasons why someone outside of my father thinks I could be a good lawyer. I breathe in deeply and look around the office. There must be another way I can get some information from him.

"Rembrandt?" I ask, pointing to the large framed image behind his desk. The painting is a famous self-portrait Rembrandt made later in his life. His face is sunken and wrinkled from the turmoil of life, with his untamed curls popping out of his brown beret. Each detail is perfectly realistic with vibrantly dull colors.

"Awh, yes, nice eye. But why should I be surprised as I sit across from a trained artist?"

My eyes shimmer like a child who finally gets a compliment on their scribbled picture. "You know about art school?"

His face becomes puzzled. "Of course. It was actually one of my favorite things about your application. It shows me you are well-rounded and creative. A woman of passion."

*Me, a woman of passion?* I don't feel like a woman of passion but rather a woman harboring fear and anxiety. I look more intently at him. "Dean Longhorn, I don't know if I'm ready to give up art for law school."

"Why do you say that? Why not both?"

*Why not both?* Perhaps I could find a way to do both, but my heart would always be pulled to the art and burdened by the law. Instead, I ask him, "Why should I do both when there is only one I truly want?" I get up from the chair and pull down on the skirt that I can't wait to take off and never wear it again. "I'm sorry for wasting your time, Dean Longhorn."

He smiles and gets up to shake my hand. "No, no. It was my pleasure, Miss Taylor. It sounds like your mind is made."

I feel shocked that he's not trying to convince me that law school is superior to art. I'm used to being pushed. My mother and father push. The Stratfords push. But Dean Longhorn is indifferent to the path I choose. "So you think I should do art?"

He shifts his body to face me and looks through my eyes directly to the scared child sitting within me. "Rachel, only you have that answer."

And for once, it feels so clear. I set down the packet that holds the answers that moments ago seemed so important to me. I shake Dean Longhorn's hand and thank him profusely for his time. It finally is starting to feel right. I just hope my family can see that as well.

---

After the meeting, I sit in Bonnie and call my dad to tell him that I won't be going to law school.

"Dad?" I start with a shaky voice.

"Hey."

I hear my mom's voice. It's unlike my mom to answer my dad's phone. "Mom, I need to talk to Dad. I met with Dean Longhorn and told him that I wouldn't be accepting the offer."

My mom's voice becomes stern, a tone she hadn't used since I was a child. "I can't let you do this, Rachel."

I feel a heat building in the back of my throat, but I try to ignore it and sound compassionate. I understand that I'm throwing a lot of change at them, but I need my mom onboard. I can't imagine my life without her support. "Mom, I'm not going to law school. I'm so sorry it took me so long to figure that out, but it's not what I want."

"What are you doing, Rachel? Why are you throwing all of this away?"

"I'm sorry. But I know I want to paint. It took me time, but I know how I want to spend my days. If there is anything Mason has taught me, and his letter reminded me, it is that my time here is limited."

"I thought we were past this. Do I need to remind you that your father and I *paid* for you to go to art school, and it didn't work out, and it was your father that had to bail you out? And in a matter of months, we're going to have to do it again."

I close my eyes and absorb the painful blow I feel from her words. While my one hand grasps the phone tighter to my ear, the other pulls at the roots of my hair. I take a deep breath. "Mom, it's not just something I can get past. My desire to paint has always been with me. I've just been hiding from it." I think of the conversation I had with Aunt Roxanne. The beautiful sets my mom created for Susie's pageant. I continue, "And I know you understand the feeling of painting. Why won't you admit it?"

I hear my mom cry on the other end. She raises her voice. "Because, Rachel, I failed at art! I failed! And art failed me! Are you happy to hear that?! It tortured me, and it broke me. And it was *my* mother who had to pick me up and put me back on my feet, and till the day she died, she reminded me of that. And I don't want that for you!"

I never knew this about my grandma. She died when I was a teenager. She was definitely your typical judgemental, old woman, but I never realized that judgment was about my mom and her decisions. "Mom, I didn't mean . . . I'm sorry . . . I just . . . I didn't know that."

"Rachel, I tried. I tried so hard with you. I saw that same creative spark in you, and I wanted you to experience it. I wanted you to get enough of it when you were young, so you could get over it when you were older. I was the one that enrolled you in ballet. In art. In pottery classes. Against my mother's wishes. Against your own father's wishes. I wanted you to experience it all when you were young so that when you were older, you would be able to move on and start a real career, but my plan backfired when you demanded that you go to art school. Your father was furious with me, and I'm sure my mother was rolling in her grave over it. It was just another failure of mine, but now as a mother, the one job I swore I would succeed at. But I told your father it was fine because you were still a child. You would learn. But, Rachel, you are not a child anymore, you are a mother, and a mother must do what is best for her children, and the instability of being an artist is not something your children need."

I shake my head. I always saw my mother as the person pulling me away from art. But it has always been my mom supporting me to express myself creatively. I guess asking me to cut back, like quitting ballet, was her way of protecting my creative spirit from the naysaying of my father and my grandparents. I have been blaming my mother for so many years for limiting me, but in reality, she was my biggest supporter. "Mom, I had no idea. I really didn't . . . But time hasn't run out for me, and it hasn't run out for you either. There is a way to make art and life work together."

I hear nothing from the other end. Finally, my mom replies, "I'm sorry, Rachel. I can't watch you do this. I need to go."

I pull the phone away from my ear and see that my mother ended the call. My muscles go weak; they crumble across the seat. I do not smile; I wail in pain. I do not force my eyes open; they close, destroying the dam that once held my deepest oases of tears. My breathing doesn't slow; it pounds rigorously. My chest no longer remains flat; it pumps up and down, unrestrained. My lungs act as convicts escaping from prison. Like victims that must relearn how to operate in a transformed world. Like astronauts adjusting to space. My fingers turn to ice. My hands squeeze the wheel, reminding me that I'm alive. I'm breathing. For the first time, I give myself permission to feel everything. I cry; I pray; I begin to create my own hope. I start to understand that freedom is the most painful thing to face, but I realize I would rather face the fear of freedom than the numbness of life imprisoned by the "shoulds" of everyone around me.

For once, I feel everything, and hidden behind all this pain, all these tears, all these trembles, is the true me that has been hidden for years. I don't know her well anymore, but I know I will like her. I used to like her. Mason used to love her. I just need more time to get to know her again. I need time to try. To play. To learn. And with those things comes self-acceptance. And from there self-transformation.

# CHAPTER 31

# Friday, January 6, 2017

*"I believe . . . I believe . . . It's silly, but I believe."*

— MIRACLE ON 34TH STREET

"KIDS! WE CAN'T BE LATE!" I shout as I scramble to collect everything we will need for today.

Susie gallops down the stairs, proudly displaying her new look. Her hair is in a low ponytail with a big ribbon in the back. She has a western-style jacket and cowboy boots with her My Little Pony in hand. "Let's goooooo, Noah!" she shouts.

"Mom, should I bring the Nerf blaster?" I hear Noah shout from upstairs as he rummages through his toy bins.

"No, honey, you cannot use the Nerf guns while on the horse."

"Fineeeeeeee." Noah marches downstairs.

I let the kids skip school today since it's the anniversary of Mason's death. Mason would want his kids facing their fears and taking grand adventures, so I decided today was a good day to take them horseback riding as promised. As we pull up to the farm Bob recommended, we see a ranch-style home across from a barn that's twice its size. Several horses frolic in the expansive fenced field. As I maneuver my car on the muddy path, I try to avoid the ducks and chickens that are roaming free.

"Mommy, look at the horses! I can't believe I finally get to ride a pony today!" Susie shouts as her legs swing rapidly in her car seat. And that smile. Every parent lives to see that smile on their child's face.

"Can I feed the horseys? I brought apples!" Susie asks.

"Let's check-in and ask," I reply. They run into the barn, nearly tripping over a duck on their way. A young girl greets us. "You must be Susie and Noah. Are you excited about your lesson today?"

Noah has become too distracted by all the animals to respond to her. Susie bashfully nods her head up and down. She jumps up and asks, "Can I feed the horseys?"

The young girl laughs. "Of course, and you get to ride a horse today, too. Sounds pretty good, yeah?"

I feel nervous. All the horses seem too big for Susie. A fall could lead to a severe injury. "Are you sure both of them are old enough . . . " I look at Susie, who isn't even four feet tall. "Do you think Susie is tall enough? If not, no worries, we can just feed and touch the horses."

Susie snaps back at me, "Mommmmmm!"

The young girl chimes in, "I can assure you they will be safe. We have some very well-trained smaller horses, and we plan to strap them into a small seat, so they shouldn't fall off."

I still feel the nerves building in my tightened shoulders. "Is it possible for me to see that seat and just make sure it looks safe . . . "

"Sure thing." She goes to get one from the tack room.

"And what about helmets?" I shout after her. I am sure the young girl thinks I am crazy, but she might be doing the same thing someday with her own kids.

"Yep, they are always required, and we have plenty of sizes that will fit the two of them."

"Mommm, we want to ride the horses!" Noah demands.

"I know. I know. It's my job to protect you, though."

As I examine the equipment and debate if this is a good decision or not, the girl asks, "Do you want to meet the horses?"

They both shout excitedly and skip along, following her to the stable right next to me. She pulls out the first horse that's about twice the size of Noah. "This here is Peanut."

"Peanut?! What a funny name!" Noah shouts.

"I love him!" Susie runs to hug his body, causing the horse to flinch. She screams just a bit and bounces back.

"Be careful!" I shout.

She quickly runs back to the horse and giggles. "He's just playing, Mom."

I breathe deeply. Mason would want this for them. Everything will be okay. Soon after, I see Susie and Noah, on the back of their horses as I sit on the bleachers surrounding the outdoor arena. The sun shines through the cloudy sky and directs itself on Susie's horse as if Mason was here guiding and protecting our child. I close my eyes like I have many times and breathe in. I hear Mason talking through the wind. I feel him with warmth on this unusually sunny January day. Mason finds his way to still be here.

I allow my worries to be pushed away with each deep breath I take, knowing Mason is guiding our babies right now. I pull out the little notebook I have in my purse and begin to doodle the scene in front of me. Perhaps, my inspiration to create is right here. I just need to trust that the kids will be okay.

After the lesson, Susie runs over to the bleachers. "Mommy, Mommy!! Peanut is my bestest friend!"

I smile wide, feeling more fulfilled than ever. "I'm so proud of you, sweetie! Your father would be so proud to see you conquering your fears today."

"I was never afraid of horses, Momma. You were." She skips away back to the horse.

I stop in my tracks. Susie is right. It's my fears of losing my two loves like I lost Mason that today is about. It's my fear of living that has me in a rut. Fear of loss. Fear of disappointment. Fear of freedom. Controlled by the fear fostered by my past preventing me from relying on the hope for the uncertain future. "Can you watch them for a minute?" I ask the instructor.

She nods and brings them over to clean the horses. I pull out the letter from Mason that I always keep in my bag. I look to my future. I pull out the two contact cards he provided.

Marsha West
Editorial Assistant
United Publishing Group
555-708-9405

Shawna Bright
Art Curator
Phillips Gallery
555-709-9345

First, I call Marsha simply because it was mentioned first by Mason in the letter. Perhaps there is a reason there. My breath trembles, but I do not look back.

"Hey, this is Marsha with United Publishing. How can I help you?" I hear from the other end.

"Hey Marsha, I'm Rachel Taylor. My . . . husband submitted some of my work to you several years ago, and I'm just now calling to see if you still have a record of that? I know it's been a long time, but I figured I would try."

"Oh, wow! Why such a long wait?"

Where do I begin? Should I start with, *Funny story, actually? My husband tried to give me the gift of hope at Christmas, but he died trying to get it to me. I never found it because I was too scared to look at the items from the scene of his death, so I never knew about this until this Christmas when I finally felt so broken, I decided to open the box.* I should probably come up with something simpler.

"That's a good question . . . I guess life got in the way. Perhaps fear."

"Fair enough," Marsha responds with a cordial giggle. "Well, Mrs. Taylor, we don't save the work from submissions for more than a year, so, unfortunately, we won't have it on file. We are not accepting new work right now. Perhaps in six months, you can resubmit?"

I look down to the gravel path. I notice the chicken pecking at my shoe, but I don't move. "Right . . . yeah . . . That makes sense. Yeah, I'll call back in six months, then."

I take the phone from my ear and press the big red button to end the call. I can't help feeling disappointed, but I try to rationalize. It's been four years. There was no way this would work. I try the other number and get a similar response.

I breathe deeply and suddenly lift my head. I remember there is another opportunity waiting for me. I hold the phone up to my ear.

"Karen?" I say.

"Yes, Rachel. Are you okay?"

"Yes! Yes! I'm doing . . . great! About your offer to paint, I want to do it! If you will still have me?"

"Oh really? I would love that! When can you get started?"

"Perhaps sometime next week, I can present you some design concepts?"

"Sounds good to me. I'm usually in the office in the morning, so you can always swing by."

"Wonderful! Thank you, Karen! I won't let you down!" *I have already let so many people down this year, but I won't fail at this too*, I vow silently.

After the call, I do a little jig. Noah and Susie see me from inside the barn. Susie says, "Mommy is going crazy out there!"

I head inside and give them both a big hug. "No, I'm just so happy to be alive today and to be here with you."

"Us too," they both add.

I just need to figure out how to get my parents onboard as well.

CHAPTER 32

# Saturday, January 7, 2017

*"I wish we could put up some of the Christmas spirit in jars and open a jar of it every month."*

— HARLAN MILLER

"I CAN'T BELIEVE we're getting cupcakes in the morning!" Noah says as we return home with a box of cupcakes at 11 AM. I want them in a good mood so that I can talk about the recent changes. It is time for them to know what I'm doing.

Last night I reviewed our finances, trying to figure out how I can make this work. I know I can't keep working at the Stratford firm and find time to take my painting seriously. Even with the Christmas bonus, our limited savings, and the gift from Mason, we can survive for about five months. I also have this temporary gig with Karen that should bring in some money. Our biggest expenses are the kids' schools and the house we bought, assuming a two-person income. I could stretch out our savings if I found a way to remove one of those larger expenses. I want the kids to be a part of deciding what changes we might need to make as a family.

They both pick up the cupcake they chose at the store, getting icing all over their fingers and faces. "Mommy needs to talk to you about something very important," I say to the kids.

Susie and Noah nod as they lick the frosting off their fingers.

I take a deep breath in and begin. "So, Mommy is going to stop working as a paralegal for the Stratfords."

"Cause of the gift from Grandpa at Christmas?" Noah asks. I have already assumed I will get a lot of questions from them.

"Not exactly. To be honest, I wasn't happy working as a paralegal."

"Why?" Susie implores.

"Well, because I don't really love it."

"But why?" Noah continues.

I realize I need to change the way I'm explaining this. "Well, you know how Susie always asks you to play with her ponies, Noah?" He nods. "But sometimes you don't like it, but sometimes you do, like yesterday?" He nods again. Perfect, he understands this line of logic. "You can do it sometimes, but not all the time? Well, I guess being a paralegal was like playing with ponies. I could do it a little bit, but I don't want to do it all the time."

"What's wrong with my ponies?" Susie shouts.

"Nothing. They are wonderful. Everyone has their thing they enjoy. And mine is not being a paralegal. I wanted to let you know that I'll be working on a mural for the Pixie Bakery instead. I know you haven't seen me painting much, but I have always loved it, and I want to do more of it. It's my version of ponies for you, Susie, and Nerf guns for you, Noah."

"Does that mean we get cupcakes every day?!" Noah asks.

I giggle. "We will see. The main reason I'm bringing this up is that I won't be making as much money with this new job."

Noah interjects, "Why?"

"Well, because it pays less, and that means we might need to make some changes in how we spend money."

"Like what?" Susie asks.

"Well, what do you guys think of downsizing to a smaller house? I found some nice apartments right next to the downtown and—"

Noah begins to cry. "NO! I don't want to move! Why can't we stay here?!"

My heart breaks. I want my kids to be happy, and I always want to put them first. Am I putting my needs before them? I think of the picture Susie made of the family with my straight-lined lips. Susie deserves to see a mom, a role model for living life boldly, that smiles every day. "Honey, this house is so big, and we could get a smaller home that will be more affordable."

"No, I refuse to move!" Noah demands.

I figured he would refuse. This house stores the memories of his father. How could I take that away from him? "Well, there is another option. What do you think of trying out a new school next year?" I ask.

"But what about my friends?" Susie asks.

"What about Marcus?" Noah yells. "Why are you doing this to us?! This isn't fair!"

"We have time to decide, but I wanted to include you in the decision. We just can't afford both the house and the schools."

"But why not?" Noah shouts. "If Daddy was here, he would never do this to us!"

I close my eyes. "I'm sorry, Noah, but we are going to either move or leave your school, and if you don't want to help decide, then I will."

Noah jumps up from the table and runs upstairs. "I HATE you!"

I can't do this. "Noah, go to your room RIGHT now!" I say sternly, even though he's halfway up to his room by then. Susie follows behind him.

I start to sob. I have lost Rick, my parents, and now my kids. I should have never done this. I should have stayed quiet. I can't do this alone. I grab my phone and text my mom.

Hey, Mom. I love you. Are you and Dad still upset?

She replies with just one word.

Yes.

I feel too drained to paint. I instead go to my room, lay in my bed, and stare at the blank ceiling blanketed by my defeat.

CHAPTER 33

# Sunday, January 8

*"My idea of Christmas, whether old-fashioned or modern, is very simple: loving others."*

— BOB HOPE

THE KIDS HAVE BARELY SAID A WORD to me since our conversation yesterday morning. My parents are avoiding talking to me as well. I have been trying to call my dad since Thursday, but he won't pick up. I ended up sending him an email about my decision that he never responded to. I never expected to be ghosted by my own parents. I decide to text my mom anyway.

Hey, Mom, I know you and Dad are still upset with my decisions, but the kids miss you. Any chance I can bring them by today, so they can see you? I can run some errands then.

Almost immediately, I see three dots.

Sure. Your father is at the office, so you won't be able to talk with him.

I reply.

That's okay. I will be there soon.

I pack up the kids and arrive at my parent's house. I can feel myself hesitating to ring the doorbell. Finally, Noah gets on his tippy toes and rings it for me.

My mom comes and provides a warm welcome to Noah and Susie. I try to go inside, and she says, "Kids, head on in. Let me talk to your mom outside."

She won't even let me in the house! I know I need to apologize. "Mom, I'm so sorry about all this. What can I do to make it better?"

She shakes her head. "I think the only thing you can do for your father is to go to law school. Have you reconsidered?"

I sigh. "Mom, I don't want to be a lawyer. I left my job, but I already have a painting job lined up."

Her eyes swim in disappointment as she looks at me. "I'm assuming that job is temporary."

"Yeah, it'll be a couple of months."

"Then what are you going to do?"

"I don't know yet, but I have savings, and, ideally, I will be able to start lining things up."

"Your father could at least help you find a proper job."

I look up to the sky. *What am I doing?* "I don't know yet, Mom. For now, though, I will have a job, and I will figure out the rest as I go."

"And Rick? You just let him go?"

I look down and rub my empty ring finger that briefly held that commitment to Rick. *Am I making a mistake?*

I look back to my mom, my head tilted and my eyes watering, "I'm sorry, Mom. I can't. It's just . . . It's not what I want anymore."

She crosses her arms and pinches her lips inward. She seems too disgusted with me to continue. "Fine. See you in a couple of hours then." She turns into the house and closes the door without looking back. Even with the door closed and my mother gone, I can't move as if my legs have become rooted here. I manage to wipe the tears in my eyes that are blocking my vision. I take another breath and finally head back to my car.

---

I pull into the gravel drive with the day-old cupcakes secured on the passenger seat. At this point, my stomach wants to hide the cupcakes so that I can eat all of them, but I know that a love of sugar is a family-wide problem.

I decided last night to reach out to Roxanne. She has lived alone in the woods for many years, essentially excommunicated from the family, except for the annual Christmas party. Somehow, though, she seems to remain cheerful when I see her. I need to learn from her how to deal with all this judgment from others.

I knock on the door, prompting the dogs to bark passionately, and soon Roxanne arrives. "Hello, dear. Come on in."

"I brought cupcakes!" I announce.

"Oh, you know I have quite a sweet tooth. Let's both have one now?"

"Of course! I was hoping you would ask!"

We grab two small saucers, and Roxanne brews coffee in her French press. We meticulously examine the variety of cupcakes and decide which one each of us will eat.

Then we sit down with our coffee and cupcakes. Our attention is solely focused on the delicious flavors. No chatter is needed when there are great tastes to observe.

Roxanne finally breaks the silence. "These are so damn good." She places the last bite in her mouth. "So, what did you want to talk about?"

"I want to know, what do you do? What do you love? How do you handle being . . . I don't know—"

She interjects, "Cut off?"

"Yeah. I want to understand how that happened."

She nods. "Well, that's a big request. Where is this coming from, Rachel?"

She has a warmth in her eyes of genuine curiosity. Eyes that permit me to finally release. In one breath, I attempt to explain everything that has happened since Mason died. That I feel trapped to do right for my parents. To be good for my children. To show others that I can function alone. That I'm whole even when I feel empty inside, I release everything truthfully for the first time. Roxanne simply nods and listens. As I reach the end of my monologue, I ask, "So what can I do to make peace with my parents and my kids?"

She lifts herself and crosses her legs as if ready to meditate. She leans towards me. "Perhaps that's the wrong question to be asking."

"What do you mean? I need to find a way to make it right with them. I can't live with their disappointment."

"Rachel, what you need to do is make it right with yourself first. Not your mother, or your kids, or even the desires of your late spouse. What do *you* want, Rachel?"

"I feel like I can only do that if I can get my family's blessing."

Roxanne smiles, uncrosses her legs, and reaches for a book on the coffee table in front of us. It is a scrapbook of pictures. She hands me the book and tells me to flip through the photos. I see two young girls close in age in almost every shot, holding each other closely with bright, youthful smiles in new landscapes and adventures. There are images of one girl teaching the other to ride a bike, the two dressed as medieval knights, and another of them rolling around in piles of leaves. I vaguely can tell that the older girl is my mom, and the other is Aunt Roxanne.

I raised my eyes from the book back to Roxanne. "You look so close in these photos."

Roxanne nods. "There was a time that Barbara and I . . . we were unstoppable." She pauses, smiles, and looks slightly up as if seeing a vision. "When your mother and I were growing up, I remember your mom needed to get a permission slip signed to go to the zoo."

I nod, letting Roxanne know I'm listening. "Of course, our mom would have signed it and said yes, but little Barbara refused. I remember asking her why, and at the prime age of eight, she said back to me, 'Because I don't need my mom to sign my permission slip for what I do.'"

My eyes are wide. "There is no way *my mother* would say that," I respond.

Roxanne chuckles, and she looks back at me. "It's crazy how much your mom has changed since then, but it's something I have always lived by. In life, you are the only signature you need to decide what you will do with your life. There are no lines for others to sign the slip. Just you, Rachel."

She reaches out to hold one of my hands. "Find your peace, and the people you love will learn to adapt."

It's hard to believe my mom said that. "What caused my mom to change?"

She frowns a bit. "At some point, I think your mom allowed society to sign her permission slip for living instead of herself."

"When did it happen?" I ask.

"I think it was a lot of small moments over time rather than one big one."

"How do you do it, Roxanne? Doesn't it bother you that the family doesn't talk to you?"

"They will *talk* to me, but only to find flaws in my decisions and lifestyle. I have chosen to surround myself with people that truly believe in me, and I have met amazing people for my support network. I would love to have your mom back in that network, but I can't force her to change, nor can I succumb to her judgments, so this distance is what is best."

"What happened between the two of you?" I ask.

Roxanne winces. "I think we can save that story for another day. For now, you should get that wandering mind of yours in isolation so that you can find your own peace."

I nod, hug her, and head back to my mom's to collect the kids.

---

I ring the doorbell and am surprised to be greeted by my dad. He looks distressed. "Let me get your mother."

"Actually, I wanted to—"

My dad stops me. "Not today, Rachel." My heart sinks. When will he be willing to talk to me again?

Promptly, she comes to the door and says, "Jeff, can you head inside and collect the kids? I want to talk to Rachel." My dad nods and walks back inside. She steps out and closes the front door behind her.

My mom looks nervous. She checks behind herself to ensure the door is closed. "Just listen, Rachel." She grabs my hand and slides a small piece of paper into my palm.

"What's this?" I ask.

She looks back at the door and then straight into my eyes. "It's for the kids. They told me about yesterday."

The door opens, and my mom whispers in my ear, "And don't tell your father about this."

The door opens, and the kids run outside, followed by my father. I slip the paper into my pocket. I know my mom is upset about my decision to paint, but my heart further sinks into its abyss, knowing I have disappointed her too.

When we get back in the car, I unfold the piece of paper. It's a check. The amount reads $10,000 and is signed by my mother. In the "purpose" line, she wrote *for Susie's and Noah's school.* My heart seems to pause.

"What's that?" Susie asks, who is now leaning forward, trying to peer into my lap.

I quickly fold it back up and place it in my pocket. I turn to look back at them. I can see that Noah is still angry with me. "I think I found a way for you guys to stay in school and keep our house."

Noah lights up. "Really?"

"Yes . . . " I pause. Should I tell them it's because of their grandmother, though? I don't want them blabbing it when they are there and accidentally telling my dad. My mother is taking a risk in her marriage to help me live my passions, something my father, at least today, would oppose. Is this my mother's way of saying she will still support me even as I change my life goals? I look back at the kids who are secure in their seats. "We just need to stop at the bank on the way home."

"Can we get lollipops there?" Noah asks.

"Let's see!" I announce. As I pull out of the drive, I see big smiles on both their faces. I feel guilty that it's not my actions that are providing them this joy.

CHAPTER 34

# Friday, January 20, 2017

*"Christmas works like glue. It keeps us all sticking together."*

— ROSIE THOMAS

"NOAH, DON'T TOUCH THAT!" I shout. I scramble over to the kitchen table to pick up the canvas that is still drying. I delicately lift it by its corners, inspecting for his little gremlin fingerprints.

"But, Mom, I need to use the kitchen table for homework," Noah demands. I never imagined a life where my son would be telling me that he wants to do his homework. Usually, it is me forcing it upon him. I look around the first floor of the house and notice more of my stuff is scattered around than my children's toys. I see my paintbrushes in the sink, my canvases covering the counters and now overflowing onto the kitchen table, and my easel blocking the TV. I guess I have just been so focused on finally being able to paint, I have forgotten it is not like the olden days where I had my own studio apartment that I could keep a mess. I have others that rely on me, and they need this space too.

"You're right, Noah. I need to clean up." I remind myself it will take time to figure out the right balance, but I finally feel so happy to be painting again.

"Yeah, Mommy," Susie chimes in as she brings her backpack to the kitchen table to work on her assigned coloring sheets, her version of homework. "You have gotten really messy. Is it cause Grandma isn't coming over anymore?"

I frown and walk over to Susie to hug her. "I'm sure you will see Grandma and Grandpa soon."

It's been weeks, and both my parents continue to avoid my calls. I have tried to set up time for them to spend with the kids, and even those messages go unanswered. In my notes app, I have a message drafted apologizing to my parents for my decisions. For the pain I have caused them. It says that I will go to law school and do the life they have planned for me. Everything would be healed with that. I have copied and pasted the message into our group text, but every time I stare at the message for minutes, even hours, and then decide to delete it. I know law school is not the right answer for me.

"But you are both right. Let me clean this all up for you guys. Mommy has gotten too messy." I start by collecting the dry canvases and take them to my closet to line them on the floor with the others. Soon I won't even be able to walk in this space. I need a better solution. I turn back to look into my bedroom.

The room is a mess. It would be generous to say I made the bed this morning. It looks more like I threw the sheet and comforter to be flat and thoughtlessly tossed the pillows on top. My dresser is covered with jewelry and various products that seduced me into thinking I could have the skin of an angel if I just bought this one more product. They never seemed to actually work. I look back in the closet. The space is actually quite large. Large enough to fit a queen-size mattress and still have some space. To the left, I look at the suits I no longer need since I left law, and to the right, Mason's clothes that haven't moved for four years.

I close my eyes and breathe in. My hand grazes the plaid shirt Mason wore on our first date. I lift the sleeve to my nose. His smell is gone. I know it's time. Mason would want me to move on. To use this space for my art instead of a memorial for the past.

I grab one of the flattened boxes Mason made us save when we moved into this house and reconstructed it. I take each shirt down and fold it, delicately placing it into the box. I shout downstairs. "Kids, do you have any toys you can donate? I think it is time for us to have a garage sale." Perhaps we can make enough to extend our living costs for a little longer.

---

That night, I hear my phone ringing on the nightstand. I roll over and pick up my phone. It's 2:30 in the morning. The call is from my mom.

I quickly sit up in my bed and place the phone over my ear. My eyes shoot open as if I was never asleep. "Mom?"

My mom's voice is quivering. "Honey, it's your father."

Immediately, I jump out of bed. "What's wrong?"

"He's in the hospital. He had a heart attack. I know it's the middle of the night, and I know . . . I know we haven't talked for a while . . . but . . . I had no one else to call."

I can't think of the last time my mom asked me for help. I'm always getting help from them. "I'll be there in ten minutes."

"No, no, Rachel. Not with the kids and everything. We can just talk on the phone."

I am already out of bed, throwing on the clothes closest to me. "Mom, no. You are always there for me. We'll be there in ten, okay? Text me where you are."

My mother doesn't try to fight the offer. "Thank you, Rachel."

"Of course! I would do anything for you."

Somehow I manage to get the kids strapped into the car with minor disturbances. When we get there, I navigate the hospital halls with Susie and Noah asleep in the wagon I usually attach to my bike. I figured it would be easier than trying to get them up and walking. When I reach the waiting room, I see my mother in the corner. Her posture is straight, her legs folded over, her neck hanging low as if trying to hide in the book she's reading.

"Mom?"

When she looks up, I see streaks of grey running down her eyes from leftover mascara. She tries to wipe her eyes with the handkerchief she pulls from her bag. "That was very fast. I wasn't ready."

Tears dampen my eyes. It's unclear if I'm crying because my dad is sick or if it's just because I finally get to see my mom again. I sit in the seat next to her and offer my arms for a hug. She leans in and holds me tightly. When I try to pull away, she doesn't let go. "Is he okay?" I ask.

She speaks softly as if too weak to speak louder than a whisper. "He's in surgery. They said they would update me soon, but I'm still waiting."

I pull away and start to look around. I want to be helpful. "Do you want me to find a nurse?"

"No, I have been asking every five minutes. I think they know me as the crazy wife in the waiting room."

There must be something I can do for her. "How about food? Or coffee? I can go out and get you anything you need."

"No, I just need your dad to be okay. I don't know how to live without him."

I wrap my arm around her shoulder. "I know, Mom. Let's hope for the best, though." I look around the waiting room. I notice a poster above the side table covered with outdated magazines that look infested with disease. *God, grant me the serenity to accept the things I cannot change, the courage to change the things I can, and the wisdom to know the difference.*

I look down into my lap. I question if this was my fault. Was there something I could have done to change things? Did my decisions cause him that last nudge of stress to push him over? “Do you think this is because of me, Mom? Because of all the stress I created for the two of you?”

She lifts my chin to meet her eyes. “No, honey, your father has been having health problems for years. He will always love you. This is not your fault.”

I smile and look down at her lap. “How can you focus on your book right now?”

She smirks. “It helps me escape from this.”

“What are you reading?”

“Actually, the Margaret Madison book you gave me. I just started it.” She sets the book on the side table and turns to me. “How did you find it again?”

“Aunt Roxanne recommended it.” Since the fight I had with my mom, I have met up with Aunt Roxanne several more times, and she kept asking if my mom has read the book, but getting my mom to read this book has been a low priority for me.

“I can’t believe I haven’t already read it. I have all her books.”

“Yeah, Roxanne said she got it on a limited release from the author. I was reading online that Margaret Madison is a pen name.”

“Yes, I have heard that too. I guess a person who writes mysteries would enjoy that extra layer of thrill for the readers. There are lots of theories online on who they might be."

I notice my mom's eyes start to twitch in exhaustion. "Mom, I think you should go home and get some sleep so you can . . . " I pause, afraid of saying too much. "So that you can come back fresh tomorrow."

She looks at the book, then at the clock on the wall. It's a little after 3 AM. "What if he gets out of surgery early?"

"I will call you mom, but you need sleep too."

She breathes deeply and grabs my hands. "You're right. Thank you, Rachel. I have missed you."

A single tear rolls down my cheek. "I have missed you too, Mom. I will see you in the morning."

"Okay." She gets up and walks away. When I look at the side table, I notice the book is still there. I turn back but can't find her. I decide to pick up the book and flip to the first page, curious why my aunt is making such a big fuss for my mom to read this book. It might be a good way to pass the time anyways.

The novel is short, with fewer than three hundred pages. I decide to give it a try. As I read the story, I feel my heart sync with the beats of the novel. The story follows a dutiful mother that fears someone will break into her home and steal her children. After each nightmare, she goes to the garage to design and install a new lock. Soon, each door and window has nearly 100 different mechanisms. But one day, she accidentally starts a fire while cooking. She tries to get her kids out, but they cannot escape because of all her locks. They all died. The mother's ghost now haunts the town's current mothers causing them to make crazy decisions to protect their children.

Does Aunt Roxanne think that my mother is that ghost? Making so many attempts to protect me that I might end up burning in her own fire of protection? Is that what my mother's mom did to her? Am I doing that to my children?

CHAPTER 35

# Saturday, January 21, 2017

*"The Christmas spirit is a spirit of giving and forgiving"*

— JAMES CASH PENNEY

"MOMMY, I'M HUNGRY!" Noah shouts into my ear, causing me to jolt out of the chair.

"Noah, don't shout."

"Why are we here?" he asks.

I shake my head and rub the back of my sore neck. Spending the night reading in this uncomfortable chair was undoubtedly a bad decision. I realized in all the commotion, I never explained to Susie and Noah what happened last night. "Come sit." I direct them both to my lap. They both attentively look up to me. "Grandpa . . . Your grandpa had a heart attack last night."

"Is he going to die?" Susie asks.

I want to say no. I want to give them some security, but the reality is I don't know. No one does. This is my moment of serenity. To accept what I cannot change. "I'm not sure, sweetie. But let's pray for him, okay?"

I grab each of their small hands and recite a prayer. I can't think of the last time I prayed, yet it feels natural to ask this higher unknown power for hope. To communicate to an entity beyond our space and time for guidance in facing the complexity of uncertainty. *Dear God, I can't lose my father. It's too soon.*

With my head down, I feel a soft touch on my shoulder like an angel coming to my side saying it will be okay. I look up and see it is my mom returning. "Mom, you're back. Did you get any sleep?"

Noah and Susie drop my hands and run over to Grandma to hug her legs.

"I tried. Any news through the night?" she asks.

"He got out of surgery about an hour ago. He's stable but not ready for visitors."

"I don't know how long I can go without seeing him."

"I know, Mom. How about we get some breakfast for now?"

"Yes! I'm hungry," Noah chimes in.

"Yes, breakfast sounds good."

---

That evening, I come back to the hospital with dinner for my mom. The kids are staying with friends. My mom is sitting in the beige recliner across from my father, who is still sleeping and recovering from the surgery. Her face is folded in her book with tears running down her face.

"Are you okay, Mom?" I go to her side and place my hand on her arm.

She continues to cry, trying to find the words. I ask, "Is everything okay with Dad?"

Finally, she mumbles, "Yes, yes, your father is okay. Just resting. It's just . . . this book." She flips the book back to its cover, *A Mother's Haunting*. "It's my town. It's my house. It's my mom."

"What do you mean?"

"The bathroom, with its gaudy red pilgrim wallpaper and crystal chandelier. That was my mother's bathroom. The book is about my family. I don't know how. I don't know if I'm going crazy, but it just feels so real, like the author has been to my home and lived with my mother."

Maybe she is on to something. Maybe Margaret Madison is closer than we all originally thought. I grab the book and read the back cover.

*There is one town in America that you don't want to move to. Bethlehem, Ohio, seems like a quaint, picturesque small town with a main street decorated for the holidays and always polite residents. But at night, all that changes. Intruders break into homes, take belongings, and at times, even take children. Yet even with these disasters, no one ever moves away. Who are these intruders? Why won't the residents leave?*

*Margaret Madison is a long-time reader and lover of mystery novels. As a kid, she would work with her sibling to solve local crimes. She now directs that energy to her books. Margret lives in a remote home with her two children, Lily and Bailey.*

It feels so obvious now. I point my mom to the author's description. "Mom, you're not so crazy. I actually think you are on to something."

She reads the passage. "I don't understand."

"Margaret Madison . . . I think Roxanne is Margaret Madison."

She looks again at the cover, and places her hand to her mouth. Her eyes dart around the room as if searching for a small fly. I stand motionless with my attention only on my mom, unsure how she will react. After a lengthy pause, her shaky hands reach into her purse and get her phone. She navigates the screen, dials a number, and puts the phone up to her ear.

"Why didn't you tell me?" she demands into the phone.

I hear Roxanne on the other end. "What do you mean?"

"You're Margaret Madison. I read the book you gave Rachel. Why did you hide that from us? From me? From our mother?"

"I never hid it. It was always right there in every book. No one ever thought to ask, though."

I can tell my mom is offended. She gets up from her chair. "What do you mean? We were always asking how you are surviving! We were worried to death that you didn't have enough to live. For God's sake, Roxanne, we thought you resorted to selling drugs to survive."

"Our mother only asked what I was doing so she could judge me. To judge my life choices. You know how she was. She did it to you, and I saw how her judgment got to you, and she found a way to push you out of art, so I wasn't going to let her do that to me. So, no, I never told anyone directly, but with every book, Barbara, I have tried to find ways to tell you it was me behind those novels. Trying to show you that I still love you and that I miss you. I never wanted to hide it from you, but I didn't know how to let you in, but protect myself from our mother."

"So the ghost in the book is our mother."

"Yes."

"And the town that is now haunted, consumed with protecting their children, hiding in fear. I live in that town?"

"Yes, but Barbara, let me help you. I can help get you out. I want to be closer with you."

"Why did you wait so long to tell me? Mom has been dead for years now."

"Honestly, I was scared. I didn't even know if you still read my books, but when I started talking with Rachel, it seemed like it was time for me to give you this book. We can't change how our mother raised us, but we can still change ourselves."

My mom looks at me. Her eyes are no longer filled with judgment but with regret. "You're right. Let me call you back?"

"Of course. I'm always here for you. I love you, Barbara."

"I love you too, Roxanne." My mom places her phone back in her bag, walks towards me, and wraps her arms around me. "Rachel, I'm so sorry for everything."

I hug her back. "I love you, Mom. Even through it all, you have always been my biggest advocate. I know that now."

We continue to stand in an embrace. Without any more words, we let go of the regrets of the past and hold onto the hope for our futures.

# CHAPTER 36

# December 2019

*"Then the Grinch thought of something he hadn't before!*
*What if Christmas, he thought, doesn't come from a store.*
*What if Christmas . . . perhaps . . . means a little bit more!"*

— DR. SEUSS, *HOW THE GRINCH STOLE CHRISTMAS!*

I CAN'T BELIEVE THIS IS HAPPENING. I lay my hand on my chest bone. My heart flutters like a dove released from its wired cage. Goosebumps dance across my forearms. I look around the space. There're no blank ceilings to torment me, just exposed pipes. There're no windows or lamps, just targeted spotlights and overhead fluorescent bulbs. The walls, a shade of white brighter than white itself, allow all the attention to settle on the art pieces scattered around the room.

At the entrance is the largest piece, larger than any wall in my home. The rainbow colors artfully waltz around the canvas as if dancers in a ballet. The colors form an abstract angel with huge spanning wings, a draping gown, and a large halo above its head.

I step closer and study the piece as if I don't know every brushstroke, every line, and every mistake the canvas holds. As if the image hasn't been living in my brain for the last several years. I examine various subcollections of strokes that form unique scenes within the larger picture of the angel. I notice a man fixing a stranger's car, a boss taking a risk on an inexperienced student, a mother shielding their child from the words of others, and a partner helping their loved one feel beautiful again. These smaller scenes are of people. They don't have wings, halos, or Grecian gowns. Instead, it's average humans doing average things for other average humans. People stepping up to be another's advocate. People choosing to become another's guardian angel.

I take another step closer to the painting. My fingers graze the porcelain title card next to the image. It reads:

THE GUARDIANS

ARTIST: RACHEL TAYLOR

My eyes become dry, forgetting to blink. I drift to the next piece in the gallery. The exhibit continues with smaller pieces of individual acts of kindness that are hidden in the large entrance piece. I stop in front of a portrait of a mother protecting her daughter from the monsters, but also shielding some good away, out of the hope of guarding her heart. The piece is called *Guardians of Innocence*. I see my initials again in the corner.

I sit on a viewing bench positioned in front of my favorite painting. The words of a prayer outline a man.

These words were a mystery to me until this angel helped me understand. *God, grant me the serenity to accept the things I cannot change, the courage to change the things I can, and the wisdom to know the difference.* The man is sitting at a desk, writing a letter. The letter I received that started it all for me. I breathe in deep. I fill my lungs fully and release the bliss I find within.

The crowd's chatter and the soft click of heels on the clean, polished wood floors pull my attention away from the art and towards the people entering the front door. There are men and women of all walks of life. One man is dressed in a black shirt and black jeans. He seems just as posh as the woman dripping in a sequined flapper dress. At the front, I see the event coordinators pouring champagne. Champagne that will be used to celebrate me and my persistence.

"Rachel!" I hear my mother shout.

I spot Roxanne and my mother walking into the show. They are both dressed in form-fitted cocktail dresses. Even their hair is curled similarly. They must have gotten ready together. They seem to do everything together these days. They are working on a joint children's mystery novel where Roxanne writes the story, and my mom does the illustrations.

I first hug Roxanne and then hug my mom. Trailing behind them is my dad, limping with a cane. Since the heart attack, he has never fully recovered physically. Even though my mother has requested many times for him to retire, he refuses. For once, I understand his desire to keep working. To live a passion. Still, whenever I see him, he seems angry with my decision to choose art. My mom reassures me that he will come around. I don't know if I believe that anymore. From a distance, he says, "I'm not as fast as them, but I'm here." And just his presence means the world to me.

I smile and ask my dad, "So what do you think of the show? What's your verdict?" Even now, I desperately search for his approval.

He clears his throat and says, "I'll need to walk around and consider the evidence."

I embrace all three of them together. "I couldn't have done it without you."

"Yes, you could have, honey. But I'm glad you didn't," my mom responds. "Where are the kids tonight?"

"Susie is at the stables, and Noah is with Marcus." After that first horseback riding experience, Susie found her passion, and as much as it scared me, I couldn't lock her away from it. Since we can't afford regular lessons, she now works on the farm to get free lessons. Noah soon realized that scooping all the manure wasn't worth it and instead spends that time with Marcus. The two of them want to become the Steve Jobs of Nerf guns. Their current invention is a whip cream sprayer that can hit someone twenty feet away. They swear it will become the next big thing. I always smile. Who am I to judge what will come from their inventions?

My eyes get caught on an unexpected face. "Rick?" I whisper to myself.

I give a quick goodbye to my family and walk in his direction. He looks exactly like the day we broke up three years ago. The same peacoat and scarf I remember he wore when he came to play with the kids. I try to amplify my voice. "Rick!"

He turns around and smiles with genuine excitement. He walks towards me and reaches out for a hug. I no longer recognize his smell. Does he have a new cologne? "Rachel! It's good to see you. Your art is amazing."

I feel lost for words and opt to stare at him as if encountering a ghost from my past. We haven't talked since our breakup. My body is pumping with so many emotions. It's unclear how I feel to see him here. Is it excitement, nerves, or some blend of the two? "How did you know about the show?" I ask.

He smiles wide. "Everyone is talking about the new talented artist in town." I give him a skeptical glare, and he continues, "My mom was talking to your mom about it."

A woman approaches Rick and wraps herself around his arm. A large diamond adorns her hand. "Rachel, this is Lindsey, my wife." His gaze turns to her. It's clear she's the greatest work of art in the room to him.

I go to shake Lindsey's hand, but she leans towards me instead. "I'm more of a hugger," she declares. *She's perfect for Rick*, I think.

"It's nice to meet you. Rick, I actually have something I want to show you?"

"Oh really? Was I a muse for your work," he jokes.

I smirk. "Actually, yeah, a little bit," I say.

I direct them to a set of two pieces hung together. The first is an angel with his wings wrapped around a crumbling woman, and the second is the same angel helping her glue her pieces back together. I look back at him. "Rick, I wouldn't be here without you. I wouldn't be here without the small and large acts of everyone I portray on these walls. You helped me in ways I didn't even know I needed and, for that, I will always be thankful."

His eyes get watery. He pulls me in for a hug. "Thank you, Rachel." We look at each other with love. I'll always love Rick, but that doesn't mean we were ever meant to be married. He places his hand on my arm. "This means a lot to me."

I nod. "Thanks, Rick. For everything."

He shakes his head and says, "Go mingle with everyone here. I don't want to hold you up."

I give him one more hug and then start to float around the space. Among the crowd, I'm just another guest. I hear guests whisper about the art, giving both positive and negative feedback. Today, though, nothing could bring me down. As I wander, I find myself in the gallery's backroom that contains a call-to-action for all the guests. An art piece we all can contribute to. On the top of the wall, I write:

*Merry Christmas, may we all create gifts that speak to the real needs of our loved ones. This Christmas, be the guardian that gives hope.*

Beneath is a table of sticky notes asking the guest what gift they plan to give this Christmas. Dozens of messages have been posted saying they will be more vulnerable with their partner; they will show up for a nightly dinner with the family or take their family on that dream vacation. One note stands out to me, though.

*Show my daughter every day*
*that I'm the proudest father in the room. —Dad*

I touch the note and close my eyes, sealing away the tears from ruining the paper. I feel a touch on my shoulder, hoping it's my dad.

I turn and see the gallery manager, Linda. I wipe away my tears. "Rachel, I have someone I want you to meet."

"Of course, who is it?"

Linda directs me to a specific painting. "I want to introduce you to someone that has taken a liking to your work. She is huge in the art scene, so she can make your career skyrocket if she likes you. This is big, Rachel!"

My body freezes. "Are you serious?"

We stop in front of a woman that seems ten years younger than me. She is notably also more stylish than me with her structured pantsuit and perfectly white, high heel boots. Linda says, "Rachel, this is Lexi. Lexi, this is Rachel."

"It's nice to meet you," I say warmly, nervous about getting her feedback. I reach out my hand, hoping it is not too cold or shaky.

Lexi points to the piece we are standing next to. "Has anyone put an offer in for this piece? I want to put in a bid."

My mouth hangs open but, otherwise, my body freezes. All words are lost except for, "Are you serious?"

She laughs with sophistication. "It's a beautiful piece, Rachel. Your eye is authentic and raw. I want to help you take this further. Would you be interested?"

My head shakes in disbelief. I let out a laugh, way less constrained than hers. "Of course, I would *love* that!" I look at the piece in front of us. The image depicts a man leaning over working on a car. Floating above him is a halo. "May I ask what drew you to this piece?"

She pauses to catch her breath. "Many years ago, I had this man pull over on the highway to help me with my car that had broken down. I was so scared and . . . He told me to wait in the car with my seatbelt on . . . and not soon after, the car got hit . . . I lived because of what this man did. He saved my life. He was my guardian angel, and yet I never learned his name. I never got to say thank you. I never got to learn why he stopped to help me."

My heart drops. "When did this happen?" I ask.

"In January of 2013," the stranger replies.

My breath becomes labored. One of my hands covers my mouth, the other drifts over my heart. "Do you know what happened to the man who helped you?" I ask.

"No, the officers never told me. I tried to search for him, but I couldn't find him."

"I . . . " I choke on my words and pause. "I think I'm your guardian angel's wife." The stranger's eyes meet mine. "The man in the image here is my husband . . . my late husband."

The stranger chokes. Her knees become weak as she reaches for my support. "Your husband . . . he died that night?"

I nod. She squeezes my hand as we pull each other closer. Our cheeks lay on each other. Our tears intertwine. My life is connected to this stranger in a way I never hoped for. Lexi pulls back. "I'm so sorry. I should have searched harder. I should have tried to find you sooner. I could have helped you."

I smile, feeling confident in my response. "I think our guardian angel knew we weren't ready to meet until now."

Her head drops, and she stares at the floor. "But, Rachel, this is my fault. I should have done something to protect him. I shouldn't have let him help me. I should have stayed outside of the car with him. I should have insisted we move the car to a safer spot. I should have—"

I cut the woman off as I maneuver my head to meet her eyes. "Hey, look at me." She lifts her eyes to mine. "You did exactly what you were supposed to. None of this is your fault. I blamed myself for years for what happened, but no amount of 'shoulds or woulds' will change the past. We move forward, thankful for the time we got with the angels in our lives. Promise me you will never blame yourself for this? Mason wouldn't want that burden on any of us. Okay?"

Her eyes close, and she shakes her head in affirmation. "I'm just so sorry. I took your husband from you."

I think back to the letter Mason wrote. His gift of hope. The gift I needed more than anything at that exact moment. My life was spiraling to a hole of insecurity and unpleasurable safety, but his hope brought me back. And Mason would want me to give that hope to others. "No, Lexi, you didn't take my husband from me. No one can. Mason's here. Not in the flesh, but I see him in my children, in my heart, in the art on these walls. He's with me, and he's so damn proud of what's happening today."

My brain attempts to process the events of the day. The fact that I finally have an art show in my name, something I couldn't even do after graduating from art school. That even my father can see the beauty on the walls. That I met the woman Mason saved. I can't believe any of this is happening, but it's my reality. It's my life, a life that once seemed unimaginable. But with braveness and action, the unimaginable became my destiny.

Acknowledgements

As I wrote this novel and listened to Christmas music for two straight years, I often asked myself, *Why do I love Christmas so much? What is pushing me to write this book?* I have always been the family member that demanded all the Christmas traditions and would spend hours watching gift wrapping tutorials, but today I know it was never really about those things. It was simply about the time I got to spend with my family.

To my brother and sister, Joe and Mary, I know you both joke about my obsessive-compulsive nature around Christmas, but Christmas was never about the activities or the gifts. None of that mattered to me. Whether it was watching 24 straight hours of *The Office* or frosting gingerbread boys with amputated legs that we ate or taking naps on the living room floor after an arguably gluttonous meal, it was always about spending time with you.

I have looked up to you in ways you probably still don't understand. When you both left for college, I missed having you at home, but I knew I would still get to see you at Christmas. And now as we each start our own families across the country, I know one thing will always be true: We will find a way to reconnect at Christmas. This book wouldn't exist without you. I love you both beyond any words I could write in this limited space.

Also, to Heather and Mitchell, my sibling's partners, thank you for letting me be a part of the Christmas traditions you establish within your own homes. Thank you for protecting and loving my two favorite people.

To my parents, Tom and Barb, thank you for taking the risk on a third child and for teaching me that family always comes first.

To my husband, Jackson, thank you for letting me live my childish wonders at Christmas and every day of the year.

Writing this book has reminded me how much support I have from my immediate network. Thank you to my family and friends who read the somewhat rough, initial versions of this novel, specifically, my husband **Jackson Taylor**, my mom **Barbara Funke**, my sister **Mary Veverka**, and my sister-in-law **Heather Funke**.

Thank you to my dear friends **Dr. Alyse Krausz**, **Dr. Abby Genco**, and **Dr. Chandler Rombes**, who gave thoughtful edits, feedback, and encouragement throughout the process. Also, congrats to this amazing group of women on finishing your doctorates as I pestered you for help, hangouts, and phone calls.

Thank you to my classmates at the **Gotham Writing School**. Reading your work and getting your feedback made the writing process feel less lonely especially during quarantine.

I also want to thank the fantastic team that helped in creating this story. Thank you to my reviewers **Kathryn Young Galla, Katia Hernandez, Ashley Nelson**, and **Tom Hansen**. **Kathryn**, thank you specifically for sharing your background in law, a world I knew little about before this book. Also, thank you **Mfena Ortswen** for helping with the promotional materials.

I want to thank my editing team **Laura Thomas**, **Paige Sanders**, and **Jade from Cover to Cover Edits**. As my line editor, **Laura** was essential in ensuring a consistent and engaging story. Thank you for going back and forth with me through my long documents of questions.

I want to thank **Estella Vukovic** for the cover design that perfectly visualized the warm and cozy feelings I hope my readers gain from the novel. Thank you, **Sandra Jurca**, for the interior design and for really connecting the inside to the outside cover. You both transformed my lines of text in a Word Document into a work of art.

And lastly to **my readers**. If you have made it to this point, you truly are above and beyond my expectations. I feel so honored that you chose this story. I hope these words helped you get in the Christmas spirit and that you will spread love and kindness to everyone in your own life. I would love to learn more about how the story impacted you. Feel free to reach out to me on Instagram **@bfunkebooks** or through my website **funkenovels.com**.

# About the Author

**Rebecca Funke** is a computer scientist turned novelist. As a lover of all things Christmas, her debut novel, *The Christmas Gift*, explores how to extend the magic of the season to everything we do. Rebecca was born and raised in Perrysburg, Ohio and now lives in Northern California with her husband and dog. For more info, visit her website funkenovels.com or follow her on Instagram @bfunkebooks.

Manufactured by Amazon.ca
Bolton, ON